TALL COTTON

**Center Point
Large Print**

Also by Lori Copeland and available from Center Point Large Print:

Yellow Rose Bride
Bluebonnet Belle
Twice Loved
Three Times Blessed
Someone to Love

This Large Print Book carries the Seal of Approval of N.A.V.H.

TALL COTTON

LORI COPELAND

CENTER POINT PUBLISHING
THORNDIKE, MAINE

This Center Point Large Print edition
is published in the year 2009 by arrangement with
Harlequin Books S.A.

The text of this Large Print edition is unabridged.
In other aspects, this book may vary
from the original edition.
Printed in the United States of America.
Set in 16-point Times New Roman type.

ISBN: 978-1-60285-624-0

Library of Congress Cataloging-in-Publication Data

Copeland, Lori.
  Tall cotton / Lori Copeland.
    p. cm.
  ISBN 978-1-60285-624-0 (library binding : alk. paper)
  1. Large type books. I. Title.

PS3553.O6336T36 2009
813'.54--dc22

2009035043

To horse owners, horse trainers
and horse lovers everywhere

Prologue

This time I'm going to do something about it,
Charlie thought as he strode to the barn and swung
open the heavy door. He paused to let his eyes
adjust to the dim interior. A nagging ache, and then
a razor-sharp pain in his chest warned him to slow
down.

"No use in killing yourself, Bailey," he muttered.
He'd lain awake all night, trying to make this decision and, now that he had made it, nothing was
going to stop him.

Absently his hand wandered across his chest.
Had he remembered to take his medicine? He
patted his shirt pocket making sure his bottle of
nitro was there if he needed it.

He'd overlooked things like that too often lately.
His mind had been on Baritone, wondering why
the colt had gone downhill despite everything he'd
done.

Last year Baritone had been a top two-year-old.
Now something was wrong. Charlie was willing to
stake his reputation on it; a reputation that had
taken him thirty years to earn.

As the pain eased, Charlie walked down the long
row of stalls, watching horses munch alfalfa and
flick their tails. He listened but found nothing
unusual in their occasional muffled stomping in
the deep shavings.

Wiping his damp palms on his jeans, he moved steadily toward a large box stall at the end of the row. When he reached out and unlatched the door, the large chestnut colt swung his head around, ears pricked alertly. Recognizing his visitor, the horse stepped forward, working his nostrils and blowing softly.

"Hi, big'un," Charlie greeted. He ran his hand over the colt's neck, down the long shoulder, over the powerful chest and down the legs. He felt each knee for heat or swelling. For an instant he thought he might have detected something in the colt's right knee, but if anything was there, it hadn't shown up in yesterday's X rays or in any X ray taken in the past year.

But Charlie's instincts still told him something wasn't right.

"We're takin' a little ride, Baritone," Charlie murmured. "Take it easy now . . . easy, boy. . . ."

After last night's frost, the ground was too slick for early workouts. It was nearly 6:00 a.m., and Charlie had sent the hands out to spread hay in the pastures. He knew there was rarely a time when the barns were completely deserted, so he'd have to work fast.

Reaching under his jacket, he took a leather lead from his back pocket and attached it to the halter. He swung the stall door open and led Baritone down the hallway.

Pausing at the open door, he glanced right then

left. No one was in sight, so he led the colt to the trailer, watching their footing as he went.

"No time to dally, boy. Let's get a move on."

Dropping his head, the colt sniffed the ramp. He gazed inside the trailer before he let out a long breath. It was the sign Charlie had been waiting for.

"Load up," he said firmly. Clucking his tongue, he tapped the colt's rump. Baritone clomped up the ramp into the trailer.

Charlie hooked the safety chain and walked to the front to snap a trailer tie to the colt's halter. As he walked back out of the trailer, he glanced around. With a groan he squatted to lift the heavy ramp that served as a tailgate. His stocky frame had always gained weight easily, and the spare tire around his middle made it hard to bend over.

"The doc would have my hide if he could see me doing this," he muttered as he struggled to hoist the ramp.

A new, sharp pain shot through his chest as he bolted the latches. He removed his sweat-stained Stetson and wiped his brow on the sleeve of his down jacket.

After a moment's pause he set his hat low on his brow and gave the brim a determined tug to secure it against the sharp breeze. He climbed behind the wheel, switched on the motor and turned in the direction of the old gravel road used by employees. A few minutes later he pulled to a stop and let the truck idle while he climbed out to open the metal gate.

As his fingers curled around the frosty metal, he heard a second vehicle approaching.

"Hold it right there, old man, I'll get it," a man's voice ordered as he strode toward the gate.

Charlie recognized the voice and turned. "No need, I can—"

The man came up behind Charlie and took a firm hold on the gate with both hands. "You're not going anywhere."

"See here!" Charlie planted himself stubbornly.

With a hard thrust the newcomer jerked the gate from Charlie's grasp and swung it shut. Baritone let out an earsplitting trumpet.

The man faced Charlie calmly. "Turn your rig around."

"You're not going to stop me—" Charlie reached again for the gate, but the man held it shut.

"Don't push your luck old man."

Charlie's heart pounded as he tugged on the gate. Suddenly his hand shot to his chest as his heartbeat jolted out of sync.

Panic seized him. "My medicine . . ." He clawed his pocket for the bottle and found it wasn't there. He began sucking in drafts of air, trying to fill his lungs.

The man's fingers hastily fumbled inside Charlie's shirt pocket where he always kept his bottle of nitro. "Where the hell is it?"

Gasping, Charlie tried to answer but he couldn't push the words past his lips. He keeled over backwards, hitting the ground with a thud. The intruder dropped to his knees and felt for a pulse while Charlie lay staring up at him sightlessly.

Springing to his feet, he rushed to Charlie's truck. He pulled the door open and ran his hands over the tools, coffee cups and tack that littered the seat and floorboards. "Where are those damn pills?" he muttered, but the frantic search failed to turn up the brown vial.

Sweat stood out on his forehead as he hurried back to Charlie's side. He pressed his fingers against Charlie's neck then slumped back on his heels.

For a long moment his gaze moved assessingly, from Charlie's lifeless body to the truck idling in the middle of the road, then to the trailer behind it.

With a weary sigh he rose and walked to the truck. Standing by the open door, his eyes wandered over the inside. His gaze lingered on a pair of work gloves on the floor. He picked them up and slipped them on.

Quickly he ran his hand over the dash until his fingers closed around a pencil and a notepad. Smoothing the top sheet with the side of his gloved hand, he scrawled a brief message, then tore off the note and tossed the pencil and pad onto the seat.

He walked back to the body, knelt in the gravel and tucked the note inside Charlie's pocket, glancing briefly at the pale, unseeing eyes as he rose to his feet.

"You were a fool, Bailey, an old fool," he muttered.

Lifting his arm, he wiped the beads of sweat from his forehead with his sleeve. Then he walked to Charlie's truck and tossed the work gloves back where he'd found them.

In a moment he was back inside his own vehicle. He made a U-turn in the middle of the road and sped quickly out of sight.

Chapter One

It was a beautifully crisp October day. The sky was azure except for a large bank of fleecy white clouds that hung above New Hope cemetery like a giant umbrella. Somewhere in the distance a mockingbird called to its mate. Somehow Kelly found the sound comforting. Charlie had loved mockingbirds.

Seeing her father's casket brought an ache to her throat. She felt paralyzed by a fear that everything important to her was dissolving into a cloud of shame. Her eyes filled with tears as she mourned the loss of the father she'd always loved but only recently known.

She felt cheated. She should have been able to share a lifetime with Charlie instead of only five years. But shortly after Kelly's birth, her mother, Margaret, had divorced Charlie. Her mother hadn't been able to adjust to the transient nature of life on the racing circuit. And, though Charlie had wished she felt otherwise, he hadn't been willing to give up the life he'd loved for her.

Eventually Charlie had permitted Kelly's new stepfather to adopt her, believing that it would make her home life more secure. But after college and a year of teaching, Kelly had set out to find the father she'd never known.

Charlie had welcomed her with open arms. He'd

been delighted to discover that she possessed his knack with horses, and Charlie had hired her as an apprentice. They were soon not only father and daughter, but the best of friends.

He'd taught her the finer points of riding, and carefully schooled her in the skills of horse care and training. He'd introduced her to his world behind the scenes at Churchill Downs, Arlington Park, and Louisiana Downs where he'd kept up to two dozen horses in training.

During the spring and summer, they'd covered thousands of miles each month, flying from one track to another, corresponding daily with his assistants at each facility.

Then, to round out her knowledge, Charlie had arranged for Kelly to work with top trainers in France and Ireland. During the past year, she'd been learning how the Europeans schooled their Thoroughbreds.

Meanwhile Charlie's poor health had forced him to slow down. He'd decided to select a small breeding farm where he could stay in one place and finally make a home for Kelly. Six months ago he had taken a job at Pinetop Farm and left his old friend Zack Bennett in charge of their other clients.

Charlie wanted Kelly to come back and follow the racing circuit. She'd planned to visit him as she crisscrossed the country. At the same time, he could train at Pinetop Farm and race colts in the spring at Oaklawn Park in Hot Springs, Arkansas.

He'd dreamed of eventually buying his own farm and raising colts for Kelly to campaign.

But fate had intervened.

The tragic news of Charlie's death had been quickly followed by speculation that his fatal heart attack had occurred while he'd been in the act of kidnapping the top colt from Pinetop. The tabloids had reported that a ransom note found in Charlie's pocket had demanded an enormous sum for the safe return of Baritone, Pinetop Farm's derby contender. The colt had been found in the horse trailer, parked beside Charlie's body. The press had theorized that the stress of committing the crime had caused the fatal heart attack.

Kelly agonized over the scandal that suddenly shadowed her father's memory. Charlie's reputation had been the cleanest in the business. For over thirty years he'd been known for his integrity as well as his horsemanship. It cut Kelly to the core to think that he'd be forever remembered as a thief. Honest, good-hearted Charlie a criminal? The trumped-up charge was ludicrous. Kelly had no idea where Charlie had been taking the horse that morning, but she was certain that he hadn't been stealing it.

Hurt and frustration were tearing her apart. She had to set the record straight. She had to go to Pinetop and find out what had really happened that morning.

She lifted her eyes to survey the crowd. It was

comforting that so many horse people had traveled to attend her father's funeral. Charlie would be pleased. But Kelly couldn't help wondering what the other mourners must be thinking. Would Charlie's friends and associates believe he could have committed the crime he was accused of?

THE AFTERNOON SHADOWS had begun to lengthen as Margaret Smith tried to persuade her daughter to leave the cemetery. "Kelly, it's time to go, dear."

Henry Smith wrapped his arm around his adopted daughter as the three walked slowly away from the grave site. "Kelly, we want you to think about staying on with us," he said consolingly. "You can go back to teaching and put all this behind you."

Kelly's arm tightened around Henry. "I can't, Dad." Noting the look of alarm in her mother's eyes, Kelly added, "At least not yet. There are things I have to do."

"Kelly," her mother began, "you simply must give up this crazy notion of going to Arkansas."

Henry shot his wife a warning look. "Now, Margaret, we agreed we wouldn't pressure her—"

"But, dear," Margaret coaxed as if Kelly was still a child who had to have her decisions made for her. "How do we know that Charlie wasn't stealing that horse—"

"Charlie wasn't stealing the horse, Mother."

"Maybe, maybe not. But you could get hurt

16

sticking your nose where it doesn't belong. Charlie's dead. Let's just get on with our lives."

Kelly shook her head and set her jaw, and a far-away look came into her eyes.

"Oh, how you resemble Charlie when you get that look!" Margaret agonized. "When he was your age, he was just as stubborn, just as headstrong as you!"

"Margaret, give it up," Henry said gently. "I understand how she feels. Send her off with your blessing, because you know she's going anyway."

Kelly rested her head on Henry's shoulder as he wrapped his arms around both women. The three formed a loving huddle.

Kelly lifted her head and sent Henry a look of gratitude and deep affection before she turned back to her mother. "Go home and get some rest, Mom." She kissed Margaret's cheek. "If you don't mind, I'm going to stay awhile."

"Kelly, don't do this to yourself."

"I'm all right, really." Kelly kissed her mother again. "Take her home, Daddy, and make her drink a thimbleful of Grandma's wine."

"But how long do you plan to stay?" Margaret asked as Henry began to lead her toward their car. "How will you get home?"

"Zack will bring me home."

Margaret looked up, grateful to find the wiry, gray-haired man striding toward them.

"I suppose you won't change your mind?"

Kelly shook her head.

"Then we'll see you for dinner?"

"Yes, Mom."

Zack and Kelly turned to walk back to Charlie's grave together. For a long moment, Kelly's throat was so tight she couldn't speak. Finally she said, "I have to go to Pinetop Farm."

Zack took a deep breath. "I'm against it."

She looked at him with red-rimmed eyes. "Someone has to find out what really happened."

"The truth will come out, Kelly. It always does."

"I'm not so sure. The authorities in Arkansas are sitting on their hands, while the press is having a field day. Someone framed my father, Zack, and I can't just stand by and let them get away with it."

Zack removed his glasses and rubbed his hand over his eyes. "Charlie wouldn't like this, not for a minute. The last thing he would have wanted was to put you in danger."

"I won't be in danger. If you'll help me get a temporary job there, whoever did this to Charlie won't even know I'm his daughter," Kelly reasoned.

"You're hardheaded, just like Charlie!" Zack complained. "Word gets around, missy. You won't be able to hide your identity for long."

"I won't have to. I'll only be there long enough to discover who did this to Charlie. Once I learn the truth, it won't matter who I am. Please, Zack, you've got to help me convince McCrey to take me on."

"Well . . . McCrey *is* looking for someone," Zack acknowledged grudgingly.

Kelly's brow lifted. "Really?"

"He asked me if I'd be interested in taking your dad's place, training for him through the Arkansas Derby."

"What did you say?"

"I told him no! I have twenty horses to manage. Most of Charlie's old clients are with me, Kelly. I'd be a fool to pull up stakes now, so would anyone who's established. McCrey knows what he's up against. It'll be next to impossible to convince anyone who's worth his salt to make a change in mid-season."

"No, it won't." Kelly's emerald eyes glinted as she watched his face for signs of relenting.

"What's that supposed to mean?"

"It means Tanner McCrey is going to be lucky enough to find a marvelous trainer who's just returned from France and is looking for short-term work."

"He might wonder about that."

"He'll accept it because it's true. I did spend the past six months on the outskirts of Paris as an assistant to the top trainer in France."

Zack shook his head worriedly. "I still don't see how we can pull it off."

"Didn't Tanner McCrey ask you if you knew of someone who could fill the vacancy—at least temporarily?"

Zack nodded reluctantly. "He asked me to recommend someone. But I'm not suggesting you—I wouldn't feel right about it, Kelly. What if something happened to you?"

"Zack, I'm going to Hot Springs—with or without your help." Kelly took Zack's hands in hers and forced him to look into her eyes. "If you'll help, I can go there as Kelly Smith, a temporary replacement trainer. That way it would be easier and safer for me to make a few discreet observations and inquiries about the previous trainer's death." She took a step back, and her voice cooled. "Of course, if Tanner McCrey knows I'm Charlie's daughter, and he had anything to do with Charlie's death, he won't hire me. My only recourse would be to show up as an unwelcome intruder pursuing a personal vendetta. That's when I could get into trouble." She glanced at Zack pleadingly. "Please help me, Zack. I have to do this for Charlie."

Zack shook his head warily. "I don't like this, not for one minute, but I guess I owe it to Charlie to cover for you if I can." He let out a sigh of defeat. "All right, I'll put in a call to McCrey in the morning—"

"Tonight. Before he finds someone else."

"All right, tonight."

"And make arrangements for me to board a horse there, too."

"You're taking a horse?" he asked.

"Happy Talk. Charlie gave her to me before I left for France, and she's in foal. I can't leave her behind."

"Okay, I'll recommend Kelly Smith for the job and make arrangements for her to bring her horse, but I still don't like it.

A relieved smile broke across Kelly's features. "Thank you, Zack." She leaned over and pecked him on the cheek. "And Charlie would thank you if he could."

The two walked to Zack's truck, parked on the edge of the grass. "Think you'll be able to get McCrey to hire me?"

"Afraid so."

Kelly smiled. "Good."

"I just hope I don't end up regretting this."

"You won't regret it. I'll be fine."

THE FOLLOWING MONDAY morning Kelly was on her way. She was anxious as she faced the prospects ahead. Tanner McCrey had swallowed Zack's story, hook, line and sinker.

After driving eight hours, the veins in Kelly's eyes were beginning to resemble the spidery lines on the state map spread across the seat of her old pickup. Around four she spotted a deserted rest stop and decided to take a break.

She slowed the truck and pulled off the highway. *It shouldn't be too much farther,* she thought as she set the brake and turned off the engine.

Slipping into her jacket, she glanced at herself in the rearview mirror. What she saw made her wince. She still wasn't accustomed to her new hair color. Dirt brown.

After the funeral, she'd decided it would be wise to change her appearance. Her long strawberry blond hair seemed a dead giveaway and, although Zack had assured her that Tanner knew nothing about Charlie having a daughter, she wanted nothing about her to raise anyone's suspicions. So, she'd gone to the store and purchased a box of hair coloring to tint her tresses a medium brown.

The results had been disastrous. The color had turned out medium brown with greenish highlights. Horrified, she went back to the store and bought a brunette tint, which produced a color close to black shoe polish—with greenish highlights. The contrast was a shock, to be sure, with her green eyes and fair skin.

Two more tries at home coloring and a trip to a beauty salon to have her long hair dyed and snipped into a short, layered cut finally produced a shade that Kelly now referred to as an ugly, but acceptable, dirt brown.

"I'm not exactly wild about it," Kelly admitted to herself as she ran her fingers through her lackluster locks. "But now at least no one should recognize me."

She sighed and opened the truck door and

grabbed her thermos bottle. After a sip of coffee she stretched a bit and walked to the horse trailer hooked behind her truck. She peeked in on Happy Talk. Charlie had believed that the mare was carrying another stakes winner. But Happy Talk was old, and each of her deliveries had been progressively more difficult. She was due to foal in a few months, and Kelly wasn't willing to entrust her care to anyone, not even Zack.

After giving her mare water and a flake of hay, Kelly wandered over to an overlook that offered a panoramic view of the Ouachita mountains. A storm was brewing on the horizon, and the approaching front was kicking up a strong wind. Kelly tipped her face upward, letting the breeze play through her hair.

Charlie had called this God's country, and Kelly had to agree as she gazed at the pine-crusted mountains and the clear-running stream winding through the valley below.

She patted the front pocket of her jeans to be sure the letter from Charlie was still there. She'd received it two days after his death, and she figured that he must have mailed it on the morning he died. The letter was vague and confusing, and she still hadn't determined whether it held any clue to his death.

Persuaded by a loud clap of thunder, Kelly got back into the truck and reached inside her purse for the map to Pinetop that Zack had sketched from memory. It showed a shortcut about three miles ahead, a private back road used by McCrey's employees. It would cut almost five miles off her trip.

She switched on the motor and pulled back onto the highway.

Kelly found the private road with no difficulty. It was an unmarked gravel road but looked as if it had been recently graded. "This must be it," she murmured as she glanced at Zack's sketch and at the odometer.

Lining the road on both sides were tall straight pines packed together as tightly as arrows in a quiver. Her old truck and trailer bumped along as she heard another rumble of thunder and the rain started to pelt down.

The slap of the windshield wipers set her teeth on edge as she strained to see the winding road. The truck motor began to whine as it started up a long grade. Kelly shifted to first and pressed on the gas.

The mare was moving back and forth restlessly in the trailer, and Kelly could feel it begin to rock. Her fingers tightened on the steering wheel until her knuckles turned white. The mare had never been a good traveler. "Hold on, Happy Talk," she said to herself.

A moment later Kelly heard a loud crash and glanced into the rearview mirror. When she failed to see the mare's head through the trailer window, her heart began to race.

Pulling to a stop, Kelly set the emergency brake. For a second the tires slid in the loose gravel.

Switching the ignition off, she hopped out and grabbed an armload of bricks from the bed of the pickup and set about blocking the wheels of the truck and trailer.

Once she had the vehicles secured, she raced to the trailer to open the front compartment and look inside. Happy Talk was down, but her halter was still snapped to the tie. Her neck and head were strained dangerously while she thrashed to regain her footing. The trailer floor was at a steep angle because of the hill, making it even more difficult for the mare to regain her footing in the narrow trailer.

Reaching inside, Kelly unsnapped the quick release trigger on the tie to free the horse. She heard the mare's neck and shoulders slide to the trailer floor with a thud.

"Easy, girl. Take it easy, Happy Talk," she soothed as she hurried to unlatch the trailer door and swing it wide.

She unhooked the safety chain, and the mare looked back at her. "Easy girl, get up easy now." Kelly reached out to gently stroke the mare's hip. Happy Talk took a deep breath and thrust her front legs forward as she sprang to her feet. She swayed for a moment unsteadily, then shook herself.

Sensing what was coming next, Kelly stepped aside as the mare backed out of the trailer like a shot.

"Whoa," Kelly ordered as she grabbed the mare's halter and snapped on a lead. She proceeded to walk the horse in small circles to try to relax her and see that she was uninjured.

The rain was coming down in sheets, accompanied by bright flashes of lightning. As the storm's fury increased, Kelly didn't notice the sound of a vehicle approaching until it was almost upon her. A huge transport truck loaded with pine logs barreled its way up the hill toward them.

Edging the mare a safe distance off the road, she took a firm hold on the lead rope. As the truck roared by, its dual rear wheels spewed a high wall of mud, drenching her and the mare. But it was the red flag flapping wildly at the end of the longest log that was Happy Talk's undoing. The mare reared and bolted, and the lead rope peeled the skin from Kelly's hands as she struggled to maintain her grip.

The mare took off down the hill, dragging Kelly in her wake. Kelly didn't dare let go of the rope. On her rapid descent downhill, Kelly muttered every bad word she'd ever heard and a few she wasn't supposed to have heard. When the mare reached the bottom of the hill, she stopped abruptly as if she'd suddenly decided that the danger was past.

Kelly skidded into the back of the horse, still cursing. She reached out to grab the mare's halter angrily. "You miserable son-of-a—"

Kelly heard someone clear his throat. "Biscuit Eater?" the man suggested.

Chapter Two

Startled by the intrusion, Kelly drew back in surprise. The deep voice had come from a man sitting behind the wheel of a silver and red Silverado, watching her.

She decided it was best to ignore him and began leading Happy Talk back up the hill. She was embarrassed by her salty language and her even more disreputable appearance. The rain was still coming down heavily, and there wasn't a dry thread left on her.

The man swung his door open and stepped out. "Hey, hold up a minute."

Kelly kept walking.

He called, "It makes no difference to me, but your wallet fell out of your jacket."

Kelly turned and pushed her hair out of her face, then took a moment to size him up. In his jeans, plaid shirt and quilted jacket, he looked like any other weary logger on his way home. He was well built and close to six feet tall. The brown Stetson pulled low on his brow cast a shadow across his face, but she could still discern strong features and a dark tan.

Praying that he meant her no harm, she led the horse toward him. "Thanks. I didn't know I'd dropped it."

"Looks like you've had a little trouble," he said as she reached to retrieve her wallet.

"A little." Kelly took a deep breath. "The storm spooked my mare, and she fell inside the trailer. Since she's in foal, I was worried that she might have hurt herself."

The man looked concerned. "Was she?"

"Excuse me?"

"Was your mare injured?"

"I think she's okay." Kelly glanced at her mare again, feeling uneasy under this stranger's scrutiny.

"Can I help?"

Though his offer sounded sincere, Kelly shrugged while she clutched the lead in her smarting palm and tried to keep her teeth from chattering in the damp cold. "Thanks. I'll just load her and be on my way."

"You sure?"

"Sure . . . I can handle it." She tried to sound more confident than she felt as she recalled the struggle she'd had with Happy Talk minutes earlier. Kelly turned and started back up the hill.

The heavy downpour slackened as Kelly reached the top of the hill. She led the mare to the back of the trailer and stepped inside to thread the long lead through a large ring in the front. Stepping out, she pulled on the rope to draw the mare inside. "Load up," she commanded, reaching back to tap the mare's flank.

Happy Talk froze, and Kelly realized with a sinking sensation that the mare had decided she'd had enough traveling for one day.

Kelly drew the rope tighter and made a clucking sound, but Happy Talk wouldn't budge. Kelly flushed with embarrassment. She was a horse trainer; she could usually coax a horse to do whatever she wanted. But she was tired and tense herself—and the mare sensed it.

"Sure you wouldn't like some help?"

Kelly glanced up, realizing that the man had followed her. "Do you know anything about loading horses?"

"Lady, I could load an elephant."

Kelly dropped her gaze to the muddy gravel. That's all I need, she though dismally, some know-it-all logger left over from a beer commercial.

She lifted her gaze, looked across the mare's back into the man's face, and felt a jolt that took her by surprise. His eyes were the palest blue and so startlingly clear that for an instant she could only stare.

She wondered if it was the directness of his gaze or his air of confidence that was sending her pulse thumping so erratically.

Kelly broke eye contact first, turning back to survey her horse. For a moment the stillness seemed awkward.

"Nice mare," he said finally.

Kelly made a sound in her throat. "How can you tell under all the mud?"

"I can recognize quality." Something in his voice told her he recognized that and more.

Leaning his elbows on the trailer gate, he looked at her, admiring the color of her eyes. *A nice green,* he thought.

He doesn't seem to know or care that it's impolite to stare, Kelly thought. Uneasy with his intent gaze, Kelly looked at the mare. "I'm afraid she's stubborn."

"The good ones usually are."

Kelly glanced up, but this time the man looked away, his expression unreadable.

"Let's load her," he suggested as he gently ran his hand down the mare's bulging side, then onto her hip.

Kelly cleared her throat and tried to sound businesslike. "All right. If you'll just step over here." She beckoned to him with her fingertips. He took a step to stand across from her on the other side of the mare.

"Give me your arm," she said, reaching around behind the mare's rump. Her brows lifted in surprise when she saw that his well-muscled forearm was already extended, waiting for hers.

As she reached out, he locked arms with her. Kelly took a deep breath as her fingers tightened around the ridges of muscle on his forearm.

They slid their locked arms under the mare's rump. "Don't give her any slack," she warned, nodding to the lead rope in her other hand. "When she gives an inch, we'll take an inch."

Together they gave a steady push, and the mare

took a small, reluctant step forward and then another and another until only her back feet remained outside.

"You okay?" she asked.

"Just fine," he returned calmly.

"Ready?" she asked.

"Ready."

"Here we go!"

Without needing to be told, he pressed his shoulder under the mare's hip and pushed forward. The mare gave up and stepped all the way inside.

"Good girl, Happy Talk," Kelly said, relieved.

The man straightened and hooked the safety chain behind the mare. "You have a fine horse there." The smile he gave her was slow and easy and full of charm.

As she smiled back, he realized that if it weren't for her hair, with those awful greenish tints, she'd be beautiful.

Her gaze dropped to their arms, still locked together, and she loosened her grip. She noticed that he held on for a second longer than she had. As if he were reluctant to let go.

She walked around him to get to the front of the trailer and reached in to snap the trailer tie securely to the mare's halter.

He gave a last appraising glance at the mare's swollen sides. "Due to foal in couple of months, I'd say."

"You do know horses." She'd suspected as much

when he'd known how to load the mare without being told. There was an air of authority about him she found attractive.

An awkward silence followed as they stood in the rain, looking at each other. "Well, thanks for everything," she said.

"Where you headed?" he asked.

"Pinetop Farm. Is it far?"

He looked surprised. "No."

"This road was supposed to be a shortcut according to my map," she mused.

"This road is private. It isn't on any map."

"I know . . . a friend drew a sketch for me."

"Is that so?"

"Yes."

"You have business at Pinetop?" He figured perhaps her mare was booked for a breeding after she foaled, or maybe this girl was looking to sell or trade her, but all of Pinetop's customers and clients used the front entrance.

"I have a job there."

"Really?"

She smiled. Everything she said seemed to surprise him. "Yes, really."

"Then I'd better introduce myself." He extended his hand. "I'm Tanner McCrey."

For a moment Kelly was speechless. This good-looking hunk was the owner of Pinetop Farm?

"I'm sorry." He smiled this time. "I don't believe I caught your name."

Hurriedly regaining her composure, she extended her hand. "Kelly Smith." They shook politely. "Zack Bennett sent me. You were expecting me, weren't you?"

"Well, I was . . . and I wasn't. Zack filled me in on your qualifications, but he failed to mention that you were a woman."

Kelly gave him a sidelong glance. "Is that a problem?" A defensive note crept into her tone.

"No . . . no problem. I'll just go get my truck and lead the way to the farm. Just wait here and follow me, Ms. Smith."

Kelly thought about Tanner McCrey as she followed him through the pines. She'd expected him to be older, but he only appeared to be in his thirties. Blatantly male, she thought, and blatantly sure of himself.

She admitted that for a brief instant she'd felt attracted to him. However, she knew that feeling was something she couldn't afford. Tanner McCrey believed that Charlie Bailey had tried to steal his horse. She was certain that if he discovered she was Charlie's daughter, he'd send her packing.

She reminded herself that the ugly incident with her father hadn't hurt Tanner McCrey any. His colt had received plenty of free publicity. Now everyone was eager to see the horse that had been the target of a multimillion-dollar ransom scheme.

Kelly noticed a road branching off to the right,

but Tanner continued straight. Another mile farther along he stopped at a gate.

He got out, swung the gate open and motioned her through. She drove ahead and waited while he drove through, closed the gate and took the lead again.

Forests gave way to white-fenced pastures. Though it was twilight Kelly could see neat white barns and sheds clustered at intervals along the way. Leggy yearlings galloped along the fence in one paddock, while in the next, brood mares stood bunched in a band. The farm was in a large valley cradled by mountains and crisscrossed by a stream.

As they wound around the last turn, Kelly saw a white, two-story colonial house, surrounded by well-trimmed hedges and flanked by towering pines. It dominated a hillside overlooking a swimming pool, a small cottage and several rows of long white barns.

Stopping at the barn closest to the cottage, Tanner got out of his truck and walked back to her. He motioned for her to follow him. "You can leave your mare here," he called as he walked to the back of the trailer.

Kelly climbed out and moved to the trailer to unsnap the tie from Happy Talk's halter. She signaled Tanner, who opened the trailer door and unhooked the safety chain.

Kelly walked to the rear of the trailer. "Back," she ordered and waited for Happy Talk to come out. When the mare had cleared the trailer, she snapped a lead rope to her halter.

Following Tanner, she led the mare into the well-lit hallway of the barn. A lean, rangy man wearing insulated coveralls stepped from a doorway. Behind him Kelly could see a modern office with a computer.

"Kelly Smith, Jim Larson," Tanner introduced. "Jim is our foreman," he told her. Tanner glanced at the man. "Kelly is replacing Charlie for the time being."

Kelly shook hands with the older man. Jim Larson—he'd given one of the interviews published in a tabloid. He'd insinuated that Charlie had been trying to steal the horse when he died. Her hand came up to smooth her hair while she studied him.

"Larson, make sure this mare is rubbed down and given some feed then get her settled for the night," Tanner said.

"Sure thing, Mr. McCrey."

"Thank you," Kelly murmured as she handed the lead to the foreman.

Tanner pointed to the doorway as they walked by. "There is your office. You can check it out in the morning. I imagine you'd like to get moved into your cottage for now."

"Yes, thank you, I would." Kelly pressed her fingers against her lower back to loosen the ache as they walked to her truck.

"I'll get your luggage," Tanner said. He hoisted

her two suitcases out of the truck bed and led the way to the white cottage.

Kelly grabbed her purse from the truck cab and followed Tanner up the three steps to the porch. He opened the door, flipped on a light and set her bags inside.

"It's nice," she said glancing around the cozy room, taking in the comfortable furniture.

"It's serviceable," he said, walking to the stone fireplace. He knelt and struck a match to the paper and kindling under the logs in the grate. Soon a cheery fire was burning. He walked to a thermostat on the wall and turned it up. "This was the original farmhouse."

"Suits me fine. I can hardly wait to clean up and relax."

"Why don't you join us for dinner tonight? Hattie will have plenty. She always does."

Kelly wandered around the room, trying to take it all in. "Hattie is your wife?"

He gave a deep chuckle. "No, though a man could do worse. I'm not married. Hattie is my housekeeper."

"Well, thanks for the invitation, Mr. McCrey, but not tonight. I'm not hungry. I'll just take a hot bath and go to bed early."

"Whatever you say, but no one skips meals around here if Hattie can help it."

Kelly smiled faintly, realizing that it was going to be hard to keep her distance from this man.

"Thanks again for everything, Mr. McCrey."

He acknowledged her gratitude with a brief nod. "We're not formal around here. Just call me Tanner."

She smiled, but she knew she wouldn't do as he asked. Referring to him by his last name would help assure a comfortable distance between them. "Thanks again . . . and good night."

He touched the brim of his hat politely. "The key to the cottage is on the kitchen table."

Once he'd gone she turned in a slow circle, taking in the overstuffed plaid chairs, the navy sofa, the walnut coffee table and the old Regulator clock ticking above the mantel. This was the last home her father had known.

A wave of loneliness washed over her. She longed for Charlie's reassuring voice, his kindness. She felt surrounded by his presence, and she ached to see him, talk to him.

She stared at the fire, imagining her joy if she could see her father walk into the room at that instant. He would tease her and make her laugh, and everything would be all right again.

She waited for a moment, as if she thought that wishing hard enough could make him return. But the minutes passed, and he didn't come. Closing her eyes tightly, she tried to stem the familiar tears rolling down her cheeks. How she wished this room could talk. Perhaps some clue to Charlie's death remained here. . . . If so, she was determined to find it.

Chapter Three

As the sound of Tanner's footsteps faded, Kelly carried her bags to the bedroom. It was an immaculate, warm, comfortable room.

She explored the rest of the cottage. There was one bath, a living room, a dining area and a kitchen. Though the cottage was old, everything looked neat and in good repair. Kelly stood in the dark bedroom and peeled out of her filthy clothes. She pulled her terry robe out of her suitcase and headed to the bathroom for a hot bath.

Later, scrubbed clean and wrapped in her robe, Kelly sat by the fire to dry her hair and think.

She knew from her father's letters that he'd entered information about workouts, feed schedules, medical info and other observations into a computer in the office she'd seen in the barn. What most people didn't know was that her father didn't trust the newfangled gadgetry, as he called it, so he'd still kept a handwritten journal of his daily activities, just as he had in the old days.

He'd given several of his old journals to Kelly, and she'd used them like textbooks to study his techniques of training Thoroughbreds so she knew what they looked like. But when his personal items had arrived from Pinetop Farm, Charlie's current journal had not been among them. Kelly assumed that it had been considered part of the training records rather than Charlie's property.

Kelly hoped it might still be somewhere in the cottage or the office, and that it might help her get to the bottom of this mystery. She rose and began searching through the bookcases flanking the fireplace. After a thorough check of every nook and cranny in the living room, she moved to the dining area. She found nothing but old Thoroughbred magazines and yearling sale catalogs in the dining-room cabinet. Piling a stack of periodicals on the round pedestal dining table, she started sorting through them for personal papers. Then she heard a knock.

She opened the front door and saw a round-faced little woman who appeared to be in her late fifties. "Hello, dear! Hope I'm not disturbing you. I'm Hattie Matthews, Tanner's housekeeper," the woman announced, tilting her head up and down slowly to inspect Kelly through each level of her trifocals. The tantalizing aroma of roast beef reached Kelly's nose.

"It's so nice to meet you, Ms. Matthews. Won't you come in?"

"Of course." The woman stepped inside and closed the door behind her. "I understand you've had a difficult trip. Here's a little something that will ward off the chill and make you feel better." Hattie's hazel eyes, magnified by her glasses, looked luminous as she smiled.

"Thanks, but you really shouldn't have come down here in the rain." When Kelly started to reach for the casserole dish, the woman quickly sidestepped her.

"I'll just pop this into the oven. It should be hot in just a little while."

Kelly opened her mouth to protest but closed it as she found herself trailing Hattie Matthews through the living room. The top hook of the woman's print dress wasn't fastened, and for an instant Kelly was tempted to hook it for her, but thought better of it.

"My, my," Hattie commented as she walked through the dining room, "you are a worker. Haven't been here an hour, and already you're cleaning out the cabinets. Wait till I tell Tanner. Our other trainers haven't been so tidy."

"Oh, please, don't mention it to Mr. McCrey, Ms. Matthews."

"That's Hattie, dear. Everyone calls me Hattie." She walked to the white stove and opened the oven door. She smoothed the foil on top of the dish and set it on a rack and closed the oven. She set the temperature and checked her watch. "Now you just sit yourself down. This'll be ready in a jiffy."

"Please don't go to all this bother, Ms. Matthews—Hattie, that is," Kelly corrected as she received a stern look. "I'm really too tired to eat."

"Nonsense. You have to keep up your strength. Why, I don't know how you trainers do it. Up at four o'clock in the morning, out in all kinds of weather . . . oh, by the way," Hattie continued, barely pausing for a breath, "I'll be in every other day to clean. Anything you need laundered, just toss it in the hamper in the hall closet."

"That won't be necessary. I do my own cleaning and laundry." Kelly saw the woman's head snap up as if she'd just been insulted. She sensed that Hattie was a woman who needed to be needed. "However, I'll appreciate your help until I see how my schedule goes," she amended lamely.

Hattie turned around and beamed. Her dark hair had strands of gray at the temples, which the rain had caused to curl around her face. She tried to smooth them back with her hands as she began, "Well, of course, if you don't want me . . . I wouldn't want to be underfoot."

"You'd just spoil me." Kelly smiled.

"Well, I'll bet you're a girl who deserves a little spoiling."

Having someone do her laundry would be a treat, Kelly realized, and she found herself softening. "I'm sure I'd enjoy the luxury," she conceded.

"Good. Now take a seat over there." Hattie set the table and stirred a glass of iced tea. "I stocked your refrigerator and cupboards, but you really should eat with us," Hattie advised as she set the glass of tea before Kelly, who was feeling awkward doing nothing while Hattie waited on her.

"Could I help you?"

42

"No, no," Hattie said, checking her watch and turning around to open the oven. She peeled back the foil and sniffed. "Dinner is ready," she announced pleasantly.

Kelly pushed the stack of magazines aside. In a moment, Hattie set a plate before her. The aroma of steaming roast beef, mashed potatoes swimming in rich gravy, and honeyed carrots filled the air. "Oh my," Kelly eyed the delectable fare, "this smells wonderful."

"Nothing like a hot meal to make you feel better." Hattie sat down across from her.

"This is delicious," Kelly murmured, after she swallowed the bite of tender beef she'd taken.

"You might as well come to the house and have your meals with Tanner and me. No sense in you cookin' for yourself. We always have plenty."

"No," Kelly refused quickly. "I mean no thanks."

"Why not?" Hattie sounded disappointed.

"My hours are too irregular . . . but thanks anyway." Kelly knew she couldn't sit across the table from a man as attractive as Tanner McCrey every night and maintain the professional distance and objectivity she needed.

"Well, Mr. Bailey came to dinner almost every night. We really enjoyed his company, God rest his soul. Such a dear man."

"I imagine you cleaned the cottage for Mr. Bailey," Kelly said.

"Yes. He told such wonderful stories, he was a

fine man . . . but he wasn't too tidy, if you know what I mean."

Kelly knew only too well. Charlie was the pits when it came to housekeeping. "I was wondering . . . did you happen to come across a journal of Mr. Bailey's after he passed away?"

"I gave all of Mr. Bailey's things to Tanner," Hattie confided. "I believe he mailed them to Shreveport."

"Do you happen to recall a journal, a large three-ring notebook among those things?"

"Hmmm." Hattie stared at the ceiling for a second. "Yes, there was a notebook. As a matter of fact, I found it on top of that cabinet. Why?"

Kelly shrugged casually. "The man who recommended me for the job mentioned that Mr. Bailey kept a training journal in a binder like that. I just thought if it was still around it might help me understand what procedures he'd been using with individual horses."

"I see. Well, I gave the notebook to Tanner. I imagine Tanner would know what was done with it."

"One would think so," Kelly murmured thoughtfully. "One would certainly think so."

THE NEXT MORNING Kelly rose at four o'clock and splashed her face with cold water. She slipped on a cotton turtleneck, a heavy sweater, two pairs of socks and jeans.

She eyed herself in the light of the small mirror, then dismally ran a washcloth over her hair. She missed her beautiful, long red hair. These shorn brown curls were almost too short to comb.

After a light breakfast, she slipped into her down jacket and sat on the back step, sipping coffee and cleaning her black riding boots.

The morning was crisp and surprisingly clear. As she watched the moon sink toward the horizon, she wondered how the other employees would accept her. Groaning softly, she pulled on her boots, her muscles aching in protest. She took a deep breath, slapped her knees with determination and stood up. It was time to get down to business.

As Kelly stepped through the doorway of the first barn and into the farm office, Jim Larson rose from behind the desk and walked around to greet her.

"Mornin', Ms. Smith."

"Good morning, Jim. Please, call me Kelly."

He nodded distractedly and led her into the hallway where he introduced her to the half dozen men and one girl who worked in the barns full-time.

Kelly watched their faces to gauge if anyone seemed to recognize her, but she detected nothing. She'd felt confident that Charlie had never referred to her as Kelly Smith because he'd always called her by her given name, Killarney, after the lakes region of southwest Ireland where he'd been born. Her mother had shortened the name to Kelly when she'd enrolled her in school, but she knew if Charlie ever mentioned his daughter, he would have told them about his Killarney, not Kelly. Although, there had still been a chance he'd shown someone a picture of her.

She didn't look enough like Charlie to be easily recognized as his daughter. Physically she resembled her mother with her slim build, copper-colored hair and fair skin, but she had inherited Charlie's expressive green eyes, so she intended to wear sunglasses as often as possible.

The six stable hands welcomed Kelly warmly. The small, dark-haired girl introduced as Marcy looked to be eighteen or nineteen. She acknowledged Kelly with a brief nod and cast her gaze downward where she was stirring the shavings with the toe of her boot.

"I guess you'll be wantin' to see our training facility . . . Kelly?" Jim Larson asked, tacking on her name awkwardly.

"Yes, Jim, I do."

They walked for a while, and Jim pointed out the various facilities to her. The extended tour ended at the white-fenced, one-mile, oval training track. "What have you been doing with the horses lately?" Kelly asked as she climbed the fence and watched as a horse and rider broke from the starting gate.

"Since Charlie died? We've just been breaking the young ones to ride," Larson admitted.

"And the horses that were racing this season? What have you been doing with them?"

Larson cleared his throat. "I run the farm and break the colts," he said abruptly. "For that matter, I could've conditioned any of those horses as well as Charlie Bailey."

Kelly remained unruffled. "I see, but the record speaks pretty well for Charlie Bailey, wouldn't you say?"

Larson shrugged and let the comment pass. "For the past couple of weeks we've ponied the race-horses every morning to keep 'em legged up."

"I'd like to see them."

"Doug," Larson called. "Saddle up and lead Keepsake out."

"I'd rather see Baritone first," Kelly said quietly.

For an instant, Larson was caught off guard by her request. "Baritone?"

Kelly's smile was polite but determined. "Yes, if you don't mind."

Larson recovered and nodded curtly. "Doug, make that Baritone instead. Larry, you help him."

"But Charlie always exercised the filly first," Marcy objected, "and the colt last."

"I'm not Charlie," Kelly reminded, though she understood Charlie's rationale better than anyone. "I know it's better to keep the fillies and the colts separate, but I have my reasons for changing the routine."

Kelly watched two stable hands lead the handsome chestnut colt from the barn. One walked on either side, each with a lead snapped to the halter.

The colt moved with big easy strides. The white star in his forehead shone like a beacon as his head moved up and down in rhythm. When they stopped the horse beside Doug's lead pony, Baritone snorted and laid his ears back.

Kelly studied the animal. His conformation was impressive, and his disposition seemed normal to her for an almost-three-year-old. As long as he was moving, he was cooperative. It was when he had to stand still that he grew impatient and feisty. That's what Charlie had called him: feisty. He was that all right, Kelly thought as she watched him gnaw on the lead pony's mane.

"Take him halfway around at a jog, then move up to a trot," she said. Doug nodded and kicked his lead pony into a canter to keep pace with the colt.

"He's got a stride as long as a Kansas well rope," Larson remarked.

Kelly watched Baritone move around the track. He seemed to cover the ground effortlessly. All year he'd been what Charlie had called a "hang on"—the jockey could just grab a handful of mane and hang on till he crossed the finish line. Until his last race.

"I want to see him under saddle," Kelly said.

From her tone, Jim Larson gathered that she wasn't making idle conversation. "Moran isn't

48

here today," Larson stated flatly. "He's the only one authorized to ride Baritone."

Kelly's eyes followed the sleek animal as Doug led him around the track a second time. "Have Baritone saddled," she said again.

Larson glanced up to confront Kelly's determined expression. "You can't be thinkin' you're going to ride him yourself?"

Her direct gaze assured him that she was.

"I'm against it! Baritone's a handful. Mr. McCrey wouldn't like it one bit."

"Mr. McCrey isn't training the colt. I am. Now let's saddle up."

Larson glared at Kelly for a long moment before he turned away, muttering under his breath as he sent Larry for a saddle. Baritone sidestepped and pranced while Doug held his head. Larson and Kelly stood on either side, struggling to saddle him.

"I'm advisin' you to forget this harebrained notion."

"I'll need you to give me a leg up, Larson." Kelly patiently overlooked his gruffness. She'd already decided that she wasn't going to worry about pleasing him.

"Okay, but I'm not responsible for what happens."

"That's right," she agreed amicably, "you're not."

The stable hands scrambled for a seat on the

fence. Kelly noticed that Marcy had quit stirring gravel with her boot and had instead found a perch on the far rail.

Kelly glanced up at Doug sitting on his horse. "Lead Baritone around in a small circle to settle him down. I'll mount up quickly, then you lead him in small circles again until I tell you otherwise."

"Yes, ma'am."

Kelly turned to Larson. "When I give you the signal, give me a leg up and then get out of the way."

"You don't have to worry about that," he muttered begrudgingly.

"Doug," Kelly called, "stop him for a second and give me room to mount."

Doug pulled Baritone to a halt and angled his horse away. Kelly and Larson moved in between the horses.

"Now," Kelly ordered. Larson grasped her left knee and ankle in his hands and lifted her into the saddle. Baritone tried to buck, but Doug kept the colt's head high, so he could only hop a little.

"Turn him in a circle," Kelly demanded as soon as she hit the saddle. For a few minutes, it was tricky, but after a few circles, the colt gave up on the idea of bucking.

"Good boy," Kelly soothed, leaning over to pat the horse's neck affectionately. "Now, Baritone, you and I are going for a little ride." Kelly wedged her feet into the stirrups as Doug led Baritone around the first turn.

"Push him into a canter," Kelly called as she stood in the irons to relax the colt. Doug pushed his quarter horse faster so that Baritone would break into a rolling canter.

Kelly felt the colt pull against the bit, reveling in his first release of motion and spirit.

As they rounded the second turn, the strong wind stung her eyes and reddened her cheeks, but Baritone threw his nose out and reached for more ground.

"Unsnap your lead, Doug, and fall back. I'll take him from here."

"Sure thing, Ms. Smith." Doug did as he was told, and as he slipped out of her peripheral vision, Kelly crouched over the colt's neck and reached up on his neck to give him some rein. Baritone surged forward, lengthening his stride.

The head wind nearly stole the breath from her lungs as the pines ringing the track flashed by in a blur.

Kelly felt alive, balancing on the edge. In the span of a few seconds, she and the horse blended into one force thundering down the backstretch. The pent-up emotions she'd stored over the past weeks were left in their wake. For the moment she was free.

On the far turn, Kelly took up on the reins to steady the colt. As they came around the final turn, she felt him begin to shorten his stride. In the homestretch, he faded altogether. She gave him more rein and pressed the heels of her hands against his neck, but the colt didn't respond. She knew something was wrong. Everything in Baritone's past, everything in his training had taught him to pour it on at this time. For all of his eagerness minutes ago, he wasn't responding now.

Kelly decided not to press him. She straightened her knees, stood in the stirrups, and gave a steady pull on the reins. Baritone slowed to a canter and then to a trot.

Kelly posted for several strides, then pulled Baritone down to a jog. She glanced around looking for Larson or Doug but was surprised when Tanner McCrey stepped into view.

"What in the hell do you think you're doing?"

Kelly watched as he crossed the track in long, angry strides. When he was next to Baritone, he grabbed the colt's bridle and snapped on a lead rope. "Are you out of your mind?" he demanded.

Baritone lunged away at the harsh sound of Tanner's voice, and Kelly had to struggle to maintain her balance. "You're spooking him," she warned.

Their eyes locked stubbornly.

"Then I suggest you get off him—now!"

When Jim Larson moved up to take the lead rope, Kelly caught a glimpse of his smug expression. On the other side of the colt Tanner's face was grim as he reached out to help Kelly down.

"I'm fine," she insisted, as her feet hit the ground. She glared at him, and he quickly released her arm.

"Cool him out, Larson," Tanner ordered curtly.

Larson motioned the stable hands to head toward the barn, and they fell in behind him as he led Baritone away.

Tanner turned and began striding away. "I'd like a word with you, *Ms.* Smith!"

Kelly glanced at her retreating staff and knew by their sheepish looks that the proverbial something was about to hit the fan.

"You're the boss, *Mr.* McCrey," she conceded as she matched his brisk, determined gait.

As far as she was concerned, now was as good a time as any to see who was going to train this horse—Tanner McCrey or Kelly Smith.

Chapter Four

A strained silence surrounded the two as they marched down the lane leading away from the barns. Tension radiated between them in waves, and an edgy restlessness echoed in their clipped steps.

Tanner flexed his broad shoulders and twisted his neck inside the collar of his flannel shirt. He was damned uncomfortable.

Tanner knew he was thinking like a male chauvinist, but he wished his new trainer were a man, a man like Charlie Bailey—a wise, comfortable old man, someone who'd use some common sense, someone he could depend on. . . . His thoughts faltered as he recalled the accusations being leveled against the deceased trainer, and his mood went from annoyed to irritated.

He stopped walking abruptly and turned to face Kelly. "I can't believe you'd ride that colt! He's thrown half the exercise boys in Arkansas. You could've broken your sweet neck!"

Kelly released a long sigh as her eyes unwillingly studied him from head to toe. Though he was dressed in denims and a blue-checked flannel shirt, there was an unmistakable quality that set him apart from the rest. Distracted the day before by her troubles on the road, she'd tried to tell herself that he was just a man, but the rationale wouldn't work today. In his lean, muscular, upright stance there lurked a confidence bred from being the man in charge.

And now the man in charge thought he was going to tell her how to do her job.

She sensed that doubt about her ability was at the root of his concern. Maybe because of her sex, maybe her age. It wasn't the first time she'd had to deal with this kind of apprehension. In the horse business she'd had to prove herself to every client and to every trainer she'd ever worked for, including her father. She should have gotten used to it by now, but today, for some reason, it bothered her more than usual. She reminded herself to be diplomatic; getting herself fired wouldn't help her accomplish her purpose.

"I think I know which ones I can handle," she said evenly, "and which ones to leave alone."

She realized that the same could apply to the way she felt about men. As a rule she knew exactly which men she could handle and which ones to leave alone. Tanner definitely fit into the latter category.

The dawning light shot gold through his dark hair, and his crystal-blue eyes were unapologetically direct. From his broad chest emanated power, a natural power without arrogance or pretense, a power born of strength and nurtured by experience.

It was a potent combination, impossible for her

to ignore. Tanner McCrey was unambiguously male. Like his handsome colt, he was outstanding. Kelly couldn't help thinking that he was easily one of the most extraordinary men she'd ever encountered.

Now, she realized that dealing with him might be the biggest challenge she would face at Pinetop. "Your colt is strong and spirited," she began, "but he isn't mean. And I had help," she added, trying to keep the defensive note from rising in her voice.

She could see a muscle working tightly in his jaw as his dark eyes surveyed her delicate cheekbones, her slender shoulders and her narrow hips. He knew Baritone's brute strength; the colt had thrown him several times when he'd helped Larson break him to ride. He recoiled at the thought of what a hard fall under twelve hundred pounds of thrashing equine could do to her.

"Look, I don't know what you're trying to prove," he said more harshly than he'd intended, "but don't try it again."

"I was merely getting a feel for the horse. The animal was completely under my control."

She suddenly found herself wishing that Tanner were like some of her former clients: absent. It wasn't unusual for an owner to leave a horse with a trainer for the entire season, seeing his horse only when it ran a race, but Kelly had the feeling she wasn't going to be so lucky.

"We pay jockeys like Jay Moran to take the

risks," he reminded. "He's used to taking hard knocks from rambunctious colts."

Her chin lifted stubbornly. "I can't see calling a jockey for a routine morning workout."

"Then ask one of our boys to ride the horse!" Tanner was not accustomed to debating with employees. As a rule his suggestions were the final say around Pinetop, and he wasn't about to treat her any differently because she was a woman.

"Physical strength is rarely necessary to ride a horse, Mr. McCrey—good judgment is. The colt isn't the problem."

Though her gaze drifted to the mountains, where autumn had turned the leaves of hard maples, white oaks and hickory trees to the color of flame, her attention never strayed from Tanner McCrey.

Drawing a deep breath, she added, "And from now on, if you don't approve of something I'm doing, I'd rather you discussed the matter with me privately."

His gaze raked her up and down. Under different circumstances she'd be a woman he'd have to know . . . thoroughly. But not this time, he thought. Not this woman. Kelly Smith was trouble. If there was anything he'd learned from his father's experience, it was never to get personally involved with female employees, especially a high-spirited, green-eyed, female employee. His life was complicated enough as it was.

"Fair enough, Ms. Smith. From now on we'll

handle our differences privately, but I will expect my orders to be followed without question," he stated.

"I can't promise that."

His head whipped around, and his eyes widened as he looked at her. The snapping green emeralds that silently challenged him made him think of the day before and how beguiling she'd looked under that layer of mud when he'd found her beside the road. Her head was tilted and her chin lifted with the same unsettling, stubborn pride he'd seen in her the day before.

His gaze slid to her mouth, and he recalled the stream of curses that had spilled from them when her mare had towed her downhill. The suggestion of a smile suddenly appeared at the corners of his mouth.

"Is there something you find amusing, Mr. McCrey?"

Kelly found his expression exasperating—but appealing at the same time. The man puzzled her; he was harsh one moment and gentle the next. She found his moods strangely exhilarating, compelling, even attractive.

"You looked like you were about to start swearing again," he said.

She met his gaze evenly. For an instant they wordlessly acknowledged the memory of yesterday with a small smile. Like sharing an inside joke, they felt warm and amused until the mood developed into a sudden feeling of intimacy.

"Keep talking that way," she warned lightly, "and I'll get there." She had a fierce temper, and she knew it.

For a moment Tanner had a strong urge to draw her into his arms and kiss her. It was a notion that could get out of hand quickly. A wave of unexpected desire rocked him, and he quickly looked away. Curiosity, he told himself as he swallowed against a dry throat. It was nothing more than simple curiosity. Clearing his throat to cover his discomfort, he avoided looking at her again, hoping she hadn't recognized the raw need that had overtaken him without warning.

It annoyed him to think that she could have read his thoughts, and he didn't pause to choose his words carefully. His tone was brusque as he sought to put some emotional distance between them. "My point is I don't need my trainer in traction or worse, and I can't afford to make another mistake at this point. From now on, you stay off the horse. Train him, but stay out of the saddle."

So that's it, she thought. So that's what it's all about? Kelly's heartbeat picked up tempo as her temper surfaced again. He doesn't want another business setback. Was that all her father's death had been to him? A business setback?

She seethed anew when she recalled how Tanner McCrey hadn't lifted one finger to get to the bottom of the truth concerning Charlie—truth that could have spared her father's reputation. She wanted to scream; she wanted to lash out at him, but she forced her emotions in check, choking back her bitterness. Telling Tanner McCrey what she thought of him would gain nothing.

"I've been riding all my life, Mr. McCrey."

Her face was pale, but her eyes were lit with fire. Tanner had a sinking feeling she was just about to call his bluff. And there wouldn't be a damn thing he could do about it, if he wanted his horse ready to race by spring.

She took a deep breath and went on. "There are advantages to riding the horses I train, and I refuse to give up those advantages. I either ride the horse, or I walk—right now."

Tanner's brow lifted. "You wouldn't."

Her eyes met his. "Try me."

He heard the defiance in her voice, and his wiser instincts told him not to back her into a corner. He sensed that he'd get the best from her if he gave her some creative leeway, but there was something about her crisp, professional veneer that wouldn't let him leave well enough alone. "I should call you on this one, but I won't. The other trainers—"

"I'm not like those trainers, sir."

Tanner bristled at the "sir." She was making him feel twenty years older than he was.

"When I was a child, I wanted to be a jockey," she told him, "until I decided I liked training better. By then, I'd done a lot of riding."

She turned and started back toward the barns. It

gave her a measure of satisfaction when, after a second's hesitation, he fell into step beside her. "When you ride a horse yourself," she said, angling a glance his way, "you get a feel for him. You know whether his mouth is soft or hard."

She paused and looked directly into his eyes. "You learn his preferences firsthand," she continued, enjoying the grudging admiration she was beginning to see seep into his eyes, "his quirks, his strengths, his faults, rather than taking someone else's word for it. And you're able to sense when a colt is in trouble."

"Are you insinuating that something is wrong with my horse, Ms. Smith?"

"He isn't one hundred percent fit," she responded without missing a beat.

His face darkened. "You want to tell me what you mean by that?" If he didn't miss his guess, she was hopping mad at the moment and not the least bit afraid of him or anyone else, but she wasn't going to drop bombshells like that one and walk away. "The colt looked all right to me today," he challenged.

"He felt good until the final turn." They began to walk again, and her gaze drifted to the exact spot on the oval track where she'd felt Baritone let up.

"Maybe he needed more incentive. Jay would have poured it on him," Tanner accused.

"I've heard that Jay never had to pour it on until

his last race. It's my understanding that Baritone always had plenty of kick in the homestretch."

"You seem to know a lot about a colt you've just seen for the first time."

Kelly realized that she'd probably said more than enough to raise his suspicions, and she began to back off. "I've done my homework," she said, shrugging.

"You've watched him race?"

"On videotape." That seemed to satisfy him, so she broached her primary concern. "I've been thinking it might be a good idea to have the colt checked out."

"Baritone is watched more closely than any horse in the stable, but if you feel there's a problem, you have to talk to Rob about it."

"Rob?"

"Rob—my brother. He does all the vet work around here."

"And where do I find this Rob?"

"You'll meet him this evening at the barbecue. Be at the house around six." They paused at the doorway to the first barn and turned to face each other. "You'll meet a few of the people you'll be working with and a few you'll be competing against."

A command performance, Kelly thought, simmering. His invitation assumed her attendance, and she wasn't surprised. Tanner McCrey was a man accustomed to having the last word.

"I'll try to make it," she said nonchalantly, hoping to bargain for a concession to her next request. "In the meantime, I'd like to arrange for a second opinion on the colt. It couldn't hurt."

"If there's something wrong with Baritone, Rob will find it." Tanner's tone left no room for argument. "Most bighearted, hard-running horses suffer nagging injuries from time to time, the same as any good athlete."

"And you assume that's why Baritone didn't make a better showing in his last race?"

He eyed her coolly. "I make it a point never to assume anything, Ms. Smith. I suggest you do the same while you work here."

She returned his gaze just as coldly. "I want to read the notes Charlie Bailey made before and after the colt's last race. I understand your housekeeper gave his journal to you."

"I gave the journal to Larson since he's been in charge of the colt's conditioning until now." His brow lifted fractionally. "You knew Charlie?"

"I was one of his apprentices for a few years . . . before going to Europe." At least that much was true.

"Yes . . . I believe Zack mentioned that." Tanner wondered why he had the niggling feeling there was more to it than she was telling.

Kelly glanced away, aware of the growing curiosity in his eyes.

Their heads turned at the sound of metal scraping

wood as someone slid open a side door. Doug stepped into the first paddock and released a leggy black colt. The black cantered in circles, his hoof-beats thundering like a drum roll.

Kelly glanced at Tanner who was watching the horse. Before she could decide otherwise, she blurted the question that had haunted her for weeks. "Surely, you don't believe that nonsense in the rag sheets about Charlie trying to steal your colt?"

Tanner turned, and his expression was hard to read as his eyes moved over her with a practiced ease. "It's not my place to judge the man. That's up to the authorities."

"What authorities? No one seems to be doing anything to dispel the rumors."

Tanner thought that for an instant he saw a glint of outrage in her eyes, but on closer inspection, he wasn't sure. "The sheriff handled the matter," he said.

"Is he following up any leads?"

He looked at her oddly. "I believe the case has been officially closed."

Kelly felt like someone had just kicked her in the stomach. She fixed her gaze on the black as he restlessly paced the perimeter of his enclosure.

"That's unfortunate. Charlie was an honest man," she said softly.

Tanner shrugged noncommittally. "So they say. Don't forget the barbecue. Tonight—six."

She nodded absently.

Tanner left the barn and slipped behind the wheel of his truck. Kelly watched as he backed the truck around, then sped down a gravel road out of sight.

She struggled to stem the rising tears of frustration. Case closed, she thought bitterly.

Over *her* dead body.

A FEW MINUTES LATER Kelly strode into the barn and asked for Larson. Doug told her that he'd gone to the north paddock to work with the yearlings, so she spent the rest of the morning directing the workouts of two Pinetop horses that had returned from autumn racing schedules.

After lunch she climbed onto the golf cart her father had used and drove down the lane to check on the brood mares. Doug had said that Larson had turned her mare out with the Pinetop brood mares early that morning. Easing off the gas, she allowed the cart to coast to a stop as she scanned the fields for Happy Talk.

It annoyed Kelly that Larson hadn't checked with her first. Before introducing any animal to the brood mare band, he should have first quarantined it for ten days. It was a routine health procedure, one that would be enforced as long as she was the trainer at Pinetop.

Approximately twenty brood mares were bunched together grazing on what was still good pasture. Hay was available to them in a large round feed bunk nearby, but they preferred to pick at the grass that hadn't been caught yet by the early frosts.

Happy Talk was standing apart, eyeing the others from a safe distance. Kelly called to her, and the bay mare lifted her head and pricked her ears in Kelly's direction.

Bobbing her head and swishing her tail, Happy Talk walked briskly to Kelly and shoved her nose over the fence into her hands.

"Well, hello there," Kelly whispered, rubbing the soft skin on the mare's nose. "Looks like they didn't roll out the welcome mat for you, did they?"

Kelly ran a critical gaze over the horse from nose to tail. There were several places where the mare's dark hide showed signs of unfriendly teeth and hooves. She glanced up to see a large chestnut mare take a few threatening steps in their direction and stop. The boss of the herd, Kelly surmised, and probably the one who'd given Happy Talk a licking to enforce the pecking order.

Kelly frowned as she examined the nicks and cuts more closely. At least the mare hadn't been seriously injured. She returned to the cart and rummaged through a box of supplies stored in the back. Grabbing a black jar, she carried it with her as she climbed the white board fence.

Happy Talk stood patiently while Kelly gently smeared the yellow salve on her wounds.

"From now on don't get too close to them, girl,"

Kelly said as she smoothed her palm down the wide blaze that nearly covered the mare's face.

The bald-faced mare. A faint smile touched her lips as she recalled Charlie saying that Happy Talk always looked like someone had hit her in the face with a sack of flour.

Charlie had wanted this particular mare for a long time. When her previous owner had been down on his luck, he'd given the mare to Charlie to pay for a long-overdue training bill. Last year Charlie had given the mare to her for her twenty-seventh birthday. Tears pricked the back of Kelly's eyes again as she determinedly pushed the memory aside.

"Give them time," she said softly, nodding toward the band of mares who were eyeing them curiously. "They'll accept you eventually." As she spoke, Kelly realized that her advice would apply to herself as well.

"But then again," she added, "we may not stick around that long."

LATER, KELLY TWISTED the doorknob and walked inside her office. Again Larson was nowhere to be found. She wondered what the man did all day and if he ever reported to anyone.

Settling into her desk chair, she accessed the computer to read Charlie's entries on Baritone. They verified that Baritone had been thoroughly checked by Dr. Rob McCrey before and after his last race. Both checkups had included X rays of the colt's legs.

Curiously enough, Kelly discovered that there were no entries for the week before Charlie's death. That wasn't like Charlie. He'd made daily entries on the computer and in his journal. He wouldn't have skipped a week, Kelly thought. Perhaps someone had erased the information. She wondered if Charlie's journal might contain his final entries.

According to Tanner, Larson had the journal now. But where was Larson, she fumed, tossing a pencil across the desk.

She'd driven to the north paddock after seeing Happy Talk. A man repairing the fence had said that Larson hadn't shown up there.

Back at the barn Doug had told her that Larson hadn't returned yet.

"The runaround," she muttered, as she shut off the computer, "all I've gotten so far is the royal runaround." She rose and walked to the door. Slipping her down jacket off the hook, she glanced around the room, taking in the sofa, two armchairs and the scarred desk with the computer.

If only rooms could talk, she thought again as she closed the door behind her and headed toward her truck.

TWENTY MINUTES LATER Kelly pulled into the outskirts of Hot Springs, Arkansas. Glancing at the old Victorian mansions on either side of the road, she had the feeling that she'd just stepped back in time.

She passed a hospital, a small shopping center and clusters of motel cottages. Closer to the heart of the little city, she noticed that parking must be at a premium because tiny lots had been blasted into the solid stone mountains that flanked the narrow road.

Straight ahead loomed the Majestic Hotel, the first of two palatial hotels that had dominated two ends of Central Avenue since the twenties. The road took a wide turn and divided around a fountain, then widened into the broad splendor of the main boulevard.

Kelly eased off the accelerator to coast along and take in the sights. It was a city of contrasts, uniquely set within a national forest, where a string of strip joints huddled in the shadows of a cathedral. Ornate carvings on stone and wrought iron balconies defined the exquisite charm of historic buildings that housed restaurants and a kaleidoscope of tourist shops.

Standing proudly beside Hot Springs Mountain was The Arlington Hotel. Kelly pulled into a parking place on the street and gazed up row upon row of steep steps to the massive columns and sweeping veranda of the elegant turn-of-the-century hotel.

For decades, people had come here to unwind in

the thermal baths and to thrill to the racing season. The fifth season, the locals called it, February through April, when many of the nation's best Thoroughbreds raced. Charlie had called it a magical season in a magical place. Now Kelly was beginning to understand why.

After dropping a coin into the parking meter, Kelly trotted across the street. She turned to stroll beneath the dappled shade of bare-branched magnolia trees to Arlington Park. Above her the hiking trails crisscrossing the mountain wilderness were dotted with tourists snapping pictures.

She paused at a bench where an elderly gentleman sat looking drowsily at his paper in the afternoon sun. She cleared her throat. "Excuse me, could you give me directions to the sheriff's office?"

The man nodded his silver head amiably and pointed out the route. "Just down the road, young 'un."

"Yes . . . so I see . . . thank you."

Kelly turned away as unshed tears blurred her vision again. She felt a compelling need to walk until she had herself under control. The old man's gestures had reminded her of Charlie.

She set off down Bath House Row, briskly blinking back the tears. Her memories eventually eased, and she was able to turn her attention to the elaborate bathhouses.

Once resplendent with marble fountains, brass

railings and stained glass, only one bathhouse remained open to capture the thermal springs that bubbled to the earth's surface nearby. According to his letters, Charlie had been a regular there, claiming that the baths had done wonders for his arthritis.

Kelly walked to an outdoor area where one spring was left open for the public to explore. She dangled her fingertips in the steaming flow and watched a couple of children splash each other and shriek their delight.

Her thoughts returned to her purpose for coming to Pinetop Farm and Hot Springs. With a deep breath, she stiffened her resolve and strode back to her truck. Soon she was heading in the direction of the sheriff's office.

The square, one-story building was a far cry from the ornate architecture of downtown Hot Springs. Outside, a sign heralded tickets to the Halloween Spook House and charity raffle were on sale there. Inside, the smell of stale tobacco and coffee permeated the air.

Kelly approached a middle-aged, no-nonsense-looking woman sitting at the front desk. "Excuse me . . . I wonder if I could speak to the sheriff?" Her eyes wandered beyond the woman to the two office doorways. One was closed, and the other was open. She could hear a man's voice and bits of a one-sided conversation.

The woman at the desk cleared her throat,

bringing Kelly's attention back to her. "Sheriff's on the phone," she said crisply. "Your name?"

"Oh . . . he doesn't know me. I'm new in this area and I just thought I'd drop by and introduce myself."

"He's not expecting you?" The woman looked Kelly up and down and brought her curious gaze back to her face.

"No." As soon as the word was out of her mouth, Kelly could see by the woman's change in expression that she was losing ground.

"Sheriff Patterson's busy. If you'll tell me the nature of your business . . ." The woman raised her dark brows expectantly.

"Actually," Kelly began, "I won't take but a minute. If I could just speak to him—"

"Calling headquarters, this is car number two," announced a disembodied voice. A rush of static crackled from the dispatcher's control panel as the woman spun her chair ninety degrees to flip a switch. "Headquarters. Come in number two."

Kelly's eyes returned to the doorway. A heavyset man in a dark blue law enforcement uniform was leaning against the door frame watching her. Smiling, he crooked a finger to motion her to his office.

"Hold it!" the woman snapped as Kelly swung open a wooden gate and took a step. "Where do you think you're going?"

"It's all right, Gracie," the man said. "I have a minute."

"But, Sheriff, you have a meeting with Judge Feister—"

"Let me know when Harold gets here," he called over his shoulder amicably.

Kelly seized her opportunity and strode into the sheriff's office. He closed the door behind her and gestured toward a chair opposite his desk.

"Thank you so much for seeing me," she began. "I know I shouldn't barge in like this."

"Don't worry about it—coffee?"

"No, thank you."

The sheriff walked to the stained coffee maker and poured himself a fresh cup. "What can I do for you, young lady?"

"Well, my name is Smith, and—"

"You're not from around here, are you?" It was a statement, not a question. The sheriff turned his small dark eyes, shadowed by overhanging brows, to look at her. She knew that he was taking in every detail of her simple dress and low-heeled shoes, her handbag, her face. His eyes lingered on her hair and narrowed.

"I'm from Louisiana." Kelly self-consciously brought her hand up to smooth the cropped ends of her hair. "I'm replacing Charlie Bailey at Pinetop Farm." She watched for a reaction, but the mention of Charlie's name didn't faze the sheriff.

A silence fell across the room as he stirred his coffee absently. Noting her silence, he lifted his heavy brows and inclined his head, signaling her to continue.

"I just dropped in to buy some tickets for the charity raffle," she murmured, remembering her excuse.

"You could have bought tickets from Gracie."

"Yes, but I thought since I was here I would introduce myself," she said with a casual smile.

"I see." He studied her a moment before seating himself behind his desk. Leaning back in his chair, he clasped his hands behind his head and studied her momentarily. Though his posture appeared relaxed, his eyes remained sharp.

"Sheriff Patterson is it?"

He nodded.

"I was wondering where you stand on the Bailey case."

The sheriff took a sip of coffee. "You knew Mr. Bailey?"

"I worked for him a few years ago."

He allowed himself a hint of a smile as he leaned forward in his chair. "Is that Miss or Mrs. Smith?"

"Miss Smith."

He nodded. "How was it you and Mr. Bailey came to meet?"

"I'd heard he was the best horse trainer around, and I wanted to become his apprentice."

"And did you?"

"Yes, sir. For five years."

"I see. He turned his chair and rocked back to look at her from a different angle.

Kelly's nerves were strung taut. She decided to drop diplomacy and get to the heart of her visit. "Sheriff, I'm concerned about the rumors going around about Charlie." She edged forward in her chair. "There was no way Charlie Bailey would have tried to kidnap Mr. McCrey's derby contender."

"How do you know that, Miss Smith?"

"Charlie was an honest man, a man of integrity, and it's imperative that his name be cleared. I think the matter deserves a thorough investigation, including his alleged heart attack." She hadn't meant to be so blunt, but she wasn't in the mood to tiptoe around it any longer.

"Alleged heart attack?" His right brow lifted. "The man died of a heart attack. No question of that. Do you have evidence to the contrary?"

"No, but I knew Charlie. I thought if we compared notes, it might shed more light on what really happened."

"Well, I don't suppose it could do any harm, though I'll warn you, there may be some matters I won't be free to discuss."

"I understand that." She swallowed nervously, and the sheriff's eyes followed the movement in her throat.

He doesn't miss a thing, Kelly realized as a renewed feeling of frustration began to churn inside her stomach. "Where were Charlie's nitro pills?" she asked.

Marc Patterson's face softened as he attempted to appease her. "Charlie's prescription bottle was found in the area where he'd loaded McCrey's horse."

"Charlie always kept his pills in his shirt pocket in case of an emergency."

"I'm sure that's right, but an employee at Pinetop found the bottle in the yard." His gaze softened even more. "Perhaps it had fallen out of Mr. Bailey's pocket," he supplied.

Kelly's forehead knitted in a tight frown. "Who found the bottle?"

"Jim Larson, I believe."

A knot of tension rose in her throat. Jim Larson. She might have known. "Have you questioned Larson?" There was an edge to her voice, part impatience and part something else. "And what about the others—"

"Of course. I've talked with everyone concerned with the case." His tone remained noncommittal, and Kelly could see she was raising his suspicions.

"I read in the paper that a ransom note was found in Charlie's pocket," she continued.

The sheriff nodded.

"Have you ordered a handwriting analysis?"

He shook his head. "Wouldn't prove anything."

Her eyes widened in disbelief. "It could prove that Charlie wasn't involved in a criminal act. It could clear him. For all we know, Charlie may have been murdered." In spite of herself, she could feel the needling of tears behind her eyes, and she swallowed hard to push them back.

"Exactly what was Bailey to you, Miss Smith?"

"A friend." And much more, she thought. But she couldn't tell the sheriff that. "Horse people may compete, but they're a tight-knit group, and we all want to see Charlie's name cleared. No one who knew him believes that he was stealing that horse."

The sheriff rolled a pencil back and forth under his thick fingers as he studied the slender young woman with the iron will. He released a long sigh. "A handwriting analysis would be useless, ma'am. The note was nothing but a scrawl. And even if it wasn't written by Mr. Bailey, it's possible that an accomplice wrote it."

Kelly came to her feet angrily. " 'Accomplice!' The kidnapping accusation is ludicrous enough, but now he had an accomplice! A trainer can move a colt for any number of reasons without raising a suspicion of theft. So a note was found—no one can prove it was Charlie's note or that he had anything to do with it. But based on that unidentifiable scrawl, a man's reputation is tainted by scandal." She was outraged. "It just isn't fair."

"Miss Smith, no crime took place at Pinetop that day. A man died of a heart attack. Period. The coroner ruled out foul play. Now granted it is unfortunate that some members of the press tried to make news out of a note found at the scene, but as far as I'm concerned, the case is closed."

"Closed? It can't be! Someone framed Charlie. Whoever it was is covering up something—can't you see that?"

"Lady, I have twenty-seven open cases currently under investigation by our office where a crime *did* take place. Now I share your concerns over clearing a man's good name, but we're understaffed. We don't have time to probe into peculiar circumstances where no crime actually happened." The sheriff placed his palms atop his desk and leaned forward, a sure sign that his patience was growing thin. "When you bring me concrete evidence that a crime has been committed, then we'll talk."

"I don't have concrete evidence," she murmured, "I just know Charlie is innocent."

"I'm not saying he's guilty of anything. But I can't do more. I'm sure Mr. Bailey would be gratified to know he has friends who care, and if new evidence turns up, we'll reevaluate the case at that time. Until then," he looked at her emphatically, "the case is closed."

CASE IS CLOSED! Case is closed! Kelly mocked heatedly as she stood peeking between the slats of her window blinds at the crowd gathering around the pool for the McCrey barbecue. The devil it was.

She glanced at the clock on the nightstand and frowned. She should have been dressed and out the door ten minutes ago, but she was light years away from a party mood. If Tanner hadn't made it clear that her presence was required, she would gladly have eaten a peanut butter sandwich and gone straight to bed. With a groan of resignation, she walked to her closet.

Ten minutes later her gaze roamed over the sea of strangers as she made her way across the lawn. Self-consciously, she ran her fingers through her close-cropped hair and prayed that no one would recognize her.

She knew her connection to Charlie couldn't remain a secret forever. Someone, sooner or later, would realize who she was. Horse people traveled in the same circles. She just hoped she'd have enough time to unravel the mystery of her father's death before the word got around. She suspected that when Tanner found out, he'd fire her on the spot.

The sun was dipping behind the mountains, splashing the sky with an explosion of autumn colors that rivaled those in the forests. Kelly paused to stand in the shadow of a tall white pine at the periphery of the gathering. This distance and darkness permitted her to study people before they knew they were being observed.

Her eyes scanned the faces, trying to read every pair of eyes. Logic suggested that whoever had framed her father would be there.

The buzz of conversation reached her ears, sprinkled with enthusiastic speculation about the Arkansas Derby just six months away.

Rubbing her damp palms together, Kelly realized that she couldn't stand on the sidelines forever. She'd have to mingle. She advanced to the edge of the swimming pool, where a mist of steam was rising into the crisp evening air. She planned to make it a short evening. Extremely short.

Chapter Five

Smiling pleasantly at the young couples sipping drinks at the poolside tables, Kelly made her way to the large white tent set up on the lawn behind the McCrey house.

She strolled through the tent, inhaling the aromas of slowly simmered barbecued beef that came to her from the buffet. With an appreciative nod she accepted a glass of champagne from a tray as she moved through the crowd.

The guests were of all ages, their dress ranging from denim to satin. Occasional bursts of laughter interrupted the chatter, and tableware clattered at the long, white-covered tables where diners had gathered.

Failing to find even one familiar face, Kelly moved out of the tent and crossed the grass to the large stone terrace that ran the length of the house.

She glanced up to see Tanner standing above her, idly leaning against the low patio wall as he watched her. His appreciative gaze skimmed over her trim figure.

"Hello," Kelly said.

Tanner lifted his glass in a silent toast to her excellent taste in clothes. "Very nice."

She nodded demurely. "Thank you."

He realized he had been looking forward to seeing her in a dress, but the way the cashmere softly clung to her curves was even nicer than he'd imagined.

Climbing the three cobblestone steps, she joined him on the wide terrace. Even in the pale light, the Wedgewood blue of his shirt made his eyes appear more striking and his tan more pronounced. She'd never seen him in anything but rugged work clothes, and her eyes showed her appreciation of the subtle print tie and tweed sport coat he'd chosen.

He touched the rim of his glass to hers lightly. "Glad you could make it."

The irony wasn't lost on her. She was unfashionably late.

"One of your yearlings thinks he's a jumper," she said by way of an excuse. "He received some minor injuries, and I couldn't get away for a while."

"Oh? And what yearling was that, Ms. Smith?"

"High Roller. He tried to take a fence, missed, skinned his shins and knocked down the two top rails of a corral."

Kelly knew she could have been on time if she'd left after tending Roller's abrasions, but because she'd been dreading the party, she'd insisted on hanging around to oversee the fence repair. It was a task she could have easily delegated, and she realized Tanner must know it.

But he accepted her excuse with a smile and slipped his hand beneath her elbow to steer her across the terrace and into the milling crowd. Kelly soon discovered Tanner McCrey not only was handsome to a fault, but he also had impeccable manners.

He guided her through the invited guests with graceful ease, pausing occasionally to introduce her to his friends, neighbors and competitors. Had she not been so nervous about being recognized, she might have enjoyed herself. The party was well organized, the music good, the food delicious and the people friendly.

Everyone seemed to be enjoying themselves. Except for Jim Larson who stood off alone, eyeing the festivities with a jaundiced eye. He was leaning against a column, one leg crossed negligently over the other, watching. When Kelly spotted him, she smiled and nodded. She was surprised to see his jaw tense and his expression grow sour. A moment later he turned and walked off.

"I have a feeling Jim doesn't like me," Kelly commented lightly to Tanner.

Tanner glanced up to see his foreman striding in the opposite direction. "Jim? I wouldn't worry about him. Give him a little time. He'll come around."

Kelly wasn't so sure.

As they paused to freshen their drinks, a small, balding man scurried up to Tanner's side and stood shifting his weight from one foot to the other. As if curiosity had gotten the best of him, he leaned forward, peering around Tanner to study Kelly more closely. Kelly glanced up, letting her side of the conversation falter.

"Hello," he said, then gave her a swift nod.

She smiled. "Hello."

"Hello, Mr. McCrey."

"Hello, Bill. Glad you could come." Tanner could see the strange little man was making Kelly uneasy with his less than discreet perusal of her.

"Thanks . . . glad I could make it."

"Bill, I'd like for you to meet our new trainer, Kelly Smith. Kelly, Bill Bolton. Bill handles all my banking needs."

The little man leaned forward again and gave Kelly another eager nod. His movements were so jerky that he reminded Kelly of a chicken pecking at the ground. "Nice to meet you . . . nice . . . uh, Mr. McCrey . . . I thought I might have a word with you . . . privately," Bill urged in a hushed whisper.

Tanner frowned. "Now?"

"Bank business," the man added with a couple more nods.

"Well . . . I . . ." Tanner glanced at Kelly apologetically. "Is it important, Bill?"

Bill bobbed his head a couple of times again quickly. "Only take a minute."

Tanner clearly didn't like the disturbance, but Kelly noticed that he accepted the interruption graciously. "If you'll excuse me, Kelly. This shouldn't take long."

"Of course," she murmured.

Tanner turned and walked toward the main house with the little man following at his heels.

Kelly wandered alone for awhile. Tanner's meeting was taking longer than she'd expected. Crossing the terrace, she paused at the low wall and gazed up at the clear night sky alight with stars.

"Nice party."

She looked down as she recognized Jim Larson's voice below. He was standing on the lawn beside the steps. "Very nice," she agreed.

"If you fit in with these kind," he added.

Kelly was surprised by the comment. The expression in his eyes was mild, but his tone held disdain.

"I hadn't really thought about it," she said. "Do large gatherings make you feel uncomfortable?"

Jim snorted. "Always do. Most of them people got more money than sense. For instance, take a look at that gal." Jim nodded at a woman dancing the two-step with a heavyset man wearing a large white Stetson. "That gold chain she's wearing is heavy enough to tow a truck."

Kelly smiled at his colorful comparison. "Well, chains are popular."

"Point is she's been goin' on all night about her big derby horse. Thinks there's no way in hell she can lose." He spat on the ground, and Kelly winced. "Hell, she don't know a thing about that horse. She's never lifted a finger to make him what he is. All she does is have her sugar daddy foot the bills, and that's supposed to make her an authority on racing."

"And you resent that."

"Don't you?" he asked in a tone that said she was a fool if she didn't. "All these people do is pay the bills and take the credit."

"Wouldn't we be out of a job without them?"

He shrugged. "Point is people like you and me don't fit into this bunch." He cleared the phlegm in his throat and gave Kelly a sidelong glance. "Leastways, I don't." He hauled off and spat again. The spittle landed in a nasty blob at the edge of the walk. "A word to the wise, little lady. Don't trust these people. They'll be nice to you when it suits 'em, and pass you over when it don't. Course now, maybe I'm shootin' off my mouth too much. Maybe you might be plannin' on joinin' 'em one of these days."

Kelly lifted her brows. "Why would you think that?"

"If that mare of yours produces another stakes winner, she might just land you into the big time. That's what you're hoping for, ain't it?"

"No, Jim, actually I was hoping you'd be able to explain why you turned my mare out without holding her in quarantine first."

Jim Larson shrugged. "Didn't figure the rules would apply to the trainer's horse."

"Well, from now on, there'll be no exceptions to

the rules. You should have checked with me first."

His eyes turned accusingly on her again. "Yes, ma'am," he said in a mocking undertone.

"And by the way, I've been looking for you all afternoon. Doug said you were with the yearlings, but I couldn't find you anywhere."

"Are we punchin' the time clock now?"

She shook her head. "No, but I think if we're going to work together, we should have better communication."

"Don't worry. I do my job . . . but I don't answer to you. I answer to Tanner directly."

Ignoring his gibe, Kelly sat down on the low wall. The man was clearly on the defensive with her, and she wondered why. "Jim, I think we've gotten off to a bad start, and that concerns me."

"You just do your job and let me do mine, and we'll get along fine, little lady."

"Agreed, but I am curious about Charlie Bailey's journal. Tanner said he had given it to you, and I'd like to see it."

The lines around his eyes puckered with disgust. "It's in the office, just like I told you before. If you're trying to make trouble for me, you can just . . ." He caught himself before his temper spilled over again.

"I can just what, Mr. Larson?" Her eyes hardened. "Why don't you spell it out for me?"

He returned her glare for a moment, then without another word he turned on his heel and walked away. Kelly watched him stride across the lawn angrily. "That arrogant, stubborn—"

"Nasty little weasel," a breezy voice behind her supplied.

Kelly whirled in surprise. A young man who was still shrugging into his sport coat came toward her grinning.

"My tie straight?" he asked wagging the knot back and forth as he glanced expectantly over his shoulder. "Hell, where's Tanner? He's gonna chew my hide for being late again."

"Tanner's inside talking to a strange little banker named . . ." Kelly searched her memory for a name as the young man came to a halt in front of her, and her hands absently reached out to assist with the obstinate tie. The young man had the kind of boyish appeal that automatically brought out her maternal instincts.

"Bolton?" he guessed.

"Bolton." She nodded. Smoothing the perfect knot, she let her hands fall sheepishly back to her sides. "There, that's better."

The young man straightened his navy blazer and ran a hand through his blond hair, still damp from a shower.

"You look fine," she assured.

"Thanks . . . so do you." She suddenly had his full attention as he issued a low wolf whistle and took a couple of steps backward to admire her more fully. "You must be Kelly."

She grinned. "How'd you know?"

"You fit Tanner's description." From the way the young man was scrutinizing her, Kelly had to wonder exactly how precise Tanner's description had been.

"Oh, by the way, I'm Rob." He grinned. "The disreputable black sheep of the McCrey family."

"Ah, Dr. McCrey, I presume."

He looks too young to be a vet, Kelly thought, and then reminded herself that most people thought she looked too young to be a Thoroughbred trainer.

"Yeah, that's me. Dr. Rob McCrey, D.V.M. And I can see you've already met our congenial farm foreman, Jim Larson, C.O.D."

"C.O.D.?"

"Crusty Old Devil."

Kelly laughed. "Yes, I'm afraid we got off to a bad start."

"Ahh, that Larson is such a party animal," Rob deadpanned. He grinned again, and Kelly knew she was going to like him a lot. "Already taken his little red wagon and gone home, has he?"

"Yes, and I can't say that I miss him," she admitted, candidly. "I'm sorry, I guess I shouldn't have said that."

"Don't worry about it. Jim usually affects people that way."

"Then how does he keep his job?"

"Ah, personnel is big brother's department. My job is to tend the horses and annoy the help."

Kelly chuckled and shook her head. Rob McCrey was an overgrown adolescent and a welcome diversion. She hadn't realized how tense she'd been until he'd made her laugh out loud a minute ago. She couldn't help but wonder though, how effective he was in his profession. He seemed too young, too brash.

But he was easy to be with, and Kelly knew they would get along just fine. Rob was the kind of man who made her feel like a big sister, while his older brother, on the other hand, made her feel anything but sisterly.

"What say you and me step out there on the dance floor and show these stuffed shirts what it's all about?" Rob said temptingly as his eyes scanned the crowd.

"Let's do it, McCrey, D.V.M."

As Rob led her out across the stone terrace, Kelly had the distinct feeling he was looking for someone in particular. They joined the other half dozen couples dancing to the spirited number the combo was playing.

"You're too pretty to be a trainer," he called above the loud music as they moved effortlessly together across the dance floor. "And you dance like Patrick Swayze was your daddy!" he added.

Kelly found Rob to be a breath of fresh air. "Thank you, sir. Bet you say that to all the girls."

"Nah, only ninety percent of them," Rob grinned. "By the way, I took a look at your mare this afternoon. Marcy told me you'd asked because she'd taken a spill yesterday in the trailer."

"Is she all right?"

"She's fine, and so is the foal she's carrying." Kelly was relieved to hear his voice take on a more professional tone when he talked about his work. "And her bumps and scrapes should heal without any scars."

"Thank you, I appreciate it."

"No problem."

"So, what made you want to be a veterinarian?"

He flashed her another engaging grin as he whirled her around, then did a dramatic dip. He stared down at her with a devilish twinkle in his eye. "Who says I want to be one?"

"Don't you? Lots of people would love to have your degree and your skills."

Righting her again, they moved across the floor, commanding the attention of the other dancers. They made a striking couple. "Then let them have them! Just give me an island in the Pacific, a jug of wine, a hunk of cheese, a pretty woman, and just see how fast I'll give up all those degrees and skills."

"You can't mean that!"

Rob just grinned again. Kelly could see she couldn't take anything he said seriously.

"The vet business was my father's idea, not mine," he said.

The music slowed, and he gathered her into his arms as they moved to a slower beat. "I'd like to ask you something," Kelly said, momentarily changing the subject.

"I'm all yours, sweet thing."

"Baritone's record has been puzzling me. Would you mind if I took a look at the X rays you took before his last race?"

"Not at all. They should be in the file cabinet in the office. Like all our records, they're on microfilm. Do you know how to use the viewer?"

"Yes."

"Well, if you need any help, just holler."

"Thanks, I will."

He smiled down at her and cocked his head to study her face and hair. She suddenly felt an alarm go off. He had the strangest look in his eye. Was it possible that he had recognized her? Her heart hammered in her throat.

"It's not polite to stare," she said lightly.

"Did you ever think about doing something to your hair?" he asked bluntly.

Kelly's face flushed hotly, and she shook her head. "No . . . why?" she asked lamely, and knew she shouldn't have. It was obvious that she should consider a change of some kind.

"With your freckles and green eyes you'd make a hell of a redhead," he mused.

"Redhead . . . ? Oh, no. Not me. Too flashy."

"No . . . I don't know . . . what do you think, big

92

bro? Would Kelly make a great-lookin' redhead or what?"

"She'd be stunning," Tanner agreed as he claimed Kelly for the next dance. He smiled down at her, and she felt her pulse quicken with anticipation. The two brothers didn't look at all alike. One was tall, dark and handsome; the other was average height with fair hair and almost pretty features. One was a man, and the other was still a boy.

"Where have you been, Rob?" Tanner asked curtly.

"Conferring with your trainer, where else?"

"He's been filling me in on things," Kelly quickly came to Rob's defense. "Your brother is quite stimulating."

"So I've been told."

A man and woman danced past them. "Rob, Tanner, great party!" Kelly was surprised to hear such a deep voice come from the man's child-sized body.

"Hey, Jay," Rob greeted, clapping the jockey on the back.

"Have you met our new trainer Kelly Smith?"

"Don't believe I have." Jay paused and extended his hand. "Welcome aboard, ma'am."

"Kelly, this is Jay Moran, our regular jockey," Tanner introduced.

"Jay, I've been looking forward to meeting you." Jay's large, callused hand took Kelly's firmly, and she smiled back at a wizened face that looked older than its years.

"Glad to meet you, ma'am," he said.

Kelly looked into his dark eyes, trying to assess his character. Marcy had told her that Jay was one of the last men to see her father alive, and she wondered exactly what he knew about the strange circumstances surrounding Charlie's death.

"Draw any good poker hands lately, Jay?" Rob bantered.

"Nah." Jay shuffled his feet nervously. "I gave up all that gambling stuff." Jay worked his shoulders unconcernedly. "It don't mix with riding."

"You're right, Jay. Riding and gambling don't mix," Rob agreed. "Just see that you remember that when Friday night rolls around."

"Will you quit with that stuff?" Jay shot Rob a warning look. "You're gonna give Ms. Smith the wrong idea about me."

"If she's as smart as I think she is," Rob bantered, "she already has the wrong idea about you."

"Such a kidder, you know?" Jay apologized, looking from Tanner to Kelly plaintively. "Nice party. Every year, a nice party." Jay and his date merged back onto the crowded dance floor.

"Would you like to dance, or would you enjoy a glass of champagne more?" Tanner asked.

Kelly glanced up at him, surprised at how hard it was to quell the urge to flirt with him. "Champagne sounds nice."

"Well, well, well. If it isn't those handsome McCrey brothers."

Kelly tensed. She was getting a little weary of the constant interruptions. It would have been nice to spend a few moments alone in Tanner's company.

"Louise!" When Rob looked at Louise, his face brightened. "Did you just get here?"

"Forgive me, dear, but I had a late appointment. When you show real estate, your time isn't your own, you know." The attractive, fortyish brunette slid her arm through Rob's possessively as she smiled and spoke to Tanner. "I hope you don't mind my bringing Jared along."

Kelly sensed more than felt the tension in Tanner's hand resting on her waist.

"Not at all. Jared," Tanner acknowledged with a distant nod.

"Tanner." A handsome, silver-haired man in his fifties stepped from the shadows. "Long time no see."

"Yes, long time."

"Glad to see you could make it tonight, Jared." Rob reached out to clasp the newcomer's hand.

"Always a pleasure to see you, son." The trim, older man's hand came up to squeeze Rob's shoulder warmly.

Kelly saw the muscle in Tanner's jaw working again. Tanner didn't seem to like this man.

"So, Tanner," Louise said brightly, "this must be your new trainer." Louise smoothed her pencil-slim skirt and offered Kelly her hand. "I'm Louise Cabot—the lady whose horse is going to win the next Arkansas Derby."

"Hello, Louise. I'm Kelly Smith," Kelly smiled and looked Louise straight in the eye, "and we'll just see about that."

"Ah, I like that," Louise laughed. "The girl has fire, Tanner."

"Her conformation's not bad, either," Jared noted with a chuckle as he extended his hand to Kelly. "I'm Jared Huxsman."

Kelly returned his smile politely as they shook hands.

"Have we met before?" Louise prompted as she studied Kelly more closely. "You look somewhat familiar."

"I'm sure we haven't," Kelly said easily.

"Louise, how's your colt, Claimjumper," Rob inquired.

"Fit as a fiddle, getting faster all the time. You boys had better watch out for him," Louise warned. "Speaking of which, when do we get to see your great hope? I'd like to take a look at what a multimillion-dollar ransom can buy." She laughed merrily, unaware her joke had caught Kelly right in the pit of her stomach.

The callous remark stung. Kelly glanced at Tanner who looked equally unamused.

Tanner's mouth curved, but the smile didn't quite reach his eyes. "Now, Louise, you know I like to keep you guessing. You'll be eating Baritone's dust soon enough." He bowed politely. "Now, if you and Jared will excuse us, I've promised Ms. Smith this dance."

"Of course . . . dear." Louise glanced at Jared and shrugged.

IT SEEMED THAT time alone with Tanner was wishful thinking. The evening was a series of one interruption after another. Tanner had tried on two occasions to make a trip to refill their glasses but he'd been intercepted both times by someone who wanted to talk.

Kelly slipped away from the party shortly after ten. The crisp night breeze beckoned to her. She walked along the brick path, realizing that she had been lucky tonight: no one had recognized her.

She found herself wandering toward the barn, Baritone's X rays still on her mind. She slipped a key from her bag and unlocked her office door. Flicking on the light, she stepped inside. Her gaze scanned the room, but she saw no sign of the journal that Larson had insisted was there.

Moving to the file cabinet, she began sorting through the microfilm holders in search of the X rays taken of Baritone's legs before his last race. Something was wrong with the colt; she would bet on it. And if her guess was right, he hadn't been right for some time. The X rays might reveal something that Rob had overlooked.

She searched the files, then searched them again. The holders for the X rays taken that day were empty. Empty!

She sorted through the holders a third time, checking and rechecking to see if the X rays might have been misfiled.

Again she came up empty-handed. Her frustration was at the boiling point. Why was it that everything she wanted to see came up missing?

"Damn. Damn. Damn," she muttered.

"Maybe Rob is right. Red hair would suit your temperament more."

Kelly turned to see Tanner lounging against the door frame.

"What?"

He chuckled. "Did you take swearing lessons from a sailor?"

Kelly heaved a sigh of disgust. "Everything I look for around here is missing."

"What's missing?" Tanner stepped inside, and she noticed he was carrying two glasses of champagne. Extending a glass to her, he waited patiently until she finally accepted it.

Taking a small sip, Kelly waited while the bubbles scampered across her tongue. "Baritone's X rays are missing," she said.

"Oh?"

"Along with Charlie's last journal." She lifted her shoulders and let them drop in frustration. "It's maddening."

Tanner took a sip from his glass thoughtfully. "Are you sure?"

"See for yourself. The X rays are supposed to be in these holders, but they're not. And Larson said the journal was supposed to be in this office, but it's not."

"Is it possible that the X rays may still be at the microfilming company or that someone misfiled them?" He casually settled a hip on the corner of her desk.

"I don't know . . . I suppose it's possible. But they're not where they should be. I've looked through the file cabinet several times."

He inclined his head casually toward the magazine rack at the end of the sofa. "Could that be the journal you're looking for?"

Kelly distractedly set her glass on the desk and moved across the room hurriedly. Sure enough, the journal was lying on top of a stack of magazines in a wicker basket. "Why on earth would Larson put it over there?"

"You'll discover Larson is as absentminded as they come. He has a habit of leaving things in the damnedest places."

Kelly was already thumbing through the journal. Her hands paused as she came to Charlie's last entry. It was dated ten days before his death, a week before Baritone's last race.

"Some of the entries are missing," she said.

She carried the journal across the room to show

him. "See. There aren't any entries before or after Baritone's last race."

When he didn't answer, she glanced up to see that he was staring at her. She hadn't realized that they were standing so close. Her arm brushed his, and their gazes locked. "So, Charlie was never very big on paperwork." He scolded softly, "You know what they say about all work and no play, don't you?"

"My work is my play."

"Not a healthy life-style."

"My hours aren't conducive to a full social life."

"I'll take it up with your boss." They moved closer, and she heard her breathing quicken. For a moment she was tempted to throw caution to the wind and drift into his arms. She knew that if she leaned forward just a little he would kiss her. One kiss. She found herself longing for just one kiss. That would get him out of her system and let her concentrate on her work, something inside her reasoned.

The journal slipped from her fingers and hit the floor with a clatter. She blinked in surprise as she snapped out of the spell he had cast upon her. With a nervous lunge, she went to the floor, scooping up the pages that had torn loose from the binder.

"Here . . . let me help," he offered.

"No," she insisted, "I can handle it."

Breathlessly she shoved the pages inside the notebook and started upward just as Tanner bent to help her. Their heads collided with a crack.

She heard his sharp intake of breath as they both groaned. Backing into the nearest chair, she sat down and rubbed her forehead. She glanced up a moment later and tried to cover a grin as she saw Tanner rubbing his head dazedly.

"Are you all right?"

"Yeah . . . are you?" He started toward her, and she quickly raised a hand to stop him. "No, stay over there!"

He paused. "Why?"

"Just stay!" she ordered.

She set the journal on an end table and took a deep breath. "Look, this isn't going to work." She glanced back at him and realized that she found him attractive. Entirely too attractive. "What I mean is, you're my boss, and I don't . . . get involved with clients. It's a rule I follow very closely. . . ."

A slow smile curved the corners of his mouth. "Are you saying that you find me attractive, Ms. Smith?"

Their eyes met again, and she felt her heart sink like a rock. It was going to be nearly impossible to keep her distance from this man.

"Extremely, Mr. McCrey."

His brow lifted with amusement. "And that's a problem?"

"I think it could be . . . and I don't want that."

Nodding politely, he acceded to her wishes, "You're right. It would be wise for us to keep a professional distance."

She glanced up, surprised she felt such a sense of disappointment with his quick acquiescence. "Yes . . . I think so. . . ."

He lifted his glass to hers again. "I suppose I'm just not used to having a trainer who looks so pretty in pink."

They exchanged a small smile, and Kelly was relieved to let the moment pass.

"Although," he added, "I have been known to break a rule occasionally." He chuckled, giving her the most uneasy feeling.

"Surely not." She shook her head and grinned at him. Leaning back in her chair, she decided to put the incident in its proper perspective.

But she admitted that it would be difficult not to like a man who could admit fault and laugh at himself, too.

Chapter Six

Kelly rarely saw Tanner over the next several days. And she'd had no luck finding the missing training records. Whenever she walked to the barns in the dark hours before dawn, she would see his truck leaving to haul a crew to the acres of timber they were trying to harvest before winter set in. And it was usually after dark when he would pull in and walk wearily back into the house.

One morning when Kelly had finished the early workouts by midmorning and was dashing into her office to thaw out, she smelled the delectable aromas of bacon and fresh coffee.

"If you can't come to the house for a decent breakfast, then the least you can do is sit down here and eat." Hattie was standing behind the desk shaking a napkin to indicate the place she'd set for Kelly.

"Hurry up before everything gets cold," she ordered briskly as she stooped to adjust the space heater to its highest setting and aim it at Kelly's chair. "There now, this will warm you."

Kelly grinned and shrugged out of her down jacket and hung it on a peg by the door. "Hattie, you shouldn't have gone to all this trouble."

"I know it. It would be easier if you'd just come to the house and eat with the boys and me."

From the vehicles she saw parked at the McCrey

house every morning, Kelly figured that Hattie must be cooking for most of Tanner's work crew.

"I don't usually eat much first thing in the morning," Kelly admitted sheepishly, knowing as she said it that it would sound like blasphemy to a woman like Hattie.

"So I've heard." Hattie frowned as she handed the napkin to Kelly and gestured for her to sit.

"I don't like to ride on a full stomach." Kelly inhaled the fragrant aromas as she bit into a slice of crisp bacon. "I usually grab something a little later."

"I've heard—" Hattie poured fresh coffee into Kelly's thermal mug "—a sweet roll or a candy bar?"

Kelly nodded. She hadn't felt this guilty about her eating habits since she'd left home. But Hattie, bundled in her heavy cardigan and double-knit polyester pants, pouring her a glass of fresh-squeezed juice, was making her feel as guilty as her mother ever had.

"Well, I suppose your junk food beats what Charlie Bailey had every morning at ten o'clock."

Kelly's mouth turned up at the amusing memory. "A cold beer?"

"Can you imagine? When I fussed at him about it—" Hattie sniffed "—he offered to add a raw egg to it to make me feel better."

Kelly shook her head affectionately. "Sounds like him."

"You knew of Charlie?" Hattie pulled up a chair to nibble on a wedge of toast while Kelly ate.

Kelly nodded and a knot tightened in her throat. "I worked for him."

"Nice man," Hattie mused, reaching for the jam to spread on her toast. "Lousy eating habits but wonderful manners."

Kelly looked at her plate as she toyed with her scrambled eggs.

"Don't you like your eggs?"

"Oh yes," Kelly murmured, taking a bite to ease the crease in Hattie's brow. "Very good," Kelly said nodding, and Hattie's mouth curved into a contented smile.

"Marcy tells me you're putting in some long hours up here," Hattie scolded.

Kelly nodded. "We all do."

"But you stay later than everyone else."

"Marcy tell you that?"

"Jim Larson did."

"Oh." Kelly accepted a slice of toast from the plate Hattie offered. "Thank you."

"Don't let Larson's attitude bother you, dear. His bark is far worse than his bite."

Kelly wasn't convinced of that. "He doesn't seem to care much for the horse trainers around here of late."

"He's an odd duck but harmless. It's Marcy I'm concerned about."

"Marcy? Why?" Kelly had gotten to know the

stable boys, but Marcy was so quiet that Kelly knew nothing about her except that she was an excellent groom.

"The girl is only eighteen. She was hanging around the track looking for work when Charlie met her. He told me he was afraid she might fall in with a rough crowd over there, so we told Tanner, and he hired her on."

"Charlie always looked out for people."

"He sure did, and Marcy really took a shine to Charlie. He'd started teaching her to ride. Crazy girl has her heart set on becoming a jockey one day."

Kelly took a sip of juice and lowered her glass. "Maybe she will."

"I dou't know. I asked Larson to work with her, but he says he doesn't have the time."

Kelly set her glass down, and her eyes hardened. "No, of course, he wouldn't." So far, she was having a difficult time trying to figure out exactly what kept Mr. Larson so busy. He supervised the feeding schedule and broke the colts, but there were times he disappeared that he didn't account for.

Kelly looked at Hattie. "I could work with her."

"Oh my, no. I didn't mean for you to . . . why, I know how busy you are and all."

Kelly's intuition told her that Hattie had brought her breakfast just to bring up the subject, but she knew it wouldn't hurt to go along with her. If

Charlie had planned to teach Marcy, she would carry it through.

"If Marcy is still interested in riding, I'll be glad to coach her."

"Oh, thank you, dear! I'm so glad you came to Pinetop. Everyone likes you."

"Oh, I don't know about that." Kelly knew she hadn't scored any points with Larson. That was for sure.

"The farmhands look up to you, and Rob says you're 'cool.'"

Kelly chuckled. If anyone was plugged into the grapevine at Pinetop, it was Hattie.

"And Tanner looked so proud introducing you to everyone the other night." Hattie beamed with maternal pride.

"I think he'd prefer his trainer was a man."

Hattie threw back her head and hooted. "Oh my, missy, you may know a lot about horses, but you don't know nothin' about men!"

THAT AFTERNOON Kelly watched as the farrier backed his pickup into the barn. He dropped the tailgate and opened the covered camper shell that housed his blacksmith shop on wheels. He locked his powerful arms around a one-hundred-pound anvil, hefted it out of the truck and set it on the ground. Brushing his hands together afterward, he turned to Kelly and winked. "Well, who's our first customer?"

Kelly glanced at Marcy. "Get Keepsake."

Marcy nodded and went to fetch her.

"I'm Kelly Smith." Kelly extended her hand to him.

"Yes, I saw you at the barbecue, but you disappeared before I could wangle an introduction. Name's Tom Jamison." Kelly found his handshake was as firm as she'd expected. His build was wiry, and she knew he had to be strong. What she liked was his relaxed manner. She'd had her fill of hotheaded farriers who lost their tempers when working on temperamental horses.

He turned away to pull out his box of tools and slip on his leather apron.

"I want you to trim three-fourths of an inch off her back heels and drop her hoof angle to forty-five degrees." Kelly had stayed up late last night watching videos of Keepsake's races and studying Charlie's notes. The filly's pedigree was filled with speed horses, and Kelly was hoping that with a little tinkering the filly would improve.

"That low, huh?"

"I want to try caulked shoes in back and smooth plates in front."

"Whatever you say." He leaned inside the camper shell to switch on his dusty portable radio. A gentle country ballad drifted out that complained of hard-hearted women and beer-drinkin' men. "These horses are used to my tunes," he explained as he rolled up his sleeves.

"I imagine they prefer country to hard rock." Kelly smiled.

"Oh, I don't know. Occasionally I'll run across one who's partial to Bon Jovi," he said with a chuckle, "but usually they like what I like."

Marcy returned with the filly and snapped the cross ties to the dappled gray's halter, then reached up to stroke her long graceful neck. The filly began to paw the rubber mat first with one front foot and then the other.

"Thanks, Marcy. I'd like you to rub down Baritone's legs with liniment and replace the wraps," Kelly said.

Marcy smiled shyly and started down the hallway. Kelly noticed that the girl had begun to warm to her since they'd arranged a riding lesson for the next day.

Carrying his toolbox, the farrier walked quietly to stand before the filly and pet her between the eyes with his thick-gloved hand. "You remember me, don't ya, hon?"

She blew softly and relaxed as he moved to her shoulder. Setting the tools down, he bent over to pinch the back of her foreleg above her fetlock. "Give it up, girl," he said.

The filly shifted her weight to her other leg and lifted her foot. Tom Jamison drew the hoof between his legs and cupped it firmly between his knees. With his tongs, he systematically clipped the nail heads to remove her shoe.

"Tom, good to see you."

Kelly recognized Tanner's voice, and she tensed even as an unexpected thrill of excitement moved through her.

"Mornin' McCrey," the farrier responded without shifting his position.

Kelly and Tanner exchanged a polite nod. His hair was tousled from the wind, and his cheeks were bright from walking in the crisp cold air. Kelly was reminded again of how attractive he was.

Tanner's gaze briefly ran down her slim jean-clad legs before it drifted back to meet her eyes. A look passed between them that assured her that the days without seeing each other hadn't diminished their mutual attraction.

The gray filly arched her neck and tried to drop her head to take a playful nip at the farrier's backside. "Cut that out," Tom warned in a stern voice.

Tanner grinned at Tom. "You still have a way with the fillies, I see."

"Funny, I've heard the same about you, McCrey." Tom tossed the shoe aside and let the filly's hoof drop as he turned to shake hands with Tanner. "What've you been up to lately?"

"Just finished planting a load of seedlings."

"Gettin' kinda late for that, isn't it?" Tom asked as he moved to the far side of the filly and began pulling her other front shoe.

"The weather is holding. It's just so dry."

"Yeah, I've never seen a fall drought like this one," Tom agreed as he snapped the last nail head.

Tanner glanced at Kelly as Tom lifted one of the filly's back feet. "How're you planning to shoe this mare?" he inquired casually.

"She needs more reach, so I'm going to have her set lower with caulks in back. I thought I'd have some hoof removed in front and use aluminum plates."

Tanner nodded. "Sounds good." He leaned forward and took a look at the filly's front feet. "How much length you going to have taken off?"

"About an inch."

His brows lifted in surprise, and he turned back to look at her. "That much?"

She nodded. "Three-quarters to an inch."

"You know how long it takes to grow that much hoof?" Tanner asked as the farrier removed the last shoe.

There was a strained pause. Kelly knew taking that much off might sound severe, but she hoped that he wasn't going to call her on it.

Tanner finally straightened and turned to her, waiting for an answer. Her eyes cooled. "I know how long it takes."

"And you're still going to do it?"

"Yes, sir."

There was that damn "sir" again. Tanner shrugged. "All right, but if for some reason it doesn't work, you'll take full responsibility."

"It will work," she said matter-of-factly. "I believe that reshoeing the filly this way will increase her potential."

Tanner studied the gray silently. Her first season had been disappointing. Her sire was Mastercharge, the ten-year-old stallion his father had raised and believed would be the backbone of the Pinetop breeding program. The filly was a half sister to Baritone, and her performance mattered to Tanner. It mattered a great deal.

"Don't you think you could trim off, say, half that much, and see how she does before you go to that extreme?" Tanner suggested in a tone that he thought sounded diplomatic.

"I considered that, but I don't think trimming half that much would change her way of going enough to help." Kelly forced her voice to remain controlled. He had reason to question her judgment.

He stared at the horse a moment longer, then finally let out a long sigh. "It's like cutting hair," he murmured as if speaking to a child, "once it's done, you can't glue it back on."

Tell me about it, Kelly empathized, wistfully recalling her long red hair. "You're right. Once it's done, it's done," she agreed. "I'm asking you to trust me on this one."

Tom Jamison stood leaning against the filly with his arm draped over her back, his gaze switching from Tanner to Kelly as if he were watching a tennis match.

After another brief silence, Tom interrupted, "Well, folks, what'll it be?" He straightened and pressed his hands against the small of his back and stretched. "Time's a wastin'."

Tanner glanced at Kelly, and she could see he wanted to forbid her to do it. She returned his gaze, her expression unyielding.

"I can understand your reluctance," she conceded, "but I've given this a lot of thought, and I believe it's the right thing to do."

He looked away and released a long breath. He'd been afraid of this. The woman was as stubborn as a Missouri mule. His eyes moved back to the filly. If her plan didn't work, it would be a long time before the mistake could be corrected.

Tom picked up his rasp, lifted the filly's foot, and cupped it between his knees. The scraping of the rasp competed with the plaintive lyrics coming from the radio.

"How much do we take off?" Tom asked as he moved the file back and forth.

Tanner looked at Kelly and sighed. "Whatever the lady says."

Tom grinned. "I figured as much."

EARLY THE NEXT MORNING Kelly leaned over the white fence, straining to see through the fog that shrouded the pines, hovering around the oval training track. The metal stopwatch in her clammy palm made her fingers feel brittle with cold.

She realized that she wouldn't be able to see all the way around the track until the sun rose high enough to spill over the mountains and drive away the mist.

"Coffee?" Marcy walked up and pressed a thermal mug into her hand.

"Thanks." Kelly took a sip, felt the searing heat on her tongue, but failed to taste the strong brew. Her eyes were following a presence she could only hear, but could not see.

Doug was riding Keepsake down the backstretch at a jog, warming up her muscles, loosening her up. Even though the hoofbeats were muffled in the deep loam, Kelly knew the instant Doug let the filly break into a canter. Her eyes blindly followed the unseen presence around the far turn.

"Sounds good," Marcy noted, looking up at her new mentor shyly. Kelly gave her a brief smile as they listened to the filly draw closer.

"I thought you'd want to know," Marcy murmured, shooting a quick glance at Kelly, "when I was walking down here I saw Mr. McCrey leaving his house and heading this way."

"Oh, brother." Kelly had been wondering if he'd show up to see how the new shoeing was going to affect his filly.

Kelly had hardly slept a wink for turning her decision over and over in her mind. Had she done the right thing? Should she have backed off, made a safer choice?

Eventually she'd returned to square one. Horse racing was a gamble, so was horse training. The filly hadn't been winning the way she was, so it was time to try a hunch. Hadn't her father told her that success was a matter of making one adjustment after another, some unorthodox if necessary, until finally something worked?

If she was ever to discover how and why Charlie had died, she had to prove herself here as a trainer. Otherwise she could lose the job before she'd done what she'd come to do. She didn't dare ask herself if that was the only reason she was aching for Keepsake to show improvement today.

She knew from the hoofbeats that Keepsake was close. In another instant, the filly broke through the mist that had held her in its gauzy web.

She watched with rapt attention as Doug let the filly canter past them for fifty yards or more before he gradually pulled her down to a jog and brought her around in a wide turn.

Kelly felt Tanner's presence before she caught sight of him out of the corner of her eye. Turning slightly, she met his eyes directly. Marcy shrank back and moved to stand on Kelly's right as he moved toward them.

"Good morning," Kelly greeted, seeing the stopwatch dangling on a cord around his neck. He was holding a pair of binoculars in one hand.

"Mornin'," he said, nodding to Kelly, then to Marcy. Marcy nodded back shyly. As he took his place beside her, Kelly noticed that he looked hollow-eyed this morning.

"Mind if I watch?" A couple of farmhands had drifted up to stand against the fence a short distance away as Tanner stood beside her.

"Of course not. She's your filly. I thought we'd work her four furlongs out of the gates on the half-mile track this morning."

She gestured to Doug, and he guided the filly to the electric starting gates. Marcy jogged over to lead the filly into a slot. When Kelly gave a signal, Marcy activated the gates.

The filly broke well and bounded down the track. After the first turn, she disappeared into the fog. Kelly glanced at the seconds racing by on her stopwatch. Tanner did the same as they both tried to peer into the wall of vapor on the backstretch. Tanner squinted through his binoculars, but it was impossible to find the gray filly in the thick fog.

Ears straining, they listened to the soft thud of her hooves as she raced down the backstretch.

Kelly glanced down at her stopwatch and back up. For a flash of an instant, her eyes met Tanner's. And he could detect the strain, the urgent hope that her hunch was right.

They heard a change in sound and Doug's shouts of encouragement as the filly made the turn for home.

Leaning against the fence, they drew together as

they listened. Keepsake was galloping hard, her nostrils flaring with the deep breaths she was exhaling in rhythm with her strides, "Chaluff, chaluff, chaluff."

The filly exploded from the fog, her graceful front legs reaching for ground, her powerful chest and shoulders pulling, her hind legs kicking out like a jackrabbit leading a chase.

Doug was leaning over, his whip teetering back and forth in his back pocket, his windbreaker billowing out in back, his hands rubbing the reins against her neck, while his shouts mingled with cheers from the ranch hands hanging over the fence waving their fists.

As Keepsake dashed across the finish line in front of them, Kelly and Tanner clamped down on their stopwatches. Kelly's eyes widened in disbelief when she read the numbers. She thrust her watch next to Tanner's to compare them. The times were identical.

As their eyes met, they broke into grins. Kelly bounced on her toes like a five-year-old on Christmas morning as Tanner opened his arms, and she rushed into his embrace. For an instant they hugged and giggled like small children.

Tanner's hold finally loosened, and he gazed down at her, his eyes brimming with respect. "Well, son-of-a-gun, it worked."

"Well, son-of-a-gun, it did," she agreed with a huge sigh.

"I thought you never had a doubt," he protested, grinning.

"Well," she shrugged, "maybe one or two."

"Is that why your light stayed on all night?"

"How would you know?" She arched him a look and stepped back, and he ruffled her hair teasingly.

"Congratulations, Ms. Smith," he said. He casually pulled her into his arms and kissed her.

When he released her, she stepped back unsteadily, feeling shaky and light-headed. She would reassure herself later that it had only been excitement over the filly's workout that had left her tingling and momentarily disoriented.

Gripping the fence, Kelly stepped out of his embrace and turned to watch Doug pull the filly to a stop nearby.

Marcy reached to grip the bridle, and Doug kicked his feet out of the stirrups and hopped to the ground. His eyes searched for Kelly's and he gave her a cocky grin. "Better?" he asked, knowing the filly had made a big improvement.

"Better," Kelly agreed. "Good ride, Doug."

He sent her a little salute as Marcy pulled the reins over the filly's head.

"Rinse her down, Marcy," Kelly said, "and walk her till she's dry."

"Then a rubdown and wraps?"

"Yes, and after all that," Kelly said smiling, "she can have her breakfast."

"Right, boss." Marcy led the filly by, and Kelly

smiled back at the young girl. It was the first time anyone at Pinetop had called her boss. Kelly knew it was what they had called Charlie, and it made her heart swell with pride.

"Well, show's over," a disgruntled voice muttered. Kelly glanced up to see Larson standing some distance behind everyone else. "Let's get some work done around here." He turned and the ranch hands fell in behind the filly and headed toward the barns.

Tanner folded his arms and leaned back against the fence. "Nice work," he said, willing to give credit where it was due. "I'm impressed. Now what?"

She acknowledged his comment with a nod and a modest smile. "Don't you think she deserves a race?" she asked. "Can you arrange it?"

"I'll make some calls tomorrow. There should be a race she'd qualify for at Remington Park or Churchill Downs."

"See what you can line up."

Kelly sighed and began walking toward the paddock. "I wish they were all that simple."

From the tone of her voice, Tanner suspected the turn of her thoughts. "You still worrying about Baritone?"

She sighed. "I'm afraid a change of shoes won't do the trick for him."

"What do you think would?"

It gave Kelly a measure of satisfaction to hear him ask her advice. "There's something wrong, but

I can't put my finger on it. For several days he seems to improve steadily, and then he slides into a slump. I've enriched his diet. I've studied his races and his medical records. Yet there's something I'm not seeing. It has me stumped. And I still haven't found those missing records."

"Rob doesn't think he's so bad. He thinks he has the ability to be a strong contender this spring."

Kelly ran a hand through her short hair and shook her head as she gazed away. "I know . . . his bones seem solid, his muscles strong, his tendons supple, but when he really needs it, he lacks the drive. I can feel it when I'm riding him. He lacks stamina. What puzzles me is the way it comes and goes." She glanced at him. "He seems shopworn, and he's going to have to be razor sharp come spring."

"I know." Tanner's gaze moved to the barns and to the pastures beyond. "It's damned important to be ready for the Arkansas Derby."

"Then I think getting a second medical opinion should be our first step." She waited, suspecting it was a step Tanner wished he didn't have to make.

"Look, I'm aware Rob acts like he hasn't got a brain in his head, and I'll admit he lacks common sense, at times, but he's brilliant with the horses." Tanner pushed away from the fence and turned around to face her. "And when it comes to performing surgery there's no one better." Kelly saw the unmistakable flash of loyalty in his eyes. "Sure, the day-to-day grind doesn't hold his interest. He isn't punctual—" Tanner's hands tightened on the top rail "—and he procrastinates like hell, but the kid knows his stuff."

"Of course he does, but you have to admit, there could be some little something we're all overlooking. We're all so close to the horse. I'm not criticizing Rob or his work, but a purely objective viewpoint couldn't hurt. Even insurance companies ask people to get second opinions."

"I know." He heaved a weary sigh. "It's just that I trust Rob, and it's important that he knows I trust him. Just give the colt some time. I think he'll come around."

Kelly shook her head. "Tanner, listen to me. I called the company that microfilms your equine records. They said they shipped the X rays on Baritone weeks ago, and they have a receipt to prove the package was received here."

"So?"

"So, I still can't find them."

"Like I said before, they're probably misfiled. Charlie was forgetful about things like that."

Kelly stiffened. True, her father had sometimes been so absorbed in his work that he overlooked details. And true, he hadn't been the tidiest man in the world, but he would have been careful with X rays. "Charlie Bailey was a reliable trainer."

"I didn't say he wasn't. He was a great man in many ways. He could remember every horse he'd ever trained—Cinderella stories, rags-to-riches

121

stories—but he couldn't keep track of a receipt, much less a file."

"Maybe he never dreamed his integrity would be questioned."

Tanner's eyes narrowed. "What's with you about him?"

Her heart began to pound as she glanced away.

"You get so all-fired bent out of shape every time his name comes up."

She tried to shrug nonchalantly. "I just don't like to see his good name maligned, that's all—it goes against my sense of fair play. The man's not here to defend himself." She shoved her hands into her pockets, so he couldn't see that they were shaking. "I might agree that the X rays were misplaced if Charlie's latest entries weren't missing too. Don't you find all that just a bit odd?"

"Frankly, it doesn't sound odd to me at all. Are you suggesting that someone is trying to sabotage the horse and hide the evidence?"

She could tell by the way he was looking at her that he was beginning to wonder if she was paranoid.

"I'm only trying to point out that if we get a second veterinarian's opinion, and the vet finds something wrong now, then we still have enough time to correct it, that's all. And if he doesn't find anything wrong, you won't have to hear another word out of me."

Tanner removed his hat and ran his fingers

through his hair wearily. "You're not going to give up on this, are you?"

"Just promise me you'll think about it."

Settling the Stetson back on his head, he sighed. "All right. I'll think about it."

"Good." She grinned as she let out a sigh of relief. The concession wasn't much, but it was better than a flat no.

Chapter Seven

"Relax, Marcy. You're bouncing again. Just relax and move with the horse. Take up the reins a little."

"It . . . it's . . . hardto . . . relax . . . whenyou'rebouncin' . . . so . . . hard," Marcy complained between gasps.

Riding alongside Marcy, Kelly was posting the trot smoothly. "Okay, let's take a break."

Gratefully Marcy pulled her horse to a halt. For the past ten minutes, they'd been riding the farm's two steadiest mounts around the track.

Kelly ran her fingers through her horse's mane and waited for Marcy to catch her breath. The late-afternoon sun was warm on her back, but November had sharpened the breeze.

"I've tried what you told me, Kelly, but I just can't seem to get it."

"Do you like to dance?"

Marcy nodded vaguely, failing to understand why Kelly would bring up dancing at this point.

"Riding is the same principle. Relax and move with the rhythm. You're trying too hard, so you're getting ahead of your horse. Just keep your weight on the balls of your feet and let his stride lift you, hold for a beat, then come down easy and let him lift you again."

"Looks easy when you do it, but I bounce like a

sack of potatoes. Shoot, you can probably see daylight between me and the saddle. If you hadn't grabbed me, I swear I'da fallen off."

Kelly grinned. "You'll get the hang of it. Ready to go again?"

"Yeah." Marcy's determined nod snapped her long ponytail comically.

Kelly clucked to her strawberry roan, and Marcy's chestnut gelding followed. The two horses matched strides as they reached into a long trot.

Marcy's face was furrowed in concentration, and soon she was moving up and down almost imperceptibly, keeping the rhythm for a moment, then bouncing for a stride or two.

"Almost," Kelly encouraged.

"Almost," Marcy repeated, chewing on her lower lip as her bounces became fewer.

On the next round, Marcy posted the trot with hardly a mistake. "Straighten your back," Kelly called.

Marcy glanced at Kelly, then pulled her shoulders back to imitate her form.

"Now you've got it!"

"If I can just keep it," Marcy returned with a cheeky grin. "Let's go another round!"

"Sure," Kelly agreed, fondly recalling the days when Charlie had given her riding lessons. Like Marcy, she'd been reluctant to see the lesson end.

Fifteen minutes later, they finally pulled to a halt,

and Hattie applauded enthusiastically. "Good job, Marcy!"

Marcy's grin was as wide as the Texas panhandle. "Thanks." She turned on the flat English saddle and smiled at Kelly. "And thank you."

"You're welcome. When would you like your next lesson?"

"Tomorrow?" Marcy's eagerness made it sound like she might have a hard time waiting that long.

"Then tomorrow it is."

After Marcy led the horses away, Kelly walked to the bench and sat down beside Hattie.

"I brought a thermos of hot chocolate." Hattie winked. "Care to join me?"

"Sounds great."

They sipped the hot chocolate in silent camaraderie for a moment.

"Nice of you to give Marcy lessons."

"I'm enjoying it."

"She says you won't let her pay you."

Kelly shook her head. "I wouldn't dream of it. I didn't pay for mine, the least I can do is pass it on."

Hattie nodded. "Well, I'm thanking you. It means a lot to that girl, and if she's got an interest like this, she won't be chasin' the boys."

Kelly smiled, remembering that in her teenage years she'd spent so much time with horses that she hadn't had time to even think of boys.

"How's the training going?" Hattie asked pleasantly.

"It has its ups and downs."

"Tanner meddlin' in your bailiwick?"

Kelly chuckled. "Why do you ask?"

"Oh, I hear things."

I'll bet you do, Kelly thought. "Well, I've noticed Tanner's protective where his brother's concerned."

"Always has been. Tanner looks out for everybody around here. And since their father passed away a year ago, he's been trying to make Rob feel a part of things at Pinetop."

"Oh?"

"Tanner used to think his father oughta sell this farm. Years ago, he had a law practice in Little Rock, but his dad was always houndin' him to give it up and come back here like Rob."

Kelly lifted a brow. "Really? Tanner's an attorney? I'd assumed that he'd always run the farm."

"No, he went off to college and then to work in Little Rock. He only came back for visits until his daddy got real sick. Then I think he felt obligated to move back and run Pinetop Farm and the McCrey timber business."

"Do they like it here?"

"I think Tanner does, but Rob, well, let's say I don't think Rob's cut out for this kind of life. Got a bug in his britches, that boy does. He wants to see the world."

Kelly stared off thoughtfully. "Hattie, I'm having a hard time understanding why Tanner won't let me have another vet examine Baritone. I know he's loyal to Rob, and I know Rob is good at his job, but I think Tanner is shrewd enough to know that if something is wrong with the horse, it could bring disaster this spring."

"Could be he doesn't wanta rock the boat. He'd like for Rob to stay on here. I think he feels bad about the way things have been between the two of them over the years."

"The two of them . . . I don't want to pry," Kelly said quietly, but Hattie saw the questions in Kelly's eyes.

"Well, maybe you *should* know a little more about the McCreys. You see, Tanner was the only son of Alexander and Mary, but Mary died when Tanner was only three. That's when I moved in, to help Alex raise him. Tanner became the light of his daddy's life. Alex developed the timber business for him and built the stables. He had a dream of raising a Thoroughbred here that could win the Arkansas Derby and go on to win the triple crown."

"Where does Rob fit in?"

"Well, about seven years after Mary's death, Alexander got himself foolishly involved with a neighbor woman he'd known since he was a teenager. When Jenny got pregnant, Alexander wanted to marry her, but things got sticky 'cause she was already married to Jared Huxsman, and he wouldn't hear of a divorce."

Kelly's eyes grew round. "Huxsman . . . the man I met at the party the other night?"

Hattie nodded. "It took some nerve for him to show up after all these years. . . . Tanner would have shown him the door 'cept he knew it'd embarrass Rob."

"Why?"

"Well, Alexander and Jared grew up together. Jared's land joins Pinetop on the south. There'd always been a rivalry between those two, and this thing over Jared's wife made it turn real ugly. Alex thought Jared should give Jenny a divorce so he could marry her 'cause everyone knew that the baby she was carrying was his. Everyone also knew Jared had been runnin' around on Jenny for years. I heard they were man and wife in name only—course that's just hearsay—but her getting pregnant by Alexander brought out the stubbornness in Jared."

"What happened?"

"Jenny was upset and confused. She didn't want to live with Jared, and I think she was afraid to choose Alexander for fear of what Jared would do if she did, so she went to live with her mother in St. Louis. She got real depressed after her son was born. Before little Rob was a year old, she died of an overdose of tranquilizers. Alexander and Jared went to court to get custody of the baby. Everyone was surprised when the judge awarded the baby to Alexander and just gave Jared visiting privileges."

"Oh, my . . . how did that work?"

"Not too well. There was always a lot of tension. It took its toll on everybody at Pinetop. When they got old enough, Tanner went away to school, and so did Rob. And Rob became a veterinarian to make Alexander happy." Hattie sighed. "It's a real shame. They're both good boys. I never had any children of my own, but I love those two like they were mine."

"And Alexander is dead now?"

"Yeah—heart trouble. He was a hard worker and kinda high tempered. But it all caught up with Alexander. After he had his first heart attack, Tanner moved back and ran things. Two years later Alexander suffered a fatal heart attack. After the funeral Tanner convinced Rob to stay and run the businesses with him."

"How long ago was that?"

"Been almost a year. Tanner don't care much for Jared Huxsman, but Jared still checks on Rob. Tanner loves his brother, and he don't want no ill feeling between them . . . but I don't know. Rob is so different. . . ."

"I know." Kelly wrapped her wool scarf tighter around her neck and handed her empty cup to Hattie. The days were getting shorter, and the long, cool shadows had long since spilled over them. "Thanks for the hot chocolate and everything else. I guess it's time for me to be getting back to work."

Hattie laid a reassuring hand on Kelly's arm.

"Things will go better for you, honey, the longer you're here. Be patient. Tanner's got a lot on his mind."

"So you've heard we've been knocking heads."

Hattie nodded. "You know, part of the problem is he likes you, and the rest of it is he's a hardheaded man! But hang in there, he'll give you more free rein once you been here a while."

"Well, I won't be here for long, just until he can get someone permanent."

"Oh? Hmmmm. Well, we'll see. That Tanner's a nice-looking man . . . haven't you noticed?"

"Me?" Kelly winked. "Never."

"Can you look me in the eye and say that?"

Kelly turned and looked Hattie in the eye and wished she believed what she was about to say. "I have no personal feelings for Tanner McCrey."

Hattie studied Kelly through each level of her trifocals and chuckled softly.

"Satisfied?" Kelly lifted her brows.

"Satisfied that you're lying."

"Oh?"

"I can always tell when someone's lying to me, dear. After you've lived as long as I have and raised a couple of boys, you know all the tricks."

"Why do you think I'm lying?"

"Well, dear, honest people, as a rule, make lousy liars. When they tell a lie, they usually blink."

"Blink?"

Hattie nodded sagely. "Sorry, dear. You blinked."

• • •

LATE THE NEXT AFTERNOON Kelly sat behind the desk in her office, the phone cradled on her shoulder, as she neatly copied the furlongs and times of the day's workouts in her journal.

Rob opened the door without knocking and strode across the room to the window. His fingers absently began fiddling with the cord to the blinds as he stared at the patio behind the main house.

Kelly glanced at him as she hung up the phone and noticed he looked as if his thoughts were a million miles away. "Did you get the yearlings wormed today?" she asked.

He shrugged negligently. "Not yet."

"Rob, we won't have many more days we can count on to be as warm as today," she reminded. "You know we can't risk passing stomach tubes on these horses when the temperature is freezing."

"Sorry, I got a late start." He continued to gaze out the window, seemingly bored and inattentive.

She watched his fingers work knots into the cord to the blinds and wondered why he didn't put that nervous energy to more productive use.

"If the weather holds tomorrow, you should do it then. If we're forced to wait until spring, they won't grow like they should."

"I know. I know." His brow wrinkled into a frown, and his fingers kept working nervously.

"Rob, is something wrong?"

132

"Who says anything's wrong?" He sent her an annoyed glance.

"I do. You don't seem yourself today."

"Would you cut the psychology crap? You don't know anything about me," he snapped.

Gone was the charming young man she'd met at the barbecue. In his place was a cool, and not very courteous, stranger.

Her gaze met his and held it. "I'm sorry."

He shrugged and thrust his hands into his pockets. "Look, don't pay any attention to me. I'm in a bad mood today. I'll take care of the yearlings tomorrow."

"All right . . . but I need you to check on Mastercharge this afternoon."

"He's not my business."

Her brows lifted. "I was under the impression that Pinetop Farm belonged to you and your brother."

"Really?" He smiled, but the automatic response showed no sign of his usual warmth. "Haven't you heard? Father left his farm to his firstborn. But Tanner's promised I can keep my job here as long as I want it." An awkward silence followed as Rob started walking toward the door.

"Larson noticed the horse favoring his front leg," Kelly warned.

"He'll hold. I'll look at him tomorrow."

Kelly's mouth dropped open as she came to her feet. "It's your job, Rob. And it won't take but a minute. Marcy's already put him on the first set of cross ties."

"Okay. Okay!" He jerked the door open and slammed out of her office irritably. For a moment Kelly stood speechless. She couldn't believe her ears. He was acting like a spoiled brat.

She'd started around her desk when she heard a cry of anguish and a loud crash. Bolting into the barn, Kelly saw Rob slumped against the wall, gripping his shoulder, his face contorted in pain. The stallion was tossing his head, fighting the restraining ties.

A look of pure rage flashed into Rob's eyes. His fingers closed around the handle of a heavy bucket nearby, and he made a lunge toward the stallion. "You son of a—"

"Rob!" Kelly rushed forward to prevent him from striking the horse.

"Get out of my way!" Rob shoved her aside and pulled back to hurl the bucket. The stallion pulled back against the ties and lashed out with his front legs. The commotion was loud enough to wake the dead.

"That's enough!"

Out of the corner of her eye, Kelly saw Tanner move in to catch her by the shoulder with one hand and slap a restraining hand on Rob's shoulder as well. "What in the hell is going on in here?"

"Let go of me! I'm going to kill that damned horse! He bit me!"

"Drop the bucket, Rob! Just stop right now and get a hold of yourself."

The two brothers faced each other.

As Tanner's demand slowly began to penetrate his anger, Rob regained control of his emotions, and he let the bucket drop from his fingers to the floor.

"You all right?" Tanner asked, chancing a brief glance at Kelly.

She nodded wordlessly.

He turned back to Rob. Marcy was standing beside Rob, peeling away his torn shirt. He winced as her fingers gently tested the red welts that were already forming. "It's okay," she soothed. "You were lucky, his teeth didn't break the skin. I think it's just a bruise."

Rob glared at the stallion. "He's the lucky one."

"You know you can't take your eyes off him, Rob." Tanner moved quietly to his brother's side. "Let's go inside the office, and I'll take a look at that under the light."

Rob jerked his shirt back over his shoulder resentfully. "I'm all right. Just leave me alone." He raked his hair out of his face and took a deep steadying breath. "I must have brushed whatever's hurting him as I leaned to grab his foot—he went for me so fast I couldn't stop him." He swore again angrily. "He grabbed my shoulder."

Marcy, who'd witnessed the incident from the end of the hallway, nodded. "He won't get a second chance. I'll hold him from now on," she promised.

Tanner motioned toward the office. "Let me take a look at that shoulder, Rob."

"No, I'm all right." Rob's glance slid to Kelly sheepishly. "I'm sorry, Kelly." His tone was contrite, almost meek. "Hope I didn't hurt you."

"No." She tried to summon a forgiving smile. "I'm fine."

Rob glanced at his watch. "Look, I'm late for an appointment." He shot another wary look in the stallion's direction. "He'll live until tomorrow," he said dryly. "I'll have a look at him then."

"I'll go with you," Marcy offered with concern shining in her dark round eyes.

"No," Rob held up a hand to stop her, "I need some time alone."

Kelly caught the look of hurt in Marcy's eyes and wondered if the girl didn't have a crush on Rob. "Boy, what's with him," Kelly murmured as Rob left the barn.

Marcy shrugged. "He's just in one of his moods. You'll learn to stay outta his way when he gets in one. He usually snaps out of them pretty fast."

"Are you okay?" Kelly asked.

"Oh, sure." Marcy gave her a weak smile. "I better go. You want me to put the stallion up?"

"I'll take care of him," Tanner said. "You need a lift?"

"No, sir. I got my truck." Marcy's glance moved from Tanner to Kelly. "Well, see ya tomorrow."

"Take care," Kelly called as they watched the girl leave.

Kelly glanced at Tanner as he walked to the stallion. "I'll put him up," she offered.

"I'd like to help."

Kelly stepped forward and murmured soothingly as she snapped a stout lead onto the stallion's halter. For good measure, Tanner positioned himself on the other side and snapped a second lead onto the halter. The stallion shifted his weight restlessly while Kelly unhooked the cross ties and let them fall against the walls.

"I'm ready," she said. They kept a taut pressure on the lines as they led the horse to the next barn. When they reached the stall, Kelly swung the door open. "Unhook your lead," she told Tanner.

She kept a steady eye on the stallion and a firm grip on the lead as she clucked to Mastercharge. He bounded into his stall, and she gave a tug on the lead to bring him around to face her. He lifted his head as if he might like to nip, but she gave the lead a brisk tug. "Here," she said sharply, "cut that out!"

It was a warning she'd heard Charlie issue a hundred times in the same tone. The stallion immediately dropped his head.

Tanner watched Kelly efficiently unsnap the lead, swing the door shut and slide the latch into place.

She glanced up to see him watching her. "I'm

137

glad Baritone didn't inherit his daddy's disposition," she murmured.

The corners of his mouth turned up. "I believe you could still handle him if he had."

"Why, sir, is that a compliment?" She sent him a look of mock surprise.

He grinned. "I'll let you be the judge of that." He swung his lead rope back, acting as if he might give her a playful swat with it.

She shook her coiled lead at him. "Here," she said playfully, "cut that out!"

She turned and walked out of the barn as she heard him chuckle and follow her out into the chilly afternoon.

The sharp wind made her cross her arms and rub her palms up and down the sleeves of her sweater. She hadn't taken time to slip into her jacket.

Tanner opened his heavy coat, and before she could refuse, he drew her inside it as they headed into the brisk wind.

She shivered as warmth surrounded her, and she stayed pressed against him as they matched strides.

He glanced down at her and winked.

"I suppose you're going to fuss about this, too, but I'm only trying to be nice—nothing personal you understand."

She grinned up at him. "Of course."

Once inside her office her glance shifted back to his. "How do I get out of this thing," she asked lightly, trying to ignore the zing of excitement traveling through her as she stood wrapped next to his solid length.

Tanner gazed down at her and her breathing quickened. Reluctantly he released her from the confines of his coat. She hesitated for an instant before stepping out of his embrace. Though her office was heated, she felt a chill envelop her as she walked away to stand behind her desk.

He shrugged out of his sheepskin coat and slipped it onto a peg. With a careless grace, he strode across the room to open the small refrigerator in the corner. He reached beneath the shelf of injectable antibiotics and prescription drugs, beyond her cans of diet soda, to the beer he kept in the far back.

He pulled out a bottle and unscrewed the cap. Lifting it, he glanced over his shoulder at her. "Want one?"

She shook her head. "No, thanks."

With a slight move of his knee he closed the refrigerator door. He tilted his head back and took a long drink. Something about watching him made her breathing slow. With an effort she filled her lungs and glanced down to her desk top. She gave a sharp pull on the chain to turn on the green-shaded lamp.

"In all the commotion I almost forgot why I'd dropped by," he began.

"Oh? Why did you?"

His eyes moved leisurely over the attractive sight

she made in her formfitting denims. "I was curious. Did you find us a race?"

"They're holding a slot for us at Churchill Downs. The only problem is that it's on the day after tomorrow."

"That gives us a day to travel. No problem for me, if it's no problem for you," he said easily.

"No, I can manage," she said. "I suppose Larson can keep things running here."

"You confirm the race, and I'll make hotel reservations."

She glanced up. "You're going?"

He could hear a little thread of panic in her voice, though her face remained neutral.

"We finished replanting today." Tanner decided to enjoy her consternation. "I think I'll give the crew a long weekend and join you. Wouldn't want to miss a chance to see the filly put it on 'em. I suppose Rob should go along, too, don't you?"

"Oh yes," she said quickly, trying to still her pounding heart. Tanner was coming with her. The idea appealed to her far more than it should.

He took another swallow of beer. "Would you like me to walk you home, Ms. Smith?"

"No, thanks. I have some paperwork to finish."

He nodded. "Better give Jay's agent a call."

That brought her head up again.

Tanner had no trouble reading her look. When her chin lifted like that, she resembled a princess about to reprimand one of her subjects. He wondered if she knew how regal she'd looked just then and decided she had no idea. "He *is* the jockey you want to ride the filly, isn't he?"

"Yes," she said without enthusiasm.

"Well, he happens to be finishing the season at Churchill. His agent's name is Shyler. The number should be in your book."

"I'll give him a call," she said in a flat tone.

"Then I'll just say good-night." He dropped the bottle into the metal wastebasket. The clatter made her jump.

"Good night," she returned absently.

Slipping into his coat, Tanner noticed she'd looked calmer handling the nasty-tempered stallion than she did now. It was an observation he'd mull over on the chilly walk to his house.

When Tanner's steps had faded away, Kelly gave a long sigh. Her throat was dry, and her head was beginning to throb. Something about that man was getting to her, and she didn't like it one bit.

She strode to the refrigerator, opened it and grabbed a can of diet soda. She let the door stand ajar while she popped the tab and took the first sip. Her glance dropped to the medicine bottles on the top shelf.

That's odd, she thought. She could have sworn there had been more bottles in there a few weeks ago. The medicine doses came by the dozen. The box had been discarded and the remaining bottles were sitting directly on the shelf now.

She took another sip and counted them. One was missing, and another was nearly empty. The label indicated the medicine was an antibiotic. Kelly shrugged. As far as she knew, none of the horses here needed an antibiotic at present.

It was something else she'd have to remember to ask Rob and Larson about. She closed the refrigerator and carried her drink to her desk. She had lots of work to do if she wanted this first road trip to be a success.

She reminded herself again that the job here was only temporary. She was just here to clear her father's name. It shouldn't matter so much to her how the Pinetop horses performed. But it was beginning to matter—more every day.

THE FOLLOWING MORNING, Kelly awoke earlier than usual. Dressing quickly, she decided to head to the office. She could have her coffee there while she finished getting things organized for the trip.

She shivered inside her jacket as she closed her cottage door. The icy coating covering the grass crunched under her boots as she walked to the barn. Glancing up at the sliver of moon that hung in the sky overhead, she decided it was going to be a clear day.

Approaching the barn, she was surprised to see a light on in her office. As she walked through the door, Larson spun the desk chair around to look at her with a startled expression. Beyond him, the computer screen was on, a green glow filled with white numbers.

"What are you doing?" The question was out of her mouth before she shut the door.

"Working." He turned back to the screen. "Shut the door. You're letting in the cold."

She closed the door harder than she'd intended. Slipping out of her jacket, she moved across the room to stand in front of her desk peering at the screen over his shoulder. "I didn't know you used the computer."

"You figured I was too dumb for that." Larson seemed in no hurry to move.

"No." She shrugged. "I just hadn't realized you'd have a need for it."

"Well, Ms. Smith," he leaned back in the chair, "I used this office long before you came along and I'll probably be here long after you move on."

She wouldn't argue that. Turning, she moved to the coffee maker and inhaled the aroma of a fresh pot brewing. She reached for a clean mug.

"Help yourself." Larson made his sour offer without glancing up from the keyboard.

His sarcasm didn't go unnoticed. "Shall I pour you one, too?" she asked nicely, forcing aside the tempting thought of pouring it directly on him.

"No."

Kelly had the uncomfortable feeling that he'd just read her thoughts.

She listened while he tapped mechanically on the

keyboard. "What are you entering?" she asked, walking up to stand behind him.

"Checking dates."

"On what?" She'd had more success getting answers from shy seventh-graders on the first day of school.

"I'm checking which brood mares might foal early," he said evasively.

"Those are yearlings," she said checking the birth dates beside the names appearing on the screen.

"Right," he said, tapping in more information.

"What are you adding?"

"Today's date on their worming schedule."

"Isn't that premature? Rob hasn't wormed them yet."

"He will today."

"How can you be so sure?"

"Because he promised me that it would be done today."

Kelly bit her tongue. Larson never passed up an opportunity to assert his authority.

"The temperature is below freezing," she said, hoping to see his haughty confidence waver if only for a moment.

"It won't be at ten o'clock." His condescending attitude was getting to her.

"Rob is leaving with us for Louisville today," she said matter-of-factly.

Larson nodded. "I heard."

She fumed silently. Larson sure knew how to get under her skin. She walked to the window and opened the blinds while she brought herself under control.

With a few additional keystrokes, he shut the computer down, and Kelly turned to face him.

As he rose from the chair, he made a haughty sweeping gesture. "It's all yours."

Not hardly, Kelly seethed, not with your continual interference, but a brisk thank-you was all she said.

Larson was out the door an instant later, and Kelly stood for a moment rubbing her hands together to stop her trembling.

She hated unpleasant run-ins. For most of her life, she'd avoided potential confrontations. But it didn't look like that was going to be possible anymore. At least not with this man.

She wondered if Larson had been as rude to Charlie as he was to her. According to Marcy, the two men had never gotten along. She found herself wondering exactly how far Larson had gone to protect his territory at Pinetop and why.

Chapter Eight

"Are we there yet?" Rob rose on one elbow and peered groggily through one open eye at Kelly sitting in the front seat.

"Not much longer," Kelly murmured as she glanced up from the map spread across her lap.

A low canopy of clouds had blocked the sun for most of their trip to Louisville, and Rob had taken the opportunity to nap in the back seat while Tanner drove the Bronco and Kelly navigated.

Kelly pointed out the route as they wound their way through a maze of on ramps and off ramps into the city. Doug and Marcy followed behind them in a Pinetop truck pulling a trailer containing Keepsake.

Once inside the city the road signs were few, so Kelly had to trust her memory to find their way to Churchill Downs. She breathed a sigh of relief when the twin spires finally came into view.

Though it was late afternoon when they arrived, the shed rows were a hive of activity. Rob examined Keepsake while Marcy unloaded equipment. Kelly and Tanner went inside to double-check their entry in the race and pay the fees.

Kelly's heart quickened with excitement as she stood on the red paving bricks, her gaze lifting from the paddock to the eaves where the names and dates of the Kentucky Derby winners over the past century were painted.

As she and Tanner paused to watch the last race of the day, her eyes drifted to the horseshoe-shaped circle where Kentucky Derby victors had basked in glory. The honor of standing there on derby day had eluded Charlie Bailey. He'd come close a few times, but the Kentucky Derby and the Arkansas Derby were two races steeped in tradition that he'd coveted but had never won. Kelly vowed to bring those victories home for him one day.

The hotel room she shared with Marcy was quiet, but Kelly hardly slept a wink that night. She felt more comfortable on the back side of the track the next morning where she was supervising every aspect of Keepsake's race preparations.

Rob had examined the filly first thing in the morning and pronounced her fit, then he'd promptly disappeared.

An air of excitement surrounded them. People were rushing and shouting, horses were nickering shrilly or kicking stall walls. Everywhere grooms were walking horses, bathing them, or rubbing them down. Kelly made her way down the liniment-scented walkways, past horses standing in ice tubs or buckets of warm water.

Racetracks were where Charlie had taught her his craft. This was the school where she'd learned to find what would work by being adventurous enough to try things, and then wise enough to know when to modify them.

She thrived on the atmosphere. Despite the competitive aspect, a camaraderie existed. These were horse people. Their lives revolved around the animals they loved and admired. Here, Kelly was accepted as one of the gypsy band that roamed the country and the world, moving from track to track, race to race. They formed a family of changing faces.

Tanner stood aside and watched Kelly. He admired the way she took control, her face aglow with enthusiasm. At Pinetop she was quietly efficient. At trackside she was that and more: she was alive. The chaos that drove some trainers to drown themselves in antacids or liquor brought a sparkle to her eye and a snap to her step.

Tanner saw the same changes in Keepsake. Her head was up, her eyes wide open and alert. The filly had been bred for this. Perhaps Kelly had been, too.

He found himself wondering if she was as happy anywhere else. Pinetop must seem awfully tame compared to this, he thought, and it occurred to him that Kelly wouldn't be working with him for long.

She'd signed a contract to stay through the Arkansas Derby, still some five months away. After watching her as he had for the past few weeks, he'd discovered that she had talent, brains and moxie. It wouldn't surprise him to see that Kelly Smith could carve a niche for herself at any track in the country. For one thing she was young, much younger than he. Mentally Tanner figured the difference in their ages as roughly twelve years. She had her whole life ahead of her, and the racing world was open for a woman to make her mark. If Kelly Smith wanted it badly enough, Tanner had no doubt that she could make her way into the select circle of the nation's foremost Thoroughbred trainers. For some reason that realization left him with an unsettled feeling in the pit of his stomach.

"What do you think?" Kelly asked, her eyes alight with anticipation. "Does she look ready?"

Tanner's glance flicked from the filly to Kelly. "She looks great. . . . By the way, I'm watching the race from the owners' section."

"Okay. . . ." Kelly felt some of her enthusiasm ebb as she watched Tanner turn and stride away. So much for warm wishes, she thought.

Well, go ahead, she told him silently. Who needs you, anyway? At Pinetop his all-too-frequent suggestions had slowed her down like hobbles, but since they'd arrived at Churchill Downs, she'd had the distinct feeling that he valued her judgment and almost enjoyed her company.

She'd begun to think of them as a team, and now he was rushing off as if the smell of a stable was too offensive. For an instant she admitted that his abrupt departure had left her feeling lonely, and the discovery infuriated her.

Fine, Mr. McCrey, she fumed silently, go sit with the owners. You and your kind don't belong here, anyway.

With a huff, she turned her full attention to the filly and lost herself in the blur of last-minute adjustments. Jay Moran arrived at the last minute, barely in time to listen to her brief instructions.

"Keep the filly relaxed on the backstretch," Kelly reminded, pointing her finger at him as she often had at her seventh-graders, "and don't ask her for speed until you turn for home."

Jay nodded as Doug boosted him into the saddle. Kelly followed the filly out of the paddock and took her place next to the rail to watch the post parade.

She smothered the fleeting urge to turn and glance up at the owners' section. Instead she kept her gaze fixed on Keepsake who tossed her head and pranced, as an outrider led her past the crowd. Away from the grandstand, the horse dropped her head and warmed up smoothly.

Kelly glanced at the green tote board in the infield. The odds on Keepsake were high, not surprising after her dismal showings in her last two races.

For the shorter, six-furlong races, the starting gate was positioned on the far side of the track, away from the crowd. Kelly held her breath and watched through her binoculars as Keepsake was led into her slot without a fuss. When the bell sounded and the gates sprang open, Keepsake bounded forward and drove for the lead.

Jay stood in the irons and eased her back to fourth. He was poised high above the saddle and, as Kelly had told him, he held the filly steady.

On the far turn, two horses rushed up on either side of the filly, and she bolted forward. Kelly heard Marcy gasp beside her. Jay looked both ways for racing room and found that he was boxed in.

"Easy," Kelly whispered, "bide your time." On the home turn, the horse on Keepsake's right faded back into the pack. "Now," Kelly said, her voice tight with tension.

Jay's body flattened out above Keepsake's neck as his hands brushed the reins forward, urging her on. Her strides lengthened as her front legs struck out to pull the ground under her. One by one, she overtook the front-runners, until she came sailing across the finish line to win by a half length.

The crowd murmured their surprise, while a few long-shot players shrieked with joy.

With a whoop of delight, Marcy hugged Kelly's neck, and Doug clapped her on the back and pumped her hand as he shouted his congratulations.

As Jay trotted the filly back to the center of the track, Kelly stepped through a gate and sank ankle deep into the loam. She suddenly felt a supporting grip on her elbow. As she glanced up, she found Tanner smiling as he escorted her across the track.

Kelly reached for the filly's bridle, and the photographer gestured for everyone to move in closer. Tanner stepped behind her, and Marcy and Doug moved into the picture behind him. Kelly could feel Tanner's broad chest against her back, and she didn't know which was more exciting, winning the race or being pressed against him.

The filly tossed her head impatiently, and Tanner's arm quietly encircled Kelly's waist to steady her. His nearness filled her senses, and she stared blankly into the camera as it flashed.

Marcy and Doug led the filly off the track, and Tanner and Kelly followed along behind. Approaching the stables, they caught sight of Rob and Louise sitting close together on a hay bale. Rob was raking his fingers through Louise's dark hair, removing bits of hay. He was so absorbed in his task that he didn't notice Kelly and Tanner until they were next to him.

Rob glanced at the filly. "How'd she do?"

"She won!" Marcy announced, trying to hide the trace of irritation in her voice.

"Congratulations," Louise said unemotionally.

"Thanks." Kelly nodded as they moved past them to the next building.

"Bathe her and cool her out," Kelly ordered as she nodded to Doug.

"Right, boss."

Marcy's head was hanging dejectedly, and Kelly suspected that some of the young girl's joy over the race had been dampened at the sight of Rob sitting with Louise. Kelly had found the sight more puzzling than disturbing. Rob was at least a dozen years younger than Louise. Were the two of them romantically involved? She made a mental note to ask Tanner.

After Doug and Marcy had led the filly to the end of the building to the wash rack, Kelly stepped inside the empty stall that served as a tack room. "What's going on with Rob and Louise?"

"Can't you tell?" Tanner glanced up, and she could have sworn she heard amusement in his voice.

"Well, I don't get it. Rob's my age and Louise has to be pushing forty."

His brow lifted defensively. "Is something wrong with that?"

"Well, for one thing, what could they possibly have in common?"

Tanner gazed at her knowingly. "I wonder."

Kelly suddenly felt the need to busy her hands. "I just meant I . . . I guess I'm just surprised, that's all. I had no idea that Rob and Louise were seeing each other."

"Why should that surprise you?" Tanner countered, sounding more defensive than he'd intended. "They're both attractive people with a similar interest in horses."

"Well, it's none of my business." Kelly briskly rinsed the bit and wiped the filly's bridle with a rag before looking back at him. "But it seems to me that they're from two different worlds."

Tanner shrugged. "Who can explain love?"

"Love!"

"Something wrong with being in love, Ms. Smith?"

She snorted at that and turned away to hang the bridle on a hook. "Infatuation would be more like it," she muttered, thinking of how easily she could fool herself into thinking she was falling in love with Tanner McCrey, instead of admitting what it really was—pure old infatuation.

Tanner chuckled. "You think so, huh?"

"It's nothing personal. I just don't happen to believe in love at first sight—or maybe being in love at all. That's a fairy tale that only gets people into trouble." She snatched up a rag and began to wipe the saddle vigorously.

"Oh?" he asked in a tone that goaded her. "What do you believe in, 'like' at first sight?"

"Well, sure. . . . You can be attracted to someone right off, but that isn't love." She refused to meet his gaze. "That's why there are so many divorces. People get all starry-eyed and rush off to a preacher never considering for a moment that it might not last. Then before you know it, they have a baby, but even that fails to keep them together because they have no foundation, no common interests, no common goals, so they split, and their kid grows up wondering why."

"Did your parents split up when you were young?" he asked perceptively.

"Never mind," she fired back defensively, wishing she hadn't said so much, wishing that he hadn't seen the hurt inside her. "Just seems to me that real love, if there is such a thing, would take longer than 'first sight,' that's all."

"How long?" he asked, leaning negligently against the doorway.

"What?"

"How long would 'real love' take?" The lines in his cheeks deepened as he teased her.

"How should I know?" she tossed back coolly.

"Ever been in love?"

"That's none of your business," she answered sharply. She tossed the rag into a corner.

"Oh, my, I've hit a nerve, haven't I?"

"Certainly not. Don't we have more important things to talk about, such as the future of your filly, or something more productive."

"No, this subject fascinates me." He pushed away from the doorway, and she tried to shrug away as he gently tipped her chin upward. Her face looked fragile and vulnerable in the dim light filtering into the small space. "You don't believe," he began, his face moving closer to hers, "that between two people separated by more than a few years—" his warm breath fanned across her face

"—there can exist a rush of emotion, so strong and unexpected that it might be called love at first sight?"

She saw the flicker of desire in his eyes and the almost imperceptible glint of challenge. Her heart was pounding so loudly she wondered if he could hear it. She couldn't have moved away if she'd wanted to. The smolder in his eyes held her mesmerized. His brow arched, and she knew an answer was expected, but she was having a difficult time remembering the question. "No . . ." she said softly.

"No?" He saw in her eyes the confusion, the uncertainty, the fear.

Slowly he lowered his mouth to hers, slowly enough that they both knew she had time to move away if she chose. His lips brushed hers once, then lifted, and for a moment they gazed into each other's eyes.

She looked back at him blankly, her vision blurred by a need she hadn't known could be so easily tapped. An involuntary sigh rushed through her lips. It was all the answer he needed.

His lips came back down to capture hers, demanding response and receiving it. Effortlessly he parted her lips with his and lightly ran his tongue over hers.

He slipped his hands under her jacket to run his fingers up her spine, pulling her closer to him. Tremors of excitement raced through her, everywhere his fingers moved. She found herself pressed against his solid chest and was surprised to discover that she was straining even closer.

His mouth tantalized, his tongue teased and tormented as it slipped into her mouth and pulled back, inviting her to taste and explore. She gave in to temptation and followed his lead. There she discovered the dark tastes and textures that were his.

Excitement burned through her, and her fingers splayed and twined into his thick hair.

"My lovely little pessimist." His husky whisper skimmed over her face and down her neck as her head tilted back and his mouth lowered again.

A sweet warmth rose from the hollow of her throat. He inhaled the light, clean scent heated by her pulse pounding there. It filled his senses like no extravagant floral scents or spices ever had.

He ached to touch more of her as his fingertips stroked the length of her back. His frustration mounted. Her clothes were layers thick, the room was cramped, people were nearby, but his body cried for more. Just one touch, just one, his scattered thoughts demanded, and you'll know the feel of her. His hands tugged her shirttail from her jeans.

"Hey, Kelly," a voice shouted from the walkway, "you want us to soak her legs or rub 'em down with liniment?"

Kelly groaned as she was yanked from ecstasy to reality. She tried to raise her voice, but all that came forth was a croak. Tanner squeezed her shoulders and reluctantly moved her a few inches away.

"Just a minute," Kelly called.

"What?" Marcy hollered over the tumult of activity outside.

Their breath mingled lightly as Tanner searched her eyes for an instant before setting her an arm's distance away. She could see the kiss had been as unsettling to him as it had been to her.

"Dinner tonight," he said. "Knock on my door when you're ready."

"I don't think—"

"We can discuss 'the future of my filly, or something more productive,'" he said, quoting her in a tone that mocked them both.

Before she could refuse, he turned and walked out. Kelly slumped down onto a hay bale, knowing that her knees couldn't have supported her for another second. She was shaken to the core.

She hadn't thought that debating with him would have provoked such a reaction. Never had a kiss had quite such an effect on her. She knew without a shadow of a doubt that it was something she should never have allowed. Something she couldn't afford to let happen again.

Marcy poked her head in the doorway. "Kelly? You all right?"

Kelly glanced up, smiled lamely and nodded. That was debatable, she thought.

· · ·

As Tanner strode past Marcy and Doug, his heart was still pounding. He was already berating himself for kissing his trainer. He hadn't meant it to happen, but Kelly's remarks had made him want to prove her wrong.

Privately he'd figured that his brother's interest in Louise was a passing thing, but Kelly's crack about their age difference had been impossible to ignore. His pace slackened and he tried to analyze why her attitude had provoked him.

To be honest he had to admit that what had really gotten him was that he partly agreed with her. His next birthday was looming on the horizon. While he'd never thought he was vain about age, the four-oh staring him in the face had been bothering him lately. Why was that, he wondered. He'd never given his age much thought before, at least not before Kelly Smith had come into his life.

She was so fresh, so full of life. There was a certain indefinable something about her that drew him to her. But she's young, he reminded himself, too young. It was obvious after today that she belonged at the heart of the action, and he knew now what he hadn't known when he'd been her age: he belonged at Pinetop. Though he loved the races, especially when Pinetop horses were running, he knew that the gypsy life of the racing circuit wasn't for him. And he had the nagging feeling that Kelly was destined to follow it.

"Congratulations, Tanner." A deep voice broke into his thoughts, and Tanner swung around. "Didn't mean to startle you." Jared Huxsman stepped out of the lengthening late-afternoon shadows. "Quite a performance out of your Keepsake filly today. Looks like the little trainer knows her stuff."

"Thanks." Tanner turned to walk away.

"Makes one wonder if she'll have as much success with Baritone come derby time."

"I expect she will," Tanner said over his shoulder.

"Yes," Jared responded quickly. "That would be something, wouldn't it?"

Tanner never broke stride.

"Say, have you given any more thought to selling me that parcel of land that adjoins mine?"

The question had the desired effect. Tanner's steps paused. "No," he said without turning around.

"Really? I thought it was a generous offer myself."

Tanner slowly turned around. "My land isn't for sale, Huxsman. You know that."

"Oh, I see. Well, with your renewed interest in the ponies, I'd hoped you might decide to sell. That ground might be fair timberland, but it'd never make decent pasture, you know."

"But you figure it'd make a decent convention center site."

"Well, you know me. Seems I have to be building something or I get restless. Of course, if our plans work out, we'll be looking to you to supply the lumber."

"We'll appreciate your business," Tanner said dryly.

"Hell, Tanner, I consider you family. Your father and I may not have seen eye to eye, but I have no quarrel with you. On the contrary, I think of you like another son."

"Glad to hear that, Jared." Tanner turned and started walking again.

"Yes, it'd make my boy Rob real happy if we'd be more neighborly." Jared made a sweeping gesture toward the racetrack. "You're a businessman and a horseplayer. Tell you what. Let's have us a side wager on the Arkansas Derby—it'll make it more fun for both of us."

"Forget it, Huxsman."

"No, I'm serious, Tanner. I propose that if Baritone wins, I'll sell you that section that adjoins yours."

Tanner's footsteps faltered again. He didn't know what Jared was up to, but he had never been able to get him to offer to sell that particular piece of land before. The offer caught Tanner off guard.

"However," Jared continued, "if Louise's Claimjumper wins, you'll sell me that parcel of yours we discussed. In either event, the land would be sold for its appraisal price. What would you say to a gentlemen's wager?"

Tanner's jaw firmed stubbornly. "I'd say no."

"No?" Jared said, unable to hide his surprise.

"A man doesn't bet more than he's willing to lose, and I'm not interested in losing Pinetop land."

"You could, easy as not, win a section to add to it," Jared reminded.

Tanner shook his head. "Thanks anyway, but I'll confine my wagering to the betting windows."

"Nothing ventured, nothing gained," Jared said pleasantly.

"The way I see it, Jared, I stand to gain enough already if my colt wins."

"Well, if you change your mind . . ."

Tanner was already three strides away before he responded. "I won't."

KELLY STOOD and stretched, then walked outside the makeshift tack room to check Keepsake's recovery from her race. Reaching under the cooling blanket, Kelly ran her hand along Keepsake's belly to be sure that she was cooling out properly.

She smiled at Marcy and Doug. "You're done a nice job." The two of them rewarded her with grins.

"Wasn't she just wonderful, Kelly?" Marcy's eyes were bright with enthusiasm.

"She was," Kelly agreed, reaching up to rub the filly between the eyes.

"Sure done us proud today," Doug said. "I always knew she could do it."

"Give her a few sips of water every five minutes and walk her until her coat is bone-dry."

"I'll take her for a while, Marcy," Doug said. "You can spell me later."

"Okay." Marcy gratefully handed the lead to Doug. As he and the filly started off, Marcy looked up at Kelly. "Guess I better clean the tack and pack it up."

"Good idea. I started on it, but you're more thorough than I am." Kelly thought of Tanner's kiss—the reason for her earlier distraction, and felt a need to work off her tension. "I'll be back in a while."

She shoved her hands into her pockets and struck out at a brisk pace. There were rows and rows of sheds, and as wound up as she felt, Kelly planned to walk around every one of them. It felt good to move, and she could think better when she was active.

People nodded at her as she wove her way around horses standing in the aisles, some just returning from the track with steam rising from their backs and others dripping wet from their baths.

She exhaled sharply as she remembered the way she'd behaved with Tanner. Her response had been ridiculously juvenile, necking in the tack room, of all things!

She shook her head. She'd known better than to let something like that get started, but had she told him to back off? Of course not, she groaned, she'd not only melted in his arms, she'd responded passionately.

Had she forgotten the reason she'd gone to Pinetop in the first place? It certainly hadn't been to find passion in the arms of its owner. She wondered what her father would have thought of this latest turn of events.

Charlie would have been proud of her victory at the track, but she hardly thought he'd have been proud of her behavior in the tack room. He'd never cared for the liaisons that occurred on the back side of racetracks. It was only natural when people worked closely together that personal involvements would result, but he'd told her that he thought such relationships caused distractions, and distractions in any competitive sport could prove disastrous.

In spite of his failings in other areas, Charlie Bailey had run a tight ship. With a stab of regret Kelly decided that he would have thought her behavior with Tanner foolish indeed. And, while she was feeling low, she asked herself how much progress she'd made on clearing Charlie's name. With a heavy sigh, she admitted that she'd accomplished nothing so far. The thrill of victory was long gone. She was feeling downright rotten.

She paused under an overhang to pet a blaze-faced horse who thrust his nose in her direction wanting a little attention.

"Hello, fella," she whispered softly. Whenever she felt bad, the company of a horse was usually her comfort.

She caught a glimpse of two young hot walkers, leading their horses down the alley.

"Did you see the sixth race?" the tall one asked the other.

"Yeah," the smaller one replied. "Could you believe Jay Moran brought in the winner?"

Kelly's ears perked up. They had to be talking about Jay's ride aboard Keepsake. She huddled in the shadows and strained to listen as they drew nearer.

"I was surprised he could even show up today," the tall one confided. "I heard he got the tar knocked outta him last night."

"Yeah," the small one agreed as they passed by, too absorbed in their conversation to notice Kelly. "Man, he better start payin' his debts, or they'll fix him so's he can't ride no more."

Kelly leaned forward, straining to hear more, but they'd moved beyond her range. Her hands balled into fists. So Jay Moran was in deep trouble. He'd won a race for her today, but how could she count on him in the future, she wondered. She was filled with a sense of foreboding.

Then an even more startling thought occurred to her. Jay had been one of the last people to see Charlie alive. Could he have had something to do with what happened that day? She wondered if those he owed could manipulate him into breaking the law.

She wasn't sure, but she knew one thing, Jay couldn't be fully trusted. If that was the case, her instincts told her that he wasn't the man to ride Baritone in the derby.

She turned and headed back to Keepsake's stall, her thoughts in a tangle. She took a deep breath, trying to put the conversation she'd overheard into perspective. She cautioned herself not to jump to wild conclusions. Jay might be having personal problems, but that didn't mean that he had to be on the take or that he'd do anything dishonest.

Logic comforted her, so she decided to apply it to another matter that disturbed her: Tanner McCrey. True, she'd responded to him to a degree she would never have expected, but she had been under strain lately. And, she admitted, she'd been lonely. Though the Pinetop staff had welcomed her into the fold, she was still grieving for her best friend: her father. It was only natural that she'd be more vulnerable now. Her resistance was down, and it seemed she wasn't immune to the potent McCrey charm.

Her reflections hadn't solved anything, but they had made her feel better.

Suddenly she felt a tug on her sleeve.

"Kelly Smith? Are you going to walk right past my stalls without even saying hello?"

Kelly glanced up to find Louise smiling at her.

"I'm sorry . . . I didn't see you. I guess I was lost in thought."

"Still floating on a cloud after your victory today, huh?"

Kelly shrugged.

Louise was standing before her, looking smart in a trendy leather jacket and wool flannel slacks. "Don't be so modest," she said, placing her hand on Kelly's arm. "Listen to me, young lady, you enjoy your success. The men certainly do, and it's no easy trick to beat them at their own games. Believe me, I know."

Kelly smiled. Louise Cabot seemed like a straight shooter. Kelly's intuition told her that Louise wouldn't cut anyone any slack on the racetrack, but she probably wouldn't cut throats to win, either.

"Come over here, Kelly." Louise motioned her to follow. "Tell me, what do you think of the way my mare is shod? Now I want you to tell me the truth."

Kelly approached the rangy chestnut and systematically lifted her feet, checked her shoes, and then moved to stand in front of her and behind her to assess her build. "How does she run?"

Louise glanced over her shoulders to be sure no one was listening. "To tell you the truth, we're having trouble with her. Hell, if she'd run straight, she'd be dynamite, but she lugs out on the turns and loses ground. Been pickin' up thirds and fourths her last times out."

"Well, I haven't seen her travel, and I haven't ridden her, but I'd say you ought to change her back plates to caulked shoes. You might try rubber bit guards too, might make her easier to guide."

"Thanks," Louise said warmly. "Rob told me you'd have some ideas."

"No guarantees, Mrs. Cabot. It's usually a process of trial and error until you find something that works."

"Call me Louise. And thanks for your tips. My trainer is good, mind you, but he's too conservative sometimes." Louise chuckled. "I get on his nerves something fierce."

Kelly smiled; she could just imagine. "Goes with the territory."

"You know," Louise said with her eyes narrowed, "I like you. You're good and you're smart. These men can be such a pain. You have to stroke their egos, and they get all bent out of shape if you have ideas of your own."

Kelly smiled. "I guess some do."

Louise looked at Kelly with a respect in her eyes that said she found her a worthy opponent. "You're working for a good man, Kelly, but that still has its drawbacks. You know, I like to see a deserving woman get ahead." Louise smiled. "I don't like every woman I meet, of course. Most are too jealous for their own good, but I have a feeling we could work well together."

"Thanks, Louise." Kelly found the woman more

likable than she'd expected from her first impression at the barbecue.

"If Tanner McCrey doesn't pay you well enough, you ought to walk."

"Money isn't my first concern," Kelly said.

"Then you should definitely come work for me," Louise said with a laugh.

Kelly chuckled.

"No, I'm being serious now, Kelly. I suspect you're committed to Tanner through spring."

Kelly nodded.

"Well, if he doesn't nail you down with a generous contract then, you come see me. I think we could do a little business." Louise glanced around. "Of course, I'd prefer you keep that to yourself."

"I will," Kelly said. "Thanks, Louise. I have a feeling you've just paid me a generous compliment."

"Caulks on back, huh?" Louise murmured as she turned to look back at her horse. "Interesting."

"And rubber guards on her bit," Kelly reminded.

"Of course, dear . . . and rubber guards on her bit."

Chapter Nine

Tanner glanced at the clock for what seemed like the twentieth time. It was ten after seven, and Kelly hadn't knocked on his door yet. He was beginning to wonder if she would show up at all. He sat on the edge of his bed scratching his palms. He wished he had a cigarette. It was the first time he'd thought about smoking in years. He'd kicked the habit long ago, but tonight for some reason he was edgy.

He paced to the window and looked down at the parking lot. The Pinetop truck was there. He'd seen Kelly arrive with Marcy forty-five minutes ago. He assumed Doug had stayed behind to keep an eye on the filly.

Why hadn't Kelly at least called, he wondered. Would she stand him up? He strode back to the bed and loosened his tie. His blazer was hanging on the back of a chair, and he thought about removing his tie and changing into jeans. He decided to give her a few more minutes.

Stretching out on the bed, he reached for the TV remote control. For the next few minutes, he flipped through every channel twice without noticing what was on any of them.

His concentration was absorbed by the memory of Kelly in his arms. There was something about that girl. He was beginning to regret asking her to dinner. She was right—it would be foolish for them to become involved. Funny, he'd never had this problem before, and he'd worked with women before. What was it about Kelly Smith that made a difference?

The light rap at his door broke into his thoughts. He closed his eyes, and for a split second he considered ignoring the knock. He chuckled at himself. He would have answered that door if he'd had both legs broken. In two strides, he'd pulled the door open.

Kelly smiled back at him hesitantly, and he knew he was in big trouble. She was wearing a tailored silk dress of emerald green that turned her eyes the color of spring grass in the south pasture. A simple black raincoat lay draped over her arm.

She stood looking back at him realizing that she'd hoped he wouldn't answer, had hoped he'd gotten tired of waiting, had even hoped that he was out celebrating his winner and hadn't given his earlier dinner invitation to her a second thought. But here he was, his eyes a most arresting blue.

"I . . . just stopped by to say I—"

"—am really looking forward to our dinner tonight, Tanner," he said, interrupting her before she could finish.

Kelly wasn't good at lying. He could easily read the look in her eyes and knew that she had knocked on his door to deliver a polite excuse and then beat a hasty retreat. He quickly took her wrist and drew her into the room before she could get away.

"How's Keepsake?" he asked as he began to shrug into his blazer.

"Oh . . . Rob examined her and said she's fine. Doug is staying with her again tonight."

Kelly really wished she hadn't come. Tanner looked entirely too handsome tonight. She should have stayed home as she'd planned. When she'd left their room, Marcy had been propped up in bed absorbed in an action-packed movie, trying to decide what she'd order from room service. Kelly envied her. What might seem like a dull evening to Marcy seemed like sheer pleasure to Kelly. And much safer. Safer than an evening in the company of Tanner McCrey. And if she hadn't known it before, this afternoon in the tack room had proved it was going to be nearly impossible to keep her feelings for him platonic.

She watched as he absently checked the pockets of his blazer and then tried to put his tie back in order. His fingers tugged the stubborn knot back and forth, inching it up to his collar. She had an urge to reach out and help him the way she had helped Rob at the barbecue, but she didn't dare. With Tanner, even that simple a gesture would have been too intimate. She reminded herself of the long lecture she'd given herself: she had to be friendly but cautious tonight.

Tanner glanced at her, and a smile formed at the

corners of his mouth when he saw the solemn line of her lips. She looked edgy as a rabbit, ready to bolt if anyone said boo.

"I'm encouraged about Keepsake," he offered, trying to ease her concerns. "She looked real good out there today."

Good? Kelly thought, the horse had looked *great,* but she found herself slowly beginning to relax. Judging by Tanner's remarks, this would only be a business dinner. She'd yawned her way through enough of those . . . yet she couldn't imagine feeling bored in his company, whether it was business or not.

Tanner glanced at his watch and frowned. "I have dinner reservations at eight. It's seven-thirty now. We'd better be on our way." Touching her elbow lightly, he guided her to the door.

"I hope you like prime rib?"

"Unfortunately I like it too much."

Tanner glanced down at her trim figure. "One would never know it."

Kelly felt her cheeks growing warm with his unhurried perusal. "Thank you," she murmured.

They drove along the banks of the Ohio, and Kelly was fascinated by the fountain set out in the river itself. Illuminated by an array of colored spotlights, it sent a tower of spray in all directions.

For generations, Louisville, Kentucky, had watched the evolution of the riverboat on the Ohio River and the Thoroughbred on Churchill Downs.

It was a city steeped in tradition that gave Kelly a sense of a solid and enduring place.

Tanner parked the car and held her door open as she stepped out into the crisp evening air. They had to walk a block to the restaurant, and Kelly was painfully aware of his hand resting casually on her waist.

They passed through a heavily carved door and stood for a moment under the brilliant glow of a chandelier the size of a compact car. Victorian furnishings had transformed a century-old warehouse into a posh restaurant.

"This is wonderful," she murmured.

"I'd hoped you'd like it."

Kelly felt a measure of relief when they were seated at a corner table, but bits of conversation sprinkled with horse racing comments floated to her ears, and she realized that the place was filled with horse owners and racing fans fresh from a long day at Churchill Downs. Her eyes scanned the sea of faces warily, and she had to push aside the worry that she might be recognized by someone who knew she was Charlie's daughter.

That's ridiculous, she told herself. It had been much more likely that someone would have recognized her at Churchill Downs, but she had been too busy to worry about it there.

She glanced at Tanner, and his eyes met hers intimately while the server poured champagne. She noticed he had made no reference to the kiss they'd shared that afternoon, but something in his eyes told her that it was far from forgotten.

"Congratulations," he said, touching his glass to the rim of hers. "Nice win today, lady."

She nodded demurely. "You have a nice filly, sir." When she felt uncomfortable, as she did now, she always found it easier to revert to being professional. She hoped if she glossed over the awkward moments, the dinner would be more comfortable.

Tanner set his glass on the table and smiled at her. "What do you suggest we do with Keepsake now?"

"Well, the season at Churchill Downs is over, but there are still several weeks left at Remington Park, if you want to give her another race or two this year."

"That's up to you."

She wasn't sure she'd heard him right. "What?"

"I said, that's up to you. You're running the show."

She blinked in surprise, wondering when they'd passed that milestone. "No, you should decide if you want to send her," she said. "You're the one footing the bills."

"Do you think she can do well?"

Kelly leaned forward, trying to control her eagerness to show him what the horse could really do. "If your filly is placed in the right races, she can win."

"I'm all for that." He leaned back in his chair to study her. Her face was flushed, and the candlelight cast soft auburn lights through her hair. Tanner suddenly recalled Rob's earlier observation that Kelly would be a stunning redhead, and he had to agree. "What's our next step?"

"I think it would be a mistake to move her up in class too quickly. Gradual steps up to higher purses is the safest route."

He nodded, and she continued, "I think we should stick with the shorter distances, five or six furlongs. She needs to build confidence and stamina. If we push her for too much too soon, I'm afraid she'll lose heart."

"I agree," he said quietly.

"From her pedigree I think she was bred to be a sprinter."

Tanner's brows lifted. Kelly was even more thorough than he'd realized. "You're right. And I've always liked her looks and her style." His eyes drifted back to lazily move over her face. *And I could easily say the same about you,* the look in his eye added.

Kelly averted her gaze. The mood had somehow taken a turn toward the personal, or was she reading things into Tanner's gaze? Well, she decided, perhaps it was time to see just how much he actually trusted her judgment.

"I overheard something that disturbed me today."

"Oh?"

"About Jay Moran."

Tanner shrugged again. "I don't put much stock in gossip."

"Neither do I, but this isn't the first time I've heard that Jay has a gambling habit."

Tanner's glance roamed distractedly over the other diners. "I'm sure he isn't the only one."

"But it sounded like Jay's gambling is out of control. Tanner, the people I heard said he was in pretty deep to the wrong people, and those kind can play pretty rough when they aren't paid on time."

"Talk at the track is usually worth what you pay for it, Kelly. Rumors spread through the barns like wildfire. Most of it has to be discounted as just that—rumors."

She seethed when she realized he hadn't taken the unsubstantiated rumors about her father as lightly. "I'd be the first to agree with you, but we're talking about Baritone's jockey. If Jay *is* in trouble with loan sharks, what would that suggest to you?"

"If you're suggesting that Jay would throw a race, I'd say no."

"Can you afford to take the chance?"

Their eyes met in a silent challenge.

Tanner finally lifted his glass again. "I have no reason to distrust Jay."

"I know . . . and I know I'm beginning to sound

paranoid, but you've made me responsible for Baritone, and I think you should be aware of all the possibilities."

"Okay, if it'll make you rest easier, I'll look into it, but I want to warn you, I don't think there's a thing to it."

Kelly nodded. "That's all I ask."

He picked up the menu. "Shall we order?"

After dinner Kelly felt more relaxed. The meal had been quite pleasant. They'd talked about world events from opposite points of view, but they'd shared jokes and laughed together, too.

"I talked to Louise Cabot today," she said, stirring cream into her coffee. She set her spoon aside and met his gaze. "I'll have to admit I like her."

"Oh," he said with mock surprise, "even if she is pushing forty?"

His playful reminder didn't go unnoticed. "All right," Kelly grinned sheepishly, "I probably deserve that. I suppose I was wrong to question her attraction to Rob."

"Opposites do attract sometimes," he reminded dryly.

And how, Kelly thought, watching reflected candle glow flicker in his eyes. "Opposites can irritate as well," she said as she let her gaze slowly drop from his. She was determined to fight the attraction.

"Yes, but opposites can also tantalize."

"And annoy," she added defensively.

His gaze moved easily to the silk stretched

temptingly across her small bosom. "And tempt," he said softly.

"And antagonize," she countered.

His gaze traveled slowly back to meet hers, and she saw the glint of amusement in his eyes.

"Opposites really do all that?"

"That and more." Her eyes met his directly. "They can hurt each other."

He stared back at her, trying to assess the change in her mood. It wasn't hard to conclude that someone had hurt her. "I guess that happens."

"Opposites attracting is fine, if you're looking for fun and games."

"Have you had a bad experience with a man?"

Kelly felt a rush of renewed color flooding her cheeks. She knew she'd sounded too defensive. "No, why?"

"I was just wondering how you became such an expert on human relationships."

"Through observation. I just happen to think that couples who are alike have marriages that last. My parents were complete opposites, and they were miserable together. My mother's second husband was a patient, solid man, and their marriage is successful. Too bad she didn't use the same judgment the first time."

"I'm sorry she didn't, either." Tanner enjoyed the sassy spark in her eyes, but the inner core of pain he was beginning to glimpse periodically distressed him. "And what about your father?"

Kelly reached blindly for her water glass. "What about him?"

"Should he have made a wiser choice the first time, or do you suppose he was just a man in love, making choices from his heart and not his head?"

"No . . . I mean I don't know how he felt . . . I just know one day he left and never came back, and Mom said it was because they were just too different."

"And you resent him for that."

"Of course not. I loved my father."

His brow lifted perceptibly. "Loved—past tense?"

"Look, can we change the subject?" Kelly felt foolish for bringing up her past, and even more foolish for trying to explain emotions she didn't even know she had. "Mom says I'm too opinionated, and I guess she's right." She shrugged. "I'm sure there are exceptions," she added.

"But you don't think Rob and Louise will be an exception." It was a statement, not a question.

"I'm not sure. Louise seems more sophisticated than Rob, I guess because she's older."

"Back to the age thing." Tanner sighed, and she wondered if she'd hit a sore spot. Deciding to lighten the conversation, she leaned back in her chair and studied him for a change.

"By the way, how old are you, Tanner?"

"None of your business."

"Tsk, tsk. Are you sensitive?" She tried to restrain a smile but wasn't entirely successful.

"No, but I'm not a spring chicken anymore, either," he said abruptly.

She chuckled. He *was* sensitive about his age, but he didn't need to be. He looked as youthful as any man in the room.

"Tell me, Ms. Smith, where do you plan to be ten years from now?" he asked, smoothly changing the subject. The question had been on his mind all afternoon.

"Ten years?" She lifted her brows. "That's a long time."

"But you've thought about it, right?"

"Well, sure . . . somewhere at the top of my profession, I hope."

He nodded. That was what he'd presumed, too. She had her whole life ahead of her, and he could see she was eager to carve her niche in the racing world.

"The world is ready for a woman trainer to make her mark in world-class competition."

"Maybe." She was still a bit skeptical about that. A woman had to work harder than a man to prove herself, but the prospect of building her career slowly didn't bother her.

Tanner reached out and laid his hand over hers lightly. The touch had the same effect as an electrical current between them. "I can picture you a few years from now with your own staff at Saratoga, New York, or Gulfstream, Florida. They'll be interviewing you on TV. There you'll be, drenched in fame and fortune, the darling of the press."

"I doubt that," she scoffed. "The press is fickle." She remembered her father. Reporters had treated him like a venerable legend until someone had decided to cast baseless suspicions.

Tanner realized with a sinking heart that he could never hold her at Pinetop. It would be impossible to corner such a rising star; he'd been lucky to have snagged a falling star like Charlie Bailey, a man who'd been on the downside of his career, a man who'd been looking for a less demanding, less rigorous pace. Kelly had her whole career ahead of her, and from what he'd seen so far, it could be whatever she wanted to make it.

"Kelly, do you still think we should get a second opinion on Baritone?"

Tanner's question caught her completely off guard. "Yes . . . if you think Rob wouldn't take it the wrong way."

"He would, you know."

"I know, but I'd be less than honest if I recommended otherwise."

His brows knit together, and she could see signs of strain around the corners of his eyes. The last thing she wanted was to cause trouble between the two brothers, yet she wouldn't be doing her job if she pretended she believed nothing was wrong with the horse.

Leaning forward, she asked hesitantly, "Have you changed your mind?"

His gaze met hers solidly. "Yes, I'm authorizing you to arrange for Baritone to go to a second veterinarian."

Kelly breathed a quiet sigh of relief. She knew this had not been an easy decision for him. "I think it's the right thing to do."

He nodded absently. "You make the appointment."

"I had Dr. Andrews in Little Rock in mind. Would you have any objections?"

"No." He glanced away for an instant and then back. "I'm going with you."

"Of course. I'll see what Dr. Andrews has open and check with you before confirming a time."

"Thank you."

"Tanner," she reached over and squeezed his hand reassuringly, "thanks." She knew he'd given the matter considerable thought, and she appreciated his vote of confidence.

They sipped their coffee in silence for a moment. "Hattie tells me you're an attorney. Do you miss practicing law?"

"I don't give it much thought. I was a partner in a firm in Little Rock until three years ago. But now I'm content to run the businesses. There's something gratifying about owning a place like Pinetop."

A look of pride surfaced in his eyes. "But you

couldn't have convinced me of that ten years ago. I'd only come back for short visits since I'd graduated from high school. I'd always had a yen to move to the city . . . seems I just wanted to get away and be on my own."

Kelly recalled how Hattie had said there had been so much upheaval following Rob's birth. "But you came back."

"When my dad had his first heart attack, I came home and stayed on to run Pinetop for him. Two years later he passed away, and I've never left."

"Regrets?"

"No." He shook his head, but she wasn't convinced there hadn't been a few. "When I was a teenager, my dad crammed Pinetop down my throat. He demanded I stay, and like any kid that age I rebelled. But when I came back, things were different. I grew to love it."

"You don't miss the big cities?"

"No, they're nice places to visit, but I don't want to live in one. Not anymore. It's hard to explain. There's something special about being in the woods on pine-scented mornings or helping a newborn foal struggle to his feet." He smiled. "And I have to admit I get a kick out of watching Pinetop babies win races."

"So you really don't miss your law practice?"

"Well, maybe occasionally." He chuckled. "But it passes. I figure I can always hang a shingle in Hot Springs if I ever feel the urge."

"It's nice to know what makes you happy," she said.

He winked at her, and she felt her pulse flutter erratically. "I'm sure it sounds like a boring life to you."

She shook her head. "Not at all."

And it didn't. It sounded like what she'd always wanted. A nice, secure, permanent place to call home.

THEY WERE BOTH QUIET on their way back to the hotel. Tanner walked her to her door, and she turned to face him. He stood for a long moment, looking at her. "It's been a long day," she said at last.

"Are you tired?"

"A little."

His hand came up, and he gently stroked his fingertips over her cheek. Her eyes met his and mirrored the look of longing she saw there. His gaze slowly lowered to her mouth as his fingers traced a path down her throat to wrap around the back of her neck.

She closed her eyes against the need, willing herself not to respond, but she was unable to turn away. She felt the brush of his lips on her forehead. When she opened her eyes, he touched her lips with his forefinger.

"Good night."

"Good night," she whispered, aching to reach out to him.

"You're sure you want to keep this professional?"

"No . . . but that's the way it has to be."

He smiled down at her. "Breakfast in the morning?"

"All right."

He turned, and she watched him walk away. Sighing, she finally slipped inside, closed the door and leaned against it. For a moment she struggled to regain control of her mixed emotions while her eyes adjusted to the dim light in the room.

The television was still on, but Marcy appeared to be sound asleep. Kelly was startled when she suddenly lifted her head drowsily from her pile of pillows. "Nice time?" she asked.

"Yes," Kelly answered, "very nice."

"He's handsome, isn't he?"

"Who?"

"Tanner," Marcy said, annoyed to have to explain.

"I guess."

"Not as cute as Rob though," Marcy murmured, drifting back to sleep.

Kelly smiled. In her opinion, no man could compare with Tanner McCrey, much less a boy like Rob.

ON THE TRIP back to Pinetop, Rob slept the day away in the back seat of the Bronco. When he'd joined the crew for lunch, he'd seemed sullen. Kelly suspected that Tanner had told him they were taking Baritone to Little Rock for a second opinion.

186

She'd figured that he wouldn't be overjoyed about that and he wasn't. Marcy had tried to coax a smile out of him, but he wouldn't oblige her.

The day after their return, Kelly made an appointment with Dr. Andrews. He said he had an opening for the next day, and after checking the time with Tanner, she'd confirmed it.

So, the following morning, Kelly loaded Baritone with help from Doug and Marcy.

"Sure you won't need me to come along?" Marcy asked.

"Not this time," Kelly said. "We'll be back later today."

"Sure," Marcy agreed, with a saucy flick of her ponytail. Kelly was delighted to see she was coming out of her shell a little more every day. After their trip to Louisville, Kelly and Marcy and Doug shared an unspoken rapport.

"Ready?" Tanner asked as he walked into the barn.

Kelly glanced up. "All set."

Kelly opened a small door on the trailer and checked on the colt before climbing inside Tanner's Bronco. The morning sun painted the sky with streaks of pink and gold as they pulled onto the highway.

An hour later they turned down the private road to Dr. Andrews's clinic. Directly ahead, they saw an unimpressive cinder block building and a long barn surrounded by a number of paddocks.

People hauled horses to Dr. Andrews from all over. It was unheard of for the old doc to travel to one of his patients, so the horse trailers lined up outside his clinic every morning. Even with a dozen vet students for assistants, he had more clients than he could handle.

"We're in luck," Kelly said, "only two trailers ahead of us.

Tanner shut off the motor and twisted around to retrieve a basket from the back seat. "Hattie sent something along."

"What is it?"

"I don't know." He gave her a wry look as he handed her the offering. "It's a surprise."

Kelly lifted the wooden lid, and the fragrance of homemade cinnamon rolls filled the inside of the car. Beneath a cloth, she found a thermos of hot chocolate. "You are indeed blessed to have that woman for your housekeeper."

He grinned. "Don't I know it."

They ate in contented silence. When he finished, Tanner pressed the lever on his seat and leaned back.

"Do you know Dr. Andrews?" Kelly asked.

Tanner nodded. "Yeah, Dad used to bring me here with him when I was little. I'd get so restless. The trip would last most of a day since Doc and Dad were the best of friends." He glanced over at her. "Do you know him?"

"I've never met him." But Charlie and the old

doc had been buddies, too, she thought silently. "He certainly has an impressive reputation," she mused. "Rumor has it that a sheik sent Doctor Andrews a plane ticket and a sizable check to fly over to tend his favorite Arabian horse and that he turned it down."

"I've heard that story, too. It's probably true." He chuckled. "Doc's afraid to fly."

Kelly glanced into the wide rearview mirror on her door and saw another trailer pull up behind them. "They're stacking up. I think I'll check Baritone."

Half an hour later Kelly and Tanner, each holding a lead, led Baritone into the building. The smell of antiseptic stung their noses, and the colt began to prance. There was a thick rubber mat on the floor to prevent the horse from slipping.

"Bring him right in here," a small, wiry, white-coated man ordered, gesturing to a metal stanchion in the center of the room.

Kelly and Tanner eased the colt into the narrow, pipe enclosure. Two assistants took the leads from them, and Tanner turned to shake the doctor's hand.

"Hello, Doc."

"Hello, Tanner. Been a long time. I hear you've got a vet in the family now."

Tanner nodded. "Rob."

"Well, least you two boys could do is come down for a visit once in a while."

Tanner smiled and gestured toward Kelly and back to the doc. "Kelly Smith. Doctor Andrews. Kelly is our new trainer."

Kelly and the doctor shook hands. "A pleasure to meet you, Doctor," she murmured.

The doc stepped back, and his alert eyes flicked from Kelly to Tanner and back again. "Just like you to hire a pretty one."

Kelly and Tanner exchanged embarrassed looks.

"This is the rascal who scaled every fence here and hid in the hayloft when it was time to go home," the doc chuckled.

Kelly shot Tanner a wry look. "Not the version I got."

The old doc chuckled again. "I bet not." He walked over to Baritone and laid his hand on the horse's back. "Good-looking colt. What seems to be the problem?"

Tanner looked to Kelly expectantly.

"We're really here on a hunch, Doctor," she began. "The colt quit in the stretch his last time out. Rob hasn't been able to find anything wrong with him, but his workouts are erratic. He'll improve for several days, and then he'll get sluggish. We're hoping you might find something we've overlooked . . . I'm thinking it's in his legs."

"Well, that's always possible. Let's have a look."

Kelly and Tanner took a seat on a bench against a wall and waited while the doc checked the colt from nose to tail and his assistants took samples into a lab in the back. Kelly discovered that although a client had to wait to get into the clinic, he wasn't hustled out in a hurry. The vet was methodical and thorough.

"Why don't you two step into my office," Dr. Andrews suggested a little later as he washed his hands and dried them on a paper towel. They followed him into a modest but functional office. The vet clipped a series of X rays onto an illuminated panel that he switched on as he flipped off the overhead light.

"If you'll study these," he began, "you'll see that Baritone's legs are in good shape."

Kelly and Tanner stepped forward to check the X rays carefully.

"I could have sworn there'd be something," Kelly murmured. "The X rays taken before his last race are missing, and I'd thought . . ."

"Nothing there," the vet said in a crisp, professional tone as he flipped on the overhead light again. "The colt checks out okay, although his lab tests are a bit puzzling. There's a trace of something in his blood that we can't identify." The old doc slipped on a pair of half glasses and squinted to read the paper he was holding. "Is the colt on anything?"

"No . . . he's not on any drugs, if that's what you mean. Just vitamin supplements in his feed," Kelly said.

Doc Andrews shrugged. "Well, everyone comes

into contact with chemicals these days. They're in the air, in the water . . . whatever this is, and it may be nothing at all, it's not a prescription drug I'm familiar with."

Dr. Andrews looked up, removed his glasses, and gestured toward the paper in his hand. "I can run a complete lab analysis on him and send it to you. Probably take us a week."

"Thanks, we'd appreciate it," Tanner said.

Kelly wandered back to the X rays of Baritone's front legs. Although she hadn't been able to feel any heat or swelling, she could have sworn that there'd been something there, perhaps something that only hurt him toward the end of a race or workout. But there was nothing on the film. She could see for herself.

"Off the record," Tanner said, "do you think you'll find anything after more lab tests, Doc?"

Dr. Andrews shook his head. "I doubt it, son, but you can never tell about these things."

Kelly crossed the room to stand before his desk again. "Have you checked everything?"

The doctor nodded. "The horse is in fine shape."

"I know there's something bothering that colt, and I'd swear it's physical. I can feel it when I'm riding him, and when I'm watching him, I can practically tell the instant it hits him. It's like a switch goes off inside him," Kelly fretted.

Dr. Andrews looked at her kindly. "I wish there was more I could do."

Kelly shook her head in frustration. "His previous trainer was Charlie Bailey, and Charlie suspected there was something wrong with this horse. I just know it."

"Yes, Charlie was concerned about the horse," Doc Andrews agreed. "He even made an appointment here some weeks back, but he never showed up. . . . I was sure sorry to hear about his death."

"Could you check the date of that appointment?" Kelly asked. "If it's when I think it was, it might prove that Charlie wasn't trying to steal the horse." Kelly tried to keep the excitement out of her voice but failed.

The vet walked to his desk and flipped the pages in his appointment book. "How long ago would that have been, young lady?"

"A month ago—October thirteenth."

Tanner watched as Kelly hurried over to help the vet check the record book.

"Let me see," the vet said, running his finger down the pages. "Yes, Charlie had an appointment on the morning of October thirteenth. He'd called and arranged it the day before. I took the call myself. He never canceled, and I never heard from him again. I read where he died, but I didn't realize it was that same day."

"I knew it!" Kelly glanced at Tanner triumphantly. "I knew he wouldn't lie! Charlie Bailey was coming here that day, so the ransom note has to be a plant! What else could it have been?" she continued breathlessly, turning back to Tanner. "If he was bringing your horse here, he couldn't have been kidnapping him."

"He might have been bringing him here, Kelly, but—"

"But what?" she said with more than a trace of annoyance.

Tanner took a deep breath, trying to choose his words carefully. "The authorities will consider the possibility that the appointment might have been arranged as a cover, in case someone checked that day."

"Well, no one checked, did they?" Her face was flushed, and her voice was angry. "Because no one cared. A man is dead, and his reputation is in tatters, but who cares?"

"I think we're taking up the doc's valuable time," Tanner reminded, and Kelly realized that he was uncomfortable with the scene she was making.

Drawing a deep steadying breath, she turned to the vet. "It was nice to meet you, Dr. Andrews," she said. "Thank you for your help."

"My pleasure."

Kelly shot an irritated glance in Tanner's direction. "If you'll excuse me, I'll go out to load the colt."

Tanner sighed. He hadn't meant to step on her toes again. "I'll be there in a minute."

"No hurry." After she'd closed the door behind her, Tanner asked the vet to bill him. When the two emerged from his office, the next client was leading a small yearling into the stanchion.

"Hey, Doc," the man called.

"Hello, Pete," the vet returned. "How're things down Louisiana way?"

"Can't complain, except I can't get this filly to grow. Our vets have wormed her, but unless you can find what's ailin' her, she won't be big enough to race Shetland ponies much less Thoroughbreds."

"We'll see what we can do," the doc promised.

"Say, Doc, that girl that just walked outta here," the man said, stabbing his thumb toward the door, "I know I've seen her before. What's her name?"

"Kelly Smith," the doc returned, glancing at Tanner for verification.

Tanner nodded.

"Nope, the name don't ring a bell. But that face . . ." The man slapped his thigh. "Now I remember! She worked at Louisiana Downs some years back. Some kin to ol' Charlie Bailey . . . God rest his soul."

Tanner frowned. "Kin?"

"Yes, sir, can't remember if it's his kid or what," the man said pensively. "But she's got something to do with him."

"Well, I'll be." Tanner turned on his heel and strode outside.

Chapter Ten

The return trip to Pinetop was strained. Both Kelly and Tanner were lost in thought. Kelly found it hard to believe that Dr. Andrews hadn't found anything physically wrong with Baritone. She realized with a sinking heart that if he had been unable to find anything, no one else would either. The experience left her feeling drained with little to say.

The sun was muted by clouds as they unloaded the colt. While Kelly and Marcy led Baritone into the barn, Tanner drove to one of the equipment shelters to unhook the trailer.

"What'd Doc Andrews say?" Marcy asked.

"Not much. Seems Rob was right all along," Kelly admitted.

"Great!" Marcy's face glowed with pride. "Aren't you glad?"

"Sure . . . I suppose." Kelly's voice held little enthusiasm for the good news. "If you'll excuse me, Marcy, I have a mountain of paperwork to catch up on."

"Sure . . . see you later."

A few moments later, Kelly closed the door to her office and leaned against it until she heard the latch click. As she peeled off her jacket, she released a grateful sigh that Larson wasn't camped at her desk again.

In a couple of strides, Kelly was behind her desk. She slumped into the chair and dropped her forehead to her folded arms on the desk top as the events of the day closed in on her.

During the ride back to Pinetop, the silence in the Bronco had been unbearable. She recalled how easily she and Tanner had talked on the way to Little Rock. Their light bantering and teasing seemed light years away now.

She had been so certain that Dr. Andrews would find something wrong with the horse. When he hadn't, she'd felt foolish.

Each time she'd hazarded a glance at Tanner, he'd been sitting stiffly, fingers wrapped around the steering wheel, jaw set, his eyes trained on the road. She hadn't been able to think of anything clever to say, and he hadn't looked as if he would have wanted to hear it if she had tried. So the silence had lengthened.

The phone suddenly jangled, and she jumped. For a moment she considered not answering it. It rang twice more before she relented with a tired sigh and picked up the receiver. "Yes?"

"Kelly, I'm so glad I caught you." Kelly recognized her mother's voice. "I've been calling off and on all day. Where have you been?"

Kelly's glance fell to the pad beside the phone. Penciled across the top was the message: "Your mother called."

"I left a word for you to return my call. The man

who took my call wasn't very helpful," her mother continued petulantly.

"Larson?" Kelly supplied, recognizing his scrawl.

"I don't know . . . he didn't give his name. Does he work for you?" Her disapproval was clear.

"No, I can't say that he does," Kelly said dryly.

"Oh?"

"A long story, Mother. How have you been?"

"Exhausted, dear. How about you?"

"Fine. We had a winner at Churchill."

There was a strained silence, followed by, "I see."

If Kelly had hoped for approval, she realized she wasn't going to get it from Margaret Smith.

"Well, dear, I'm calling to see when you think you'll be arriving for Thanksgiving."

"Mother, I don't see how I can make it home this year."

"Oh?" Margaret's tone made it clear she'd better have a reason—a good reason for shunning tradition.

"Mom, I've been out of town for the last several days, and I have so much to catch up on here."

"We're counting on you, dear."

"I know." Kelly was torn. So far she'd accomplished nothing in the way of clearing her father, and her time at Pinetop was passing swiftly. It would only be a matter of time now before her job blew up in her face.

She desperately needed to utilize whatever opportunity she had left to unravel the mystery behind Charlie's death. Taking a few days off right now was out of the question, but it would only upset her mother if she tried to explain why. "I feel terrible about it, Mom, but I don't see how I can get away. Not now."

"Henry will be so disappointed, Kelly."

Margaret had always been able to make her daughter feel guilty. It annoyed Kelly that even after Charlie's death, she could still feel torn between them. However, she assured herself, there would be other Thanksgivings to spend with her mother. "Give Henry a kiss for me, Mother, and I hope you both have a wonderful holiday."

Margaret sniffed. "I hardly think that will be possible knowing you're off down there, doing who knows what."

"Mother, please."

"Don't disappoint me at Christmas, Kelly."

"I'll do my best, I promise."

"See that you do. We miss you, dear."

"I miss you both, Mother, and I'll try to make it home for Christmas."

"Kelly . . ."

"Yes?"

"I'm afraid I have some unpleasant news."

Kelly slumped lower on her chair. "What . . . nothing's wrong with Henry, is there?"

"No . . . Charlie's lawyer contacted me this

week. Your father's records were in a terrible mess, and, well, I don't know how to say this over the phone. I'd hoped you'd come home so I could soften the blow."

Kelly sat up straighter. "What is it, Mother?"

"Well, dear, your father's estate is in the red," she said in a rush. "He was hopelessly in debt. I don't know how he thought he'd ever get his head above water."

"How can that be? Charlie made good money."

"And he spent every penny he made. I always told him, 'Charlie, you have to save some of your money for a rainy day,' but did he listen to me?" She sniffed self-righteously. "Of course not."

"You mean he was broke?" Kelly asked.

"Flat as Kansas. The truth is he died owing more than he could repay, unless he was banking on winning that blasted lottery he always threw his money away on."

Kelly rubbed her temple. She couldn't believe it. Charlie broke? Why hadn't he told her?

"The lawyer is still trying to untangle the mess your father left, but I'm heartsick. I'd hoped your father would leave you a nice nest egg."

"Mom, that doesn't matter to me."

"I know, but I'd feel a lot better about this career of yours if you had a cushion to fall back on."

Kelly didn't want to get into that again. She and her mother would never see eye to eye about job security or the lack of it in the horse business. Her mother's idea of a suitable profession for her daughter was teaching school. That could only be further improved by a good marriage and children. Horse training would be her mother's last choice for her.

"Mother, I'll have to get back to you later."

There was a long-suffering sigh on the other end of the line. "All right," Margaret relented. "But should you get to thinking about it and change your mind about Thanksgiving, we'll have a place set for you at our table."

Kelly felt a renewed stab of guilt. "I can't promise anything, but I'll give you a call later in the week if I see that I can get away."

"Yes, dear."

After she'd hung up, Kelly stared at the door, trying to absorb the unsettling news. At the time of his death, Charlie had been in financial trouble. She recalled how he had talked of retiring in a few years. He'd told her of the horse farm he wanted to buy, one the size of Pinetop. The way he'd talked, she'd assumed that he had saved the money, that he had the cash to see his dream realized. He hadn't been an extravagant man, but apparently he hadn't been able to manage money, either.

She was still reeling from the shock of Dr. Andrews's clean bill of health on the colt, and now this. . . . None of it made sense.

Kelly was suddenly flooded with nervous energy. Something was terribly wrong, but she couldn't put her finger on it. She stood up and began to pace. Nothing added up the way she'd thought it would.

She paused in front of a sagging bookcase and stared at the half dozen shelves crammed with books and periodicals devoted to horse racing and horse care.

Her gaze fell on a volume that looked as if it didn't belong with the rest. A brightly colored paperback was wedged above the top row of books. She reread the title. It was a how-to book on money management.

Reaching up, she removed it from the shelf. As she flipped through the pages, something slipped out and sailed to the floor. Bending over, she saw what it was, and her heart began to pound in her ears.

With trembling fingers, she picked them up, one by one, six in all, little squares of microfilm. Even before she held them to the light, she knew what they were. A sick feeling in the pit of her stomach warned her that she had found Baritone's missing X rays.

Reading the names and dates printed on the cardboard edges, she felt her heart plummet. The X rays belonged to Baritone all right; they were the ones taken before his last race.

Moving across the room, she sank onto her chair. Slipping the film into the microfilm viewer, she carefully adjusted the focus. She wasn't a vet, but the film looked as clear and trouble free as the X rays Dr. Andrews had taken just hours ago.

She sat back in her chair and closed her eyes tightly, feeling the acid churn in her stomach. The X rays hadn't been stolen or misfiled, she realized. They'd simply been misplaced, carelessly and foolishly misplaced. She could picture Charlie viewing the X rays and then, without thinking, using them to mark his place in the book. He'd probably had all good intentions of putting them in the proper place—later.

Charlie had always been forgetful when it came to mundane chores, like filing and paying bills. She picked up the book again as a new thought assailed her. Perhaps someone else owned the book. Perhaps someone else had carelessly tossed the X rays inside it.

But her renewed surge of hope was quickly dashed as she discovered the price reduction sticker on the front cover. The book had been a clearance item at a bookstore in Shreveport, Louisiana.

Kelly leafed back through it and found notes in the margin in Charlie's handwriting. She scanned that section and discovered that the subject was on filing bankruptcy. Shaking her head sadly, she closed the book.

It was time she faced a few ugly facts. Charlie had been in dire financial straits. He'd purchased a book and read up on declaring bankruptcy.

With that still on his mind, he'd probably stuffed the X rays in the book inadvertently.

A horrible thought lay at the edge of her mind now. It was something that she hated to face. Was Charlie guilty as accused? Restlessly she came to her feet. The office seemed unusually stuffy and small. She dropped the book and X rays on the desk top and strode to the door, grabbing her jacket off the peg on her way out.

The cool air stung her eyes as she walked briskly to the third barn, where the saddle horses were kept. Striding to the second stall, she lifted a halter from a hook and swung the door open. A tall palomino gelding flexed his neck to peer over his shoulder at her.

Kelly clucked her tongue, and the horse turned around, his ears pricked with curiosity. With deft ease, she slipped the halter over his nose and buckled it.

"C'mon, lazy," she muttered as she tugged the Tennessee walker down the hallway to cross tie him next to the tack room. Goldigger was her favorite, and his smooth gait and easy disposition were just what she needed at the moment.

She grabbed a hoof pick and cleaned his hooves. When she stroked a body brush along his spine and down his sides, dust particles rose to float in a shaft of sunshine. It felt good to do something physical, to block her thoughts and to give herself fully to a task she could do automatically.

She spread a small fuzzy pad onto the horse's back and set the English saddle on top of it. Reaching under him, she caught the girth and drew it up snugly to buckle it.

The old gelding opened his mouth and accepted the bit without a fuss. She straightened his brow band, drew the reins over his head and mounted up.

Gathering the reins, she squeezed his sides with her legs, and he moved into an easy, ground-eating stride as she guided him to the road.

As she approached the paddock, a band of weanlings trotted to the fence for a closer look. When she drew near, they bolted away, bucking. Like children watching a scary movie, they relished the thrill of alarm.

Kelly reined the palomino toward the pine-crusted mountains where he began a steep climb. Halfway up, he plunged with her down a steep embankment. As he lunged on the other side, a covey of quail burst to flight under his nose. Goldigger snorted and shied. "Easy," Kelly said, reaching under his heavy blond mane to reassure him.

Ahead rough, scaly pines massed together in a tight cluster. The dark branches combing the wind above made an ominous whirring.

Kelly pulled Goldigger to a stop and glanced down at Pinetop Farm, nestled in the wide valley below. She realized that she had already grown to love it here. It represented all she had ever longed for in a home, all she would never have.

Switching directions, she angled back toward the road. Guiding Goldigger along the shoulder, she continued aimlessly, seeking solitude.

She rounded a bend and to her surprise she saw Tanner bent down on one knee in the middle of the road. He was raking his fingers through the gravel as if he was looking for something. Her eyes moved to his truck parked in the ditch alongside the road.

She applied leg pressure, and Goldigger responded. Tanner glanced up as he heard the sound of horseshoes striking the hard-packed gravel.

"Lose something?" she asked as she reined the horse to a halt.

Tanner stood up and dusted his hands on his jeans. For a moment he stared back at her silently, trying to see if she understood the significance of where she was. But her expression registered nothing.

Kelly wondered why he was staring at her. There was an awkwardness between them that made her almost wish she'd headed in another direction.

"What are you doing?" she asked again.

Tanner glanced over his shoulder at the pipe gate. "It's funny, but whenever I stop to open and close this gate, I take a moment to look around. I guess it's become a habit."

Kelly swung to the ground in a fluid motion and walked over to him. "Looking for something in particular?" she asked, glancing at the ground.

"I don't know . . . I check this spot after every rain, hoping I might find something that was missed."

Kelly absently rubbed the horse's jaw as her eyes moved to the gate and to the spot near it where Tanner had been looking. "After every rain?"

"A good rain will wash arrowheads and stones to the surface. I thought it might wash up something else one of these days."

Their eyes met, and the meaning of his words suddenly hit her. This was the spot where her father had died. For some reason, she'd assumed that his body had been discovered closer to the highway, but now she remembered that he'd been found beside a gate. This gate.

Her eyes glazed with pain, and she recoiled as she visualized Charlie lying here in the cold, afraid and dying.

Somewhere deep in her throat she made a sound that started as a sigh and ended in a moan. In two strides, Tanner was beside her, enfolding her in the haven of his strong arms.

Her vision blurred as she leaned her head against his shoulder, fighting her tears. It all came rushing in on her: Charlie's death, Dr. Andrews's report, the news of Charlie's financial disaster, the discovery of the X rays . . . and now fate had brought her to the place Charlie had drawn his last breath.

Her body crumpled against Tanner as her defenses lowered. The possibility she'd been holding at bay, engulfed her. What if the tabloids had been correct? What if Charlie had been so broke that he'd planned to extort a ransom from Tanner McCrey?

Kelly felt a searing stab of guilt. How could she, of all people, entertain that idea? It was that very premise she'd come here to dispel, and now she was giving it credence.

Tanner's arms held her tightly against his broad chest. Her shoulders trembled with sobs too long denied as his fingers absently traced and retraced the tight ridge along her spine. He had a nice masculine scent of pine and outdoors and soap and water. His wool shirt was rough against her cheek, but she welcomed it.

He held her for a very long time, saying nothing until her crying eventually slowed and her shudders eased. With a gentleness he hadn't expected to feel, he stroked his fingers through her short cap of curls and wished he could ease her pain.

Kelly began self-consciously digging into the pockets of her jacket and then her jeans, searching for a tissue. She found a clean handkerchief pressed gently into her hand. "Thanks," she whispered as she dabbed her eyes and face. She pressed the damp cloth to her forehead, trying to clear her mind. "I don't know what's wrong with me today."

Her guilt burgeoned as she thought about the way she'd been deceiving Tanner since she'd arrived. For the first time she wondered if her lies to him had been justifiable. Until now she'd been certain that the end would justify the means. Clearing Charlie's name had been her only purpose for coming to Pinetop, but now she wasn't so sure she'd been right to come.

She took a step away from Tanner, moving out of his embrace. Clearing her throat, she inhaled slowly, allowing her breathing to come faster. "I'm sorry," she stammered, unable to look at him directly. "I . . . owe you an apology."

She glanced up at him, taking in his serious expression. She looked away quickly as her heart filled with shame. She hadn't been fair to him, but it was time to change that.

She walked to the board fence a few feet away. Her fingers still held the end of the reins tightly, so the horse followed her and lowered his head to pick at the grass beside the road.

Kelly took a deep breath and pushed her hair off her forehead. "I owe you an apology, Tanner. But more than that, I owe you the truth."

He walked up to stand beside her. She could feel his gaze on her, and she closed her eyes tightly, willing herself not to cry again. Opening her eyes, she stared at the sky. The sun on its journey toward the mountains had dropped below the cloud bank, casting soft, purple shadows across the valleys.

Drawing on her reserves of courage, Kelly said softly, "Charlie Bailey was my father. I arranged to come here so I could find out what happened and clear his name."

When Tanner didn't reply, she continued, "I didn't tell you who I was because I thought you'd send me packing if you knew."

"Smith . . . couldn't you have thought of something a little more original?"

Kelly bowed her head. She figured she had that coming. Naturally he'd be angry. She shook her head, amazed that she'd been so sure of her cause. Now, she wasn't sure at all. "Kelly Smith *is* my legal name. My mother's second husband adopted me."

"When Charlie spoke of his daughter, he called her Killarney," Tanner said.

She lifted her eyes to meet his. "Only Charlie called me that. My mother preferred Kelly, so Kelly it was. I didn't know my real father until five years ago." She exhaled wearily and struggled to suppress the tears that pricked her eyelids. "Maybe I didn't even know him then."

"Why do you say that?" Tanner reached out and gently brushed away a tear that had managed to escape.

"I've found out a lot can happen in a day. Today, I've learned that before his death my father was deep in debt, and that his creditors were nipping at his heels. And you know the X rays I thought were stolen?"

"Yes."

"Well, it seems Charlie had just misplaced them. Used them for a bookmark." She sighed. "He was horribly careless and forgetful."

She dropped her forehead into her palm. "Oh, Tanner, I was so sure that Dr. Andrews would find something wrong with Baritone. And if he had, I thought sure it would prove that Charlie had been framed." She gazed at the sky to steady herself. "I had visions of vindicating him. But to be honest with you, the evidence I've uncovered so far doesn't prove Charlie's innocence. On the contrary, it only makes him look more guilty."

She glanced up, her face ravaged with anguish. "But I still don't believe that my father intended to steal your horse and extort money from you." Her eyes pleaded mutely for his understanding.

"Neither do I."

"You don't?" she said, her voice barely above a whisper.

"Frankly, I've had a hard time believing all along that a man like Charlie would do something so foolish."

She sighed. "Until today, I'd had no idea that Charlie might have had any reason to commit such a crime." She looked away, hating herself for voicing such treasonous thoughts. "I don't know . . ." she reasoned aloud, "maybe he . . ."

"You don't believe that," he stated flatly.

She glanced up at him, and the first hint of a

smile touched the corners of her mouth. "No, I don't."

A moment passed while she tried to sort out what she did believe. "Tanner, I'm sorry I deceived you. Until today I only considered Charlie. I only thought about learning the truth and clearing his name. It wasn't fair to you. You deserve a trainer who'll give you one hundred percent—nothing less."

"I agree."

Her heart was pounding. She braced herself for his rage. When it didn't come, she tried to prepare herself for something worse. He was going to fire her on the spot. Perhaps it would make it easier if she suggested it herself. "I wouldn't blame you if you told me to pack up and leave."

"I've given it serious thought."

She turned to leave gracefully, but he laid his hand on her shoulder to restrain her. "That was my initial reaction when I first found out who you were."

Her eyes were round when they lifted to meet his again. "You knew," she whispered hoarsely, "you already knew who I am?"

He reached under the flap of his shirt pocket and pulled out a magazine clipping. He unfolded it and passed it to her.

Kelly looked at the color photo. It showed her standing arm in arm with Charlie, both of them beaming. The story beneath it had appeared in a national racing magazine when Charlie had announced he was hiring her as an apprentice. The caption read "Like Father, Like Daughter."

With trembling fingers, she passed the clipping back to him. "How long have you known?"

"I wasn't certain until this morning, but I've been looking into Charlie's past since the day he died. Somehow the idea of his kidnapping my horse never fit my image of him. He was a living legend, a man I'd admired for years. I thought I'd pulled off a real coup when he agreed to come here. Call it what you will, maybe I don't like to give up my heroes." He shrugged. "Like you, I won't be satisfied until I know what really happened that day."

"Thank you," she said quietly. "It would make me happy if we could work together to clear Charlie's name . . . but how did you find out that I was Charlie's daughter?"

"A man at the clinic recognized you this morning. After we got back, I searched through my files and examined the picture again. When I'd first clipped it, I'd been more interested in the article than the photo." He glanced at the picture and back at her. "You've lost weight and changed your hair since then."

He reached up to touch her short locks and noticed the color of the roots matched her hair color in the photo. "Let your hair grow out. I like your natural color better."

She nodded. "So do I." Her eyes met his. "I'm sorry about lying to you," she said. "I figured that I'd be recognized sooner or later, but I hadn't considered how it could affect you."

"It didn't come as a total surprise. When the sheriff told me you'd been asking about Charlie, I'd started keeping a close eye on you already."

"When did you talk to the sheriff?"

"At the barbecue."

"You've known all this time?" She leaned her back against the fence.

He shook his head. "I had my suspicions, but I didn't know for sure until today. Although I couldn't figure your motive, I didn't believe you'd come here to do me harm. I decided to wait and watch you play your hand."

Understanding came into her gaze. "That's why you were always on my case, always questioning my judgment. You were really questioning my motives, weren't you?"

"And your methods," he added. "I wasn't sure if you were trying to improve Keepsake or set her back."

Kelly shook her head, remembering their argument over changing the filly's shoes. "You suspected I might be trying to sabotage your filly?"

"Can you blame me? Things didn't work out so well with my last trainer. Can you see why I'd be reluctant to trust the next one?"

She nodded, wondering if he fully trusted her

now. Whether he did or he didn't, she decided it was time to lay all of her cards on the table. "The reason I insisted on getting a second opinion was because the colt really didn't seem fit to me. And he still doesn't, no matter what Doc Andrews said this morning. I thought if the horse wasn't fit Rob would have to know it, and when the X rays came up missing, I immediately suspected that perhaps Rob was trying to cover up something."

"And now?"

"I don't know what to think anymore. It seems that Rob's findings were correct. Maybe I'm on the wrong track."

"If you're accusing Rob of doing any wrong, then you are."

"But can't you see what you're doing? You're as reluctant to admit that your brother could be at fault as I was to admit that my father could be the culprit."

"Personal feelings can get in the way," he admitted, "but I trust Rob."

"Yes, personal feelings can get in the way." It amazed her that, somewhere along the way, what happened to Tanner McCrey had begun to matter to her—more than it should. She wanted to clear Charlie, yes, but she was beginning to realize that that wasn't all she wanted. Looking away, she resorted to anger to fight feelings she still didn't want to acknowledge. Her eyes sparked with determination when she looked back at him. "I'll admit I've been angry with you," she said, deciding to make a clean slate of it. "Every time I felt guilty for deceiving you, I reminded myself that you hadn't protected Charlie, hadn't lifted a finger to stop the ugly rumors circulating about him."

"Or so you thought. Why didn't you come to me and tell me what you suspected?"

"Would you have listened?"

Their eyes met and held.

"Yes."

"Then I'm sorry I didn't—and even sorrier for deceiving you the way I have."

With a mixture of surprise and regret, Kelly realized that she was going to be sorry to leave Pinetop. She'd wanted to bring Tanner success. Winning the Arkansas Derby for him would have made her proud. But she refused to face her personal feelings about leaving him. She'd gone into this relationship with her eyes open. The same couldn't be said for him. He hadn't known who she was when he'd hired her, and that offended her sense of fair play.

The only thing she could do was bow out gracefully, if he would let her. A small part of her prayed he wouldn't. "You have a fine horse and a good shot at the derby." She pushed herself away from the fence and managed a ghost of a smile. "I wish you luck."

"With what?"

"Finding a new trainer and winning the Arkansas Derby."

"Oh no you don't. *You* signed a contract to train at Pinetop through April, lady. That contract is binding on both parties."

"That contract can be nullified by the consent of both parties," she amended. "Don't worry, Tanner, I won't hold you to it."

"Well, I'm holding you to it."

Her jaw dropped. "Why?"

"Because we both want the same thing." His eyes locked obstinately with hers. "We both want to know what happened to Charlie, and we both want to win that derby come April. Agreed?"

She nodded. "Agreed."

"We'll work together instead of against each other," he suggested. "With a little luck we should be able to come up with the truth surrounding my horse's problem and Charlie's death."

"All right, but we may not like what we discover," she warned. She knew from her mother's unsettling news that it was possible that Charlie had made a dreadful mistake, but she also knew that it was possible the truth could involve someone else, someone close to Tanner.

"Anything would be better than not knowing, wouldn't it?" he asked quietly. "Can you handle it if we find out that it was Charlie?" He thought she was strong enough to accept the truth, but he'd feel better hearing her say it.

She met his questioning gaze with one of her own. "Can *you* handle it if it proves to be someone *you* love?" Her eyes held the same sparkle of challenge.

"Yes."

"So can I," she returned. "I guess that brings us to the most important question—are you willing to trust me with your horse?"

After a brief pause, he nodded. "I won't question your judgment, but from now on, no more secrets between us. However, I don't think we should disclose your identity. People here will probably tell you more if they don't know you're Charlie's daughter."

"Agreed." She extended her hand. A handshake between honest horsemen was as binding as a legal document. And from the look in her eye Tanner could tell this one was strictly business.

His hand engulfed hers as they shook firmly.

She smiled a little, feeling her spunk return. "You can start by showing me what you've learned about Charlie." She tugged the reins to draw the horse closer. With practiced ease, she drew the reins over his head and swung into the saddle. Glancing down at him, she nodded toward his truck. "Coming?"

"Lead the way."

Chapter Eleven

Tanner followed Kelly back to the barn and waited while she unsaddled the horse and instructed Doug to take care of him.

"Let's go into my office," Tanner suggested, "and we'll go over what I've learned so far."

"Good," Kelly agreed.

The sun had just dipped behind the mountains, sharpening the air as they strode up the walkway to the McCrey house. Kelly was still surprised that he'd offered to share what he knew about Charlie with her.

Tanner led Kelly through the back door and ushered her into his office. Taking a key from his pocket, he unlocked a deep drawer in his mahogany desk, then lifted out a stack of folders and set them on his desk.

"You may look these over in private," he said. "When you're finished, let me know. I'll be across the hall."

"Thanks." Kelly waited as he crossed the room and closed the door behind him.

She took a seat in the leather chair behind his desk and opened the folder on top, the one bearing Charlie's name.

As it turned out, Tanner's inquiries had been consistent with his other work, discreet but thorough. His file on Charlie Bailey contained a few specifics that Kelly wasn't already aware of.

Charlie had invested more than he'd owned in the recent syndication of a racehorse. The syndication had not panned out, and Charlie had been left with monstrous debts.

Kelly recalled Charlie talking about his retirement, and how she had always assumed he had prepared for it even though he'd always been looking for a big score that would provide him an even bigger nest egg.

Apparently getting in on the ground floor of a major syndication had seemed to him like a perfect opportunity. A successful racehorse had been retired to stud, and Charlie had figured that the annual stud fees would provide him with a comfortable retirement and something to leave his grandchildren.

However, the stallion's expenses had been larger than he had anticipated. When the horse had failed to prove himself in the breeding shed, Charlie had lost all that he'd won from his share of racing purses, and then some.

In another folder, Kelly discovered that Tanner had made various inquiries about Jay Moran that had confirmed rumors of the jockey's gambling habit and substantial gambling debts to men with probable connections to organized crime.

She was even more surprised to find a folder containing information about herself. His facts about her were also unsettlingly accurate.

In other folders, she found various bits of information about Pinetop farm employees. She discovered that when Larson had been in his late teens, he'd been arrested for burning down a neighbor's haystack and other adolescent pranks.

A file revealed that Marcy had run away from a foster home and been hanging around Oaklawn Park looking for work when Charlie had taken her under his wing. Tanner had hired her, and Hattie had let the girl live with her in a cottage close to the main entrance.

Thirty minutes later, Kelly closed the last folder and leaned back in the chair to try and absorb all she'd read. Her eyes roamed absently about the room as she surveyed a small part of Tanner McCrey's personal world.

This room suits him, she thought, admiring the carved fireplace mantel flanked by built-in bookcases. Hanging against the birch library paneling were framed oil paintings of Thoroughbreds. In front of the fireplace was a glass cocktail table with a sofa on one side and two leather wing chairs on the other.

She gazed through the round-top window at the rows of green and white barns and the sprawling hillside beyond. The room gave her a tranquil feeling. It was a haven from the storm raging inside her.

Somehow Tanner never failed to surprise her. She'd never have guessed that he was carefully researching the employees at Pinetop in search of the truth behind Charlie's death. Instead she'd have sworn that he couldn't have cared less about her father. Evidently Charlie had occupied Tanner's thoughts nearly as much as he'd occupied hers.

A few moments later Kelly stepped into the hall and saw Hattie walking toward her.

"Oh, there you are!"

"Hi, Hattie. Have you seen Tanner?"

"He said to tell you he'd be right back. Are you going home for Thanksgiving?"

"No, I—"

"Good. Then you'll be having dinner with us and don't say you can't because if you're not going home, there'll be nothing to stop you. Everybody will get here about ten o'clock, so don't be late."

Kelly opened her mouth to decline, "I—"

"We always have a real good time," Hattie interrupted, making it plain that she wasn't going to take no for an answer. "After the meal we all walk over to the track and watch the training races."

"The training races?" Kelly asked dumbfounded.

"Hasn't anyone told you?" Hattie paused long enough to whisk away an imaginary speck of dust from one of the hall tables with the cloth that could always be found in her apron pocket.

Kelly shook her head wordlessly.

"Training races are part of the Thanksgiving tradition at Pinetop, when the weather permits. We spend the whole day together. Horse people gather here like a big family to share a meal and enjoy each other's company. Sometimes folks haul a colt or two over to give them some experience away from home. The workouts are for fun, and it gives the young horses some practice. We're counting on you to join us."

"Well, I . . ."

Tanner suddenly appeared in the doorway. "Yes, Ms. Smith, we're really looking forward to your being here," he bantered, winking knowingly at Hattie.

"Ah, go on with you—you know if I didn't insist on her coming, this little mite would spend the day in her cottage eating tuna and cottage cheese." Hattie was used to Tanner's good-natured ribbing, and it didn't bother her a bit. "Tell her to be here at ten o'clock sharp Thanksgiving morning, Tanner."

"Ms. Smith, you're to be here at ten o'clock sharp Thanksgiving morning," Tanner repeated obediently.

Glancing from Hattie to Tanner, Kelly realized when she was outnumbered. "Well . . . is there any-thing I can bring?"

Tanner winked at her. "Anything but cottage cheese and tuna."

THE WEEKS BEFORE Thanksgiving passed unevent-fully while Kelly settled more deeply into a routine at Pinetop. Each day she'd make sure she was in her office when Tanner dropped by, shortly after sundown.

The weather had been unseasonably dry, and he was busy heading a crew to clean up the roads and service the equipment.

The cutting season was over for another year. Pinetop timber employees were leaving or finding temporary work nearby until they were needed again in the spring.

Every evening Kelly found herself looking forward to seeing Tanner. Sometimes he would talk her into coming to his house for one of Hattie's home-cooked meals. On Hattie's evenings off, they would drive into Hot Springs for a barbecue sandwich or a hot fudge sundae. Kelly was horrified to discover that she'd put on three pounds, and Tanner close to five, from their late night ice cream excursions.

On Thanksgiving Day Kelly called her parents to apologize again for being away this year. Christmas, she promised, and she wondered why she felt a sense of loneliness when she thought about spending the holiday without Tanner. Later she walked to the McCrey house, carrying a plate of deviled eggs she'd made from her mother's recipe.

She was amazed to see Hattie hadn't been exaggerating when she'd said everyone would be there. The assorted vehicles parked in the drive suggested that, indeed, everyone from miles around was at the McCrey house that day. She recognized

Jay Moran's pickup and Jared Huxsman's Mercedes parked in front. She wondered how Tanner would feel about spending the day with Jared under his roof, but then the man had been kind to Rob. And Tanner would put up with a lot for Rob's sake.

"There you are!" Marcy greeted warmly as Kelly walked through the back door into the breakfast nook. Marcy slipped a deviled egg from the plate and popped it into her mouth. "Super!" Marcy commented. With a wink, she took the plate from Kelly's hands and set it on the round table laden with festive dishes.

Kelly followed her into the crowded kitchen. Some people were cutting cakes and pies, others were tossing salads that they'd brought, and some were munching the snacks that Hattie had placed everywhere.

Larson walked into the kitchen twisting the cap off a beer and tossed it into a wastebasket. "Sure you won't have one of these?" he prodded, extending the bottle to Jay.

"No thanks," Jay refused good-naturedly. "After I eat Hattie's home cookin', I'll have to spend three hours in the sweatbox as it is."

"I'll take that as a compliment." Hattie was bent over the oven, basting the turkey, her ample bottom protruded out into the kitchen. Jay grinned and popped her playfully on the rump with a rolled-up dish towel.

"Jay Moran!" The oven door clattered shut, and Hattie's hands came up to her hips indignantly. "You go on and git!"

"Do you watch your weight that closely?" Marcy asked as Jay wandered out of harm's way.

"Have to. I'm not a kid anymore. I can gain weight just smelling food. I'm living for the day I retire from this sport, and I can eat anything I want."

"You're not old enough to retire," Marcy scoffed.

"Ah, you never know, I might get lucky and win a couple of big ones one of these days."

Doug grabbed a piece of celery stuffed with cheese and bit into it. "Hey, Moran, I heard old man Sims chewin' you out last time we were at Churchill Downs."

"Yeah," Jay's face clouded, "he's under the false impression that his horse can't lose."

"But you showed him differently, didn't you." Doug grinned as he took another bite of celery.

"What was it this time?" Larson asked.

"Well, after the race," Jay explained, "Sims hauls me aside and says 'Didn't you see that hole between horses up ahead of you? Why didn't you go through it, man?' And I says, ' 'Cause the hole was movin' a lot faster than I could, man!' "

Louise entered the kitchen and was caught up in the good-natured gibing. "Well, boys, as they say, that's the sport of kings."

"Yeah," Jay said offhandedly, "easy for you to

say, Louise. You don't have to ride those critters."

Louise wagged her finger at him piously. "Paying the bills for those critters isn't easy, either, my friend."

"Dinnertime," Hattie sang out.

Everyone filed into the dining room, and Tanner took his place at the head of the table. With an almost imperceptible gesture, he invited Kelly to take the seat beside him. She smiled and accepted the invitation as Marcy moved onto the chair beside her. Across from them Louise chose a place between Tanner and Rob, and Jared Huxsman sat on the other side of Rob.

The dinner progressed pleasantly. As Kelly had always known, horse people put their differences aside in hard times and on holidays.

Kelly noticed that Rob's attention was centered more on Louise than on his meal. Occasionally Kelly caught Marcy watching the handsome young vet, and she decided that the girl's crush on Rob hadn't faded. Later, as Tanner handed Kelly a bowl of mashed potatoes, their fingers touched. When she glanced up, he smiled at her, causing a familiar flutter in the pit of her stomach. That feeling hadn't faded, either.

The dinner conversation consisted of lighthearted banter. Even Larson managed to be civil after he'd twisted the cap off his fifth beer.

"I do hope we get to see Baritone work out today," Louise goaded Tanner petulantly.

Tanner glanced at Kelly. "That's up to his trainer." Kelly could see an expression of trust in his face, a trust that had been growing over the past few weeks. It warmed her to know that he was leaving the decision to her and willing to let his family and friends know it.

"Baritone's getting to be a real ham," Kelly admitted. "I think he'd love to run for you today." The colt had been steadily improving, and she figured that now was as good a time as any for people to see what he could do.

After coffee and dessert, everyone slipped into their jackets and drifted outside to walk off the huge meal.

Later that afternoon the entertainment began. Louise's trainer drove her horse van to the training track and busied himself with a two-year-old he was training for her.

Larson and Marcy were in the hallway of the barn, saddling two Pinetop colts that Larson had been breaking to ride.

Tanner was off somewhere, so Kelly stepped into the tack room to find a leather punch that Louise had requested.

Jay was leaning insolently against a stall door, watching the proceedings. "Who's gonna ride these outlaws?" he heckled.

"Who do you think?" Larson grunted, slipping a small flat saddle on the back of one of the two-year-olds.

"I'll be racing them one of these days," Marcy volunteered.

Jay's eyes grew round in mock surprise as he sent Larson a wink. "That so?"

"Yes, that's so!" Marcy snapped. "Kelly's been teaching me to ride. She says I'll be ready to apply for my apprentice license this summer."

"No kiddin'," Jay goaded. "Sounds like you'll be puttin' me out of a job."

"I wouldn't worry if I was you," Larson said, nodding at Jay. "I'm bettin' that our Ms. Smith won't stick around that long."

"What do you mean by that?" Marcy asked curtly. "Kelly hasn't said anything 'bout leavin', leastways not until after the Arkansas Derby."

"Just a hunch," Larson said offhandedly, "but I'll lay you odds that your highfalutin lady trainer will skedaddle long before spring gets here."

"No she won't!" Marcy denied heatedly. "If she was leaving, she'd tell me."

Larson snorted. "They's a lotta things she don't tell you. Ever notice how chummy she's getting with the boss man?"

"You gonna work one of these babies, Marcy?" Jay asked, realizing it was time to change the subject.

"Kelly said I could ride the bay," Marcy tossed back defensively.

"Promise you won't make me look too bad?" Jay bantered.

Marcy sniffed. "We'll see."

229

Kelly stepped into the hallway with the leather punch in her hand, and Marcy scurried to Kelly's side and said loudly enough for all to hear, "Larson says you're going to leave us before long." The girl's eyes held more than a hint of concern.

Kelly sent Larson a cool stare. "Wishful thinking on his part, Marcy. I wouldn't pay much attention to it if I were you."

Larson's grin was nothing short of smug as he turned away and walked out of the barn. Kelly watched him go, seething inside. She didn't know why he disliked her so. As far as she knew, she'd done nothing to cause it.

Kelly gave Marcy a leg up and led the colt outside where Doug was waiting on Goldigger. Handing him the lead, Kelly smiled, "Pony her around the track at a trot."

"Okay, boss."

Twenty minutes later, just before the colts were led to the starting gates for their five-furlong workout, Kelly waded through the track's deep soil to Marcy's side. She stroked the bay's black mane as her eyes met Marcy's earnestly. "Don't let these boys rattle you." Kelly glanced at Jay and Louise's rider nearby. "You stay calm and ride your own race."

"Okay," Marcy agreed, her eyes shining with eagerness. Jay passed by and grinned down at Kelly. "Any instructions for me, boss?"

"Don't crowd her, Jay. I mean it."

Jay nodded, his grin widening. "Yes, ma'am."

Doug and two other outriders led the colts to the starting gates, and two farmhands stepped up to load them. Since Marcy's colt was the steadiest, the boys loaded him first.

When the gates sprung open with a clang, the colts bolted forward to sprint down the backstretch. Kelly was relieved to see Marcy holding the colt in a steady position on the outside.

When they came around the track and turned for home, Marcy leaned forward and urged the colt on with her voice and hands, her whip still wobbling in her back pocket.

"Let him go, Marcy!" Kelly shouted.

The horses came thundering down the track as the spectators waved and cheered them on.

Jay's colt and Louise's colt were matching strides, but Marcy's bay was a half length ahead and pulling away. Marcy flattened out over the bay's neck and urged him to open his lead.

As the three colts neared the finish line, Jay hollered, "Hey, Marcy, pull him up! Pull him up!"

Marcy glanced worriedly at Jay, and he shouted again, "Pull him up, I tell you! Now!"

Marcy hauled on the reins, and Jay shot past her to finish first. Barreling across the finish line third, Marcy's bewildered gaze searched for Kelly on the rail. Their eyes met, and Kelly shook her head.

Marcy's chin fell as she realized that she'd been tricked.

Jay pulled his colt down to a trot and turned him around. Marcy reined in her bay beside him.

"You tricked me!" she accused heatedly.

"I educated you," Jay corrected calmly.

"You made it sound like there was something wrong with my colt," she flared. "I thought you were trying to help me!"

Jay shrugged casually. "Let it be a lesson to you, girl. I helped myself to an easy win, and don't think it can't happen in a real race." His gaze pinpointed hers. "It's a tough game, Marcy. You've learned to ride, but you're gonna have to get track wise. Remember what Kelly told you? Ride your own race. If you're smart, you'll learn to listen to your trainer and forget everybody else."

"I'll never listen to you again, Jay Moran!"

"Now you're catchin' on." He sent her a devilish wink as he trotted off, and her face flushed scarlet.

Sliding off her horse, Marcy stalked toward Kelly with her chin down. "Don't take it so hard," Kelly soothed. "It was just a workout."

"If I would've listened to you, I could've won." Kelly saw bright tears shining in the girl's eyes, but she knew it was more from embarrassment than hurt.

Kelly put her arm around Marcy's shoulders as they walked away from the others. "I know you feel foolish and what Jay did was unfair, but he just taught you a lesson you'll never forget. Now take the lesson and learn it well. Don't listen to anyone when you're out there on the track. You ride your own race, Marcy."

"Makes me mad he could fool me so easy." Marcy shook her head furiously. "I hate him!"

"He was showing you the ropes in his own way. Most of the jockeys will try you. It won't be easy."

Marcy glanced up to meet Kelly's eyes. "You're not mad at me?"

Kelly laughed and draped her arm around the girl's neck as they walked back to the paddock. "No, I've fallen for their stunts too, if it makes you feel any better." Kelly looked over and grinned. "We'll get even with him."

"You better believe we will." Marcy glared in Jay's direction. "I'll beat that little bully yet."

"Atta girl." Kelly gave the girl's shoulder a reassuring squeeze. "Now go make sure the boys have Baritone ready. Let's show these people what a real horse can do."

"You bet!" Marcy impulsively leaned over and hugged Kelly around the neck tightly before jogging off toward the barns.

Fifteen minutes later, Tanner gave Jay a leg up, and Kelly walked along beside Baritone as he pranced sideways. She looked up at Jay. "Work him out of the gate for five furlongs," she said. "Then ask him for speed at the top of the stretch."

"Okay, boss."

"And don't be playing any more of your little tricks."

"Is Marcy going to be around?"

"No."

Jay grinned. "Then I'll behave."

A few minutes later Kelly took a place beside Tanner on the rail and watched anxiously as Baritone broke from the gate and galloped down the backstretch.

Her fingers gripped the top board until her knuckles were as white as the fence. Tanner reached over and laid his hand on top of hers, but they both kept their eyes on Baritone.

At the top of the stretch Jay urged him, and the colt flattened his ears and surged forward. Baritone's hooves flew across the dirt, and Kelly thought he looked good. Darn good. Jay asked the colt for more, but after a few promising strides, the colt began to slow. His body was bathed in sweat, and he looked strained beyond his limit. He was losing momentum all the way to the finish line, and Kelly's face clouded with disappointment.

Leaning over to check Tanner's stopwatch, she already knew his time was poor.

She heaved a heavy sigh. Why, she thought, did he have to fold today? He'd been improving with every workout—until now. She had the horrible feeling that she was back at square one.

Louise walked to Kelly's side to offer her sympathy. "Aren't these sophomores a pain? After such a wonderful season last year, you'd think they'd have this game down cold, but even my Claimjumper has his good days and off days."

Kelly nodded absently. She was sure Baritone's poor performance had to be more than just an "off day."

Turning, Kelly headed for the barn as Louise made her polite farewells to Tanner. When Kelly reached the barn, she unsaddled Baritone herself, looking him over carefully as she ran a scraper over his body to remove the foamy sweat.

She lifted his mane to draw the scraper down his long neck, and her gaze fixed on a lump rising from the flat muscle there.

Frowning, she ran her fingers over the lump, and Baritone moved away from the pressure. "Get Rob," Kelly called to Marcy.

Minutes later Rob examined the colt, and he was frowning as he turned to face Kelly and Tanner. "There's the tip of a needle embedded in his skin."

"A needle! How did that happen?" Tanner demanded.

Rob shrugged. "Looks like someone broke a needle off while giving him an injection. There's nothing to worry about. I can give him a local and remove it."

"Did you give him a shot?" Tanner asked incredulously.

"Of course not," Rob replied curtly. "Baritone isn't on any medication."

Tanner glanced questioningly at Kelly, and she shook her head. "The colt hasn't been receiving any medication from us."

"The needle tip wasn't there this morning when I examined him." Rod stepped back and faced Tanner for the first time.

Kelly nodded. "I was right here with Rob this morning. The colt was fine then."

"Find out what was shot through that needle," Tanner snapped as he stepped over to run his hand down Baritone's sides.

"I'll send it to the lab," Rob said, "along with blood samples. They should be able to tell us."

Tanner turned and walked away, and Kelly followed him. When they were standing in the open doorway of the barn, out of earshot, he turned to her. "What do you think?"

"Sabotage. Someone got to him today. My guess is the same thing happened before his last race and all the other times he's run poorly."

"But *nothing* showed on his lab tests."

"Dr. Andrews said there was something, but it couldn't be identified," Kelly reminded.

"The labs are closed today because of the holiday." She noticed his face was lined with worry as he stared thoughtfully at the peaceful countryside. "I think I'll give Doc Andrews a call. If he's there, he might be willing to run a few tests for us."

"I think that's wise," she agreed.

"The time has come to put guards on Baritone

round the clock. Some of my men on the logging crew could use the work. They're strong, and they're loyal—they'll see that no harm comes to the horse."

"All right," Kelly murmured. Her troubled gaze met his. "Who do you think could be doing this?"

He shook his head. "I don't know."

Their eyes traveled down the long hallway to Jay and Larson who were standing by, watching Rob as he worked on the colt. Beyond, they saw Louise's horse van pull out and Huxsman's Mercedes following behind it. Tanner glanced back at Kelly briefly, realizing that she was one of the few whom he could still trust.

She looked up at him, her eyes filled with concern. The culprit was most likely someone who'd sat at his dinner table just hours ago. With a cold chill, Kelly realized that the injection could have just as easily been fatal.

"I'll check around—maybe someone will be able to find the syringe," she said encouragingly.

"I doubt anyone would be foolish enough to leave it behind, but it won't hurt to look."

Tanner turned, then suddenly turned back. "Are you okay?"

She looked at him. "Yes."

His gaze softened. "I don't like this, Kelly. I don't want anyone getting hurt, particularly you."

"I won't—but thank you for your concern."

"I'm always concerned about you."

His words took away the chill momentarily.

"Is there anything you want me to do?"

"No, I'll need to use your office to call Doc Andrews. I'll be there if you need me."

She nodded. "All right."

After Tanner left, Kelly checked the trash containers and the aisle of the barn, but found nothing. Uneasy, she checked on Baritone again. Rob had removed the broken needle without a problem and drawn the blood samples they would need. Marcy and Doug were cooling the colt.

Kelly walked to Baritone's stall and stepped inside the deep cedar shavings. Leaning over, she began picking up the alfalfa hay that the colt had strewn carelessly about.

"How's it going?" She glanced up to find Tanner standing in the doorway.

"I didn't find anything," she admitted, noting that his eyes were dark and shadowed with fatigue. Her heart went out to him, and she wished she could make things better. He didn't deserve this. "Your horse is a slob, you know," she teased, hoping to lighten his spirits. "He pulls his hay out of his feeder and strews it all over and then just picks at it."

The corners of Tanner's mouth turned up. He knew what she was trying to do, and he appreciated it. He stepped aside to let Marcy and Doug lead Baritone into his stall.

Kelly ran her hands over the colt to be sure he was cool and dry. As soon as Doug and Marcy unsnapped their leads, Baritone walked to the automatic waterer in the corner of his stall and took a long drink.

Kelly moved back to his side and lifted his mane. Rob had done a good job. She noted that the swelling from the needle was already beginning to lessen. In a few days the knot would disappear, but not the threat.

Her gaze returned to Tanner, and he seemed to read her thoughts. Walking out of the stall, she latched the door behind her.

Tanner motioned toward a heavyset man wearing a plaid jacket who quietly stepped to his side. "Kelly, Bob Hendricks. Kelly is our trainer, Bob. She can come and go as she pleases."

Kelly shook Bob's hand and felt the incredible strength of his grip. Tanner worked fast, she thought, the guard is already in place.

"Larry Harrold will be here at six," Bob said.

"All right," Kelly acknowledged. "Bob, if you need anything, just let me know."

"Sure thing, ma'am."

Kelly watched Bob open a folding chair and set his water jug beside it. She did a double take when she saw him set an ax handle beside him.

"I'm headed to Doc Andrews with the blood samples," Tanner told her. "You're welcome to ride along if you want."

"I'd like that," she said, following Tanner down the hallway.

Hours later, Tanner and Kelly watched as Dr. Andrews emerged from his lab. "Well, I don't know what to tell you. I found more traces of a substance that my tests can't identify. I suspect that it's the same substance we couldn't identify in the lab tests we did on the colt some weeks ago."

"This is crazy," Tanner snapped. "I'd love to get my hands on the person responsible for this."

"If I were you, I'd send the samples to California. I know a lab there that's better equipped to handle this sort of thing. Let them work on this and see if they can come up with something."

"In the meantime, what am I supposed to do?" Tanner asked.

Doc Andrews's face was unusually somber. "Keep a close eye on that horse, son."

On the way back to Pinetop, Kelly and Tanner said little. Both were lost in thought, tumbling the events over and over in their minds, trying to figure out who would do such a thing and why. How far, they wondered, would someone go to keep the colt from winning?

Kelly realized that it was too soon to draw any definite conclusions, but it seemed likely that whoever had injected Baritone had also been involved in Charlie's death.

They arrived back at Pinetop after dark. After checking on Baritone, Tanner insisted on walking Kelly to her cottage.

The harvest moon was full, and the air was cold and still. As they passed a paddock, they heard a clatter of hooves on the frozen ground. Tanner drew Kelly protectively against his side as they moved to the fence to view the horses.

The startled yearlings edged closer until one of them took a playful nip at another, initiating a game of tag.

For a moment they leaned against the fence watching the colts gallop and spin and leap at each other.

"I wish I could know which one has the courage to give it all," Tanner mused.

"Which one did Charlie like best?" Kelly asked.

Tanner pointed to a chestnut colt. He wasn't the largest yearling, but he was aggressive enough to move the others out of his way.

"Figures," Kelly grinned. "Charlie could usually pick them."

"He had a knack, all right," Tanner agreed, "for picking a good one and then finding the key to unlock his full potential. Which one do you like?"

Kelly had looked at the yearlings every morning and every evening on her way to the barns. She sometimes thought she found more satisfaction working with the youngsters on the farm than fine-tuning them on the track. "I like the chestnut colt and the black filly. He's got the moves, but watch her sometime."

"What's so special about her?"

"Well, she rules the roost for one thing. She goes to the water first, and they all wait until she's had her fill before they move in. I figure she'll be aggressive enough to get to the finish line before the rest of them, too."

"I hope you're right." He didn't tell her, but the black filly had always been his favorite. "I need a winner."

"You'll have a lot of winners," she promised optimistically. "You have a good breeding program here."

"We should have the best. My father spent every spare nickel he had trying to build his brood stock. Now we need a winner or two to bring in some buyers. We're close. I believe Baritone can do it if we can keep him healthy."

"We can do it." Kelly gazed up at him in the moonlight.

"We can?"

She smiled. "Yes."

"I kind of like the sound of that," he admitted, drawing her closer.

"So do I." Her reply was barely a whisper.

His fingers reached out to stroke her cheek. Her eyes looked dark and her skin luminous in the pale moonlight. He brushed the tousled curls from her forehead. Right now she looked fragile, vulnerable, and he felt an overwhelming urge to protect her. Pressing his lips to her temple, he gathered her in his arms. "Oh, Kelly, I wish things weren't so complicated."

Cupping her face in his hands, he slowly lowered his lips to hers. His mouth took hers without pressure, gently, lovingly. She stood very still as the rhythm of their breathing quickened. His warm lips roamed over her face and returned to her lips to taste, to savor their sweetness.

He lifted his head and looked for a long moment into her eyes. As they stood in silence, they both knew something was happening between them.

There was a pull between them, something basic, something elemental. It was a force she had denied and avoided for too long. Tonight she didn't want to fight it.

His gaze held hers for a long moment, and she sensed a struggle inside him. His finger moved to trace the outline of her lips, but his gaze never strayed from her eyes.

"Will you answer one question for me?" he asked quietly.

She nodded, unable to deny him anything.

"If you hadn't come here because of your father, would you have considered accepting the training job at Pinetop? Be honest," he added when she didn't reply right away.

"I . . . it's hard to say," she admitted, finding it hard to think when he looked at her so intently.

"Think about it," he urged, and she sensed that

her reply really mattered. "Having a career . . . moving all over the country to train horses—that matters a lot to you, doesn't it?"

She struggled to find the answer. Yes, in many ways her career mattered very deeply to her, but in other ways she knew she would gladly trade it all for some semblance of a normal life with a man like Tanner. Was that what he wanted her to say? "I don't know if I would have considered taking a job I knew was a temporary replacement," she said, wanting to be honest. She owed him that much. "But I don't regret taking this job, if that's what you're asking."

"But it isn't the big time," he said quietly.

She looked at him, confusion clouding her eyes. "Who said I wanted the big time?"

His fingers stroked her cheek as he gazed at her, searching her face for the truth.

"Does my age bother you?"

She shook her head, grinning. "I don't know how old you are."

"Just take a guess. How old do I look?"

"I don't know—maybe thirty-four, thirty-five?"

He smiled, relieved she had guessed young. "That's flattering, but a little low. Guess again."

"Eighty-six?"

"A little high. I have a feeling I should have accepted the thirty-four and run like hell."

She laughed and kissed him again. "Nothing about you bothers me—at least not in the way

244

you're thinking, and we couldn't be over ten or twelve years apart."

They kissed again, and she wondered why he was suddenly so troubled.

"It's getting late," he murmured. Gently he turned her in his arms and walked her to her cottage.

They exchanged one more long kiss before they whispered good-night.

She watched him cross the lawn, a solitary figure casting a long shadow in the moonlight.

What answers had he been searching for when he'd probed for her motives for taking the Pinetop job? Why had he mentioned that it wasn't the "big time"?

Turning, Kelly walked inside her cottage, feeling as if she had somehow let him down and not having the vaguest idea how.

Chapter Twelve

As the weeks passed, the changing of the guards outside Baritone's stall at the end of each eight-hour shift became another facet of Pinetop's daily routine. The guards Tanner had assigned were quiet, watchful men who were careful not to get in the way any more than necessary. And Tanner had left a pager so that he could be summoned at a moment's notice. The guards passed the pager as they rotated duty throughout the day and night.

Kelly was pleased to note that Baritone continued to improve a little each day. The lab report from California came back marked "Substance: Unknown." They agreed that a depressant of some sort had been injected into the horse, but they were unable to identify it.

One morning about ten o'clock, after Kelly had finished half the workouts, she walked down the hallway to a stall where Marcy was assisting Rob in worming the yearlings.

"How's it going?" she asked.

Rob tossed her a smile. "You want to be next?" He made a face.

"Believe I'll pass."

Marcy was holding the colt's head up while he tried as hard as he could to spit out the sticky medicine Rob had squeezed onto the back of his tongue. Finally the colt gave up and swallowed.

"Mm-mm good," Rob teased, "but for some reason, they never ask for more."

Kelly chuckled. "Why are you working inside a stall?"

"The colts seem more relaxed in here than cross-tied in the hallway."

"And it's easier to let one out and bring another in through the paddock door," Marcy said, gesturing toward a walk-through from the stall to the paddock.

"I see."

"Want me to take Baritone off the automatic walker and bring him in?" Marcy asked.

"You're busy. I'll get him," Kelly offered easily.

She walked to the next barn and threw the switch to stop the walker. As she snapped a lead to the colt's halter, the guard rose from the bench. Sam McKenna was the man on duty.

"The colt seems gentle as a pup after a workout and an hour's walk on that thing," Sam remarked.

"It takes the steam out of him all right," Kelly agreed.

She led the colt outside with Sam following behind. Entering the barn, Kelly glanced into the stall where Rob was working. He was leaning against the wall, waiting for Marcy to bring in his next customer.

Kelly was headed toward the opposite end of the barn to Baritone's stall when she heard a scraping sound overhead. The barn was two stories high, but above the stalls on both sides was a floored storage area. During the winter, the loft was packed solid with fifty-pound bales of alfalfa. She glanced up and saw a wall of hay shift and tremble. With a rush of terror, Kelly watched as the bales leaned and tilted. Within a fraction of a second, the bales were tumbling toward her.

Kelly choked on the scream rising in her throat. A hand closed over her left arm and jerked her roughly, dragging her to the left through an open stall door. With the lead still gripped firmly in her right hand, Baritone was following on her heels.

Kelly felt the colt crashing into her back and someone spinning her out of the way.

Rob shoved Kelly into a corner of the stall and moved to shield her from Baritone who was thudding against the stall walls in sheer panic.

The guard scrambled over the fallen bales in the hallway. "Kelly! Are you all right?" Sam shouted.

"She's in here," Rob yelled.

Sam began shoving bales out of his way to get to them. He glanced overhead but could see nothing in the loft. A thick cloud of dust fogged the air making it nearly impossible to see.

"Easy, boy, easy," Rob said over and over as he held on to Baritone's halter, trying to bring the animal under control.

Kelly's eyes were burning, but she retained a firm hold on the lead. Drawing the horse closer, she grasped his halter. With Rob on the other side, she managed to hold the colt steady.

Marcy cracked the door from the outside. "Are you all right?" she called. "What was all that noise about?"

"Stay where you are," Kelly cautioned, "and keep that door closed. Can you move the yearlings to another lot?" she asked as an idea occurred to her.

"Sure," Marcy said.

"Then do it quickly."

In a minute, Marcy was back at the door.

"Is the paddock secure?" Kelly asked.

"Yes," Marcy called, "gate's latched."

"Then open the door and stand back. We're bringing Baritone outside."

Marcy swung the gate back, and Kelly signaled Rob to move with her as they led the colt into the late-afternoon sunshine.

Baritone snorted and tried to rear. "Let go, Rob," Kelly ordered. When Rob stepped back, Kelly swung the horse in a tight circle around her, keeping her elbow angled against Baritone's neck so he couldn't step on her. She placed the lead in Marcy's hands and stayed next to her. "Move him in small circles," Kelly told her, "until he settles down."

"Got him," Marcy said, taking over.

"Keep an eye on her, Rob," Kelly said, moving to his side and touching his arm. His troubled blue eyes met hers. "Thanks for pulling me into that stall," she added softly.

"Anytime," he returned absently.

"I owe you one," she called over her shoulder as she hurried back inside. She glanced around on her way to the stall door. "Sam?" she called.

"Kelly, are you all right?" Sam shouted, sweat streaming down his face as he paused to listen.

"Yes, are you?"

"I'm okay," he answered, returning to the task of clearing a path to the stall.

Kelly heard the grinding of tires on gravel and the slam of a door.

"Kelly!"

Kelly recognized Tanner's voice. Never had she been so glad to hear any voice in her life.

"Kelly!" Tanner was climbing over bales, trying to reach her.

"In here," she called. "We're okay."

"What in the hell happened?" Tanner roared as he hurled bales aside with almost Herculean strength.

Sam had almost cleared a path to the stall when Tanner joined him. "Am I glad to see you, boss. I switched on the pager as soon as it happened," Sam said breathlessly.

Together they removed the last bales, and Tanner rushed into the stall to haul Kelly into his embrace. Sam moved discreetly past them into the paddock to check on Baritone.

"What happened?" Tanner demanded, smoothing Kelly's hair back from her forehead. His serious gaze probed hers.

"I was leading Baritone into the barn, and the bales started tumbling down on us."

"Were you hurt?"

"I'm okay. Luckily Rob was working in this stall, and he reached out and dragged me inside. Baritone followed me. I think he's all right. He's in the paddock." She rested her cheek against Tanner's chest. With his arms wrapped around her, she felt safer than she could ever remember.

"I don't know what I would have done if something had happened to you," Tanner said, admitting the chilling fear that wrenched through him. The passion in his voice surprised them both, and Kelly felt a curious warmth flood through her. She closed her eyes and hugged him tighter.

Rob stepped into the doorway. "You okay?" Tanner asked him.

"Yeah." Rob glanced at their embrace and looked away. "Thought we'd take the colt over to the next barn to examine him."

"Go ahead."

Rob disappeared, and Tanner rested his cheek on top of Kelly's head.

"What happened?" Larson approached from the hallway, climbing over bales with catlike stealth.

The last thing Kelly wanted was to move out of

Tanner's arms, but she could feel Larson's gaze, and the moment was spoiled.

Tanner didn't seem any happier about Larson's interruption than she. "Where were you when this happened?" he snapped.

"Checkin' on the brood mares," Larson replied easily. "Looks like you had an accident. Anybody hurt?"

"Not like they could have been," Tanner admitted, sounding every bit as irritated as he felt. "Who stacked that hay anyway?"

"The boys packed a truckload up there this morning. We strung ropes across the opening to keep everything in place. Checked them myself. They were secure."

"Doesn't look secure to me," Tanner said, stepping over two bales in the hallway and climbing into the loft to check it out himself.

"Maybe someone messed with them later," Larson said, calling up to Tanner. "All I know is when I left, the cables were secure."

Tanner knelt to examine the ropes on the floor of the loft and found where the ends were cut and frayed. Moving to the back of the loft where the eaves sloped to a narrow crawl space, he found another rope. It was tied by one end to a vertical support; the other end was dangling through the boards into an empty stall.

Tanner reasoned that someone had severed the ropes that restrained the bales and had strung another rope behind the wall of hay. That rope had served as a trip wire. Tanner climbed down the ladder and stepped into the empty stall. He concluded that someone in the empty stall had pulled on the end of the rope dangling in the stall, forcing the bales to topple at the moment that Kelly and Baritone were in the aisle below.

Tanner's blood ran cold. Stepping into the hallway, Tanner looked at Larson and gestured at the bales. "Leave everything exactly as it is." Tanner motioned for Kelly to join him. He kept his hand on her elbow as he guided her through the narrow maze to the office.

Inside, Kelly drew in several deep breaths. "Larson gives me the creeps," she said.

"He's an odd one." Tanner took a deep breath as he reached for the phone.

"Why don't you replace him?" Kelly knew when she said it that Tanner probably wouldn't appreciate her suggestion.

"He's strange, but there's no proof he's disloyal," Tanner said as he dialed. "I can't afford to break in someone new at this point."

Kelly couldn't help wondering if the same logic applied to her as she listened to Tanner summon the sheriff.

"Kelly, this is serious," Tanner said after he'd replaced the receiver. "I'm adding more guards, armed guards. You could have gotten hurt today." He looked her in the eye. "I'm convinced that what happened was no accident. Someone rigged those bales to fall when you and the horse were in position."

"Who would've done that?" she asked, feeling sick to her stomach.

Tanner shook his head. "Until the sheriff has him in custody, I want you to stay in the main house."

"Your house?" Kelly asked.

He nodded. "I don't want you staying in the cottage alone."

"I'll be fine," she said.

He gave a sigh of exasperation. "Look, just do this for me. I'll feel better knowing you're safe."

"Tanner, this could have happened no matter where I was staying at night," she argued.

"If you're concerned about your reputation," he continued, ignoring her protest, "Hattie can move in, too."

Kelly held up her hands. "I'd rather stay where I am. Okay?" From the expression on his face, Kelly concluded that Tanner McCrey was not happy about being turned down.

"Why, for heaven sakes?" he demanded.

"I don't want to lose the respect of my staff." And she didn't want to lose her heart to him. Living under the same roof would make it impossible for her to remain immune to him. Kelly turned on her heel and started toward the door.

"We'll discuss this again later," he warned.

Kelly swallowed hard and opened the door.

She'd just stepped into the hallway when Rob rounded the corner.

"How's the colt?" she asked, trying to ignore Tanner's presence behind her.

"Amazingly well. He's shook up, of course, and he may fret off a few pounds, but he's going to be all right."

Rob glanced at her. "How are you?"

"I'm fine," Kelly responded automatically as Rob fell into step beside her as she headed to the next barn to see the horse.

Kelly stood outside the stall for a moment. Baritone was pacing back and forth, ignoring Marcy's efforts to soothe him. Kelly nodded to Sam who'd already taken his position outside the stall.

All at once Kelly felt totally drained. She turned around to say something to Tanner and saw that he wasn't there. For some crazy, feminine reason, she felt abandoned and close to tears.

"You don't look fine," Rob said beside her. "Everything is under control here. Why don't you go on home."

Normally she would have protested, but this time she gladly accepted his offer.

"Okay." She glanced at Rob briefly. "Thanks."

"Don't thank me. You're okay, Smith." He glanced at her again and smiled, and Kelly saw genuine fondness in his expression. "Take care of yourself," he said gently.

"I will . . . good night," she returned, nodding at Marcy before she walked into the piercing cold that seeped into the valley after sundown.

Feeling lonely and weary, Kelly shuffled toward her cottage. When she reached the steps, she did a double take. A guard was sitting in the shadows on the porch.

"Hope I didn't alarm you, Kelly. It's Bob."

Kelly's hand covered her heart. "I didn't know you'd be here," she said, climbing the steps slowly. Bob was bundled up in a blanket, in the red rocker, with a shotgun across his lap. "Are you going to be warm enough?" she asked.

"I've got hot coffee in my thermos, miss. I'll be fine, thanks."

Kelly nodded. It hadn't taken Tanner long to arrange for protection. She unlocked her door and switched on the light, unaware that Tanner, in the house up on the hill, was standing at his window watching her, longing to ease her misery.

During the next few weeks Tanner kept after her to move into the main house for security reasons, and Kelly kept turning him down. Because of his continuing insistence and her stubborn refusal, an awkwardness developed between them. Tanner ceased to drop into her office just to visit at the end of each day, and Kelly didn't hang around waiting for him.

But she missed him. She missed looking up from her desk to see his broad-shouldered frame filling the doorway, a teasing light shining from his eyes, a lock of his windblown hair hanging on his fore-head, his tanned face reddened from the wind. She missed watching him shove the door closed, shrug out of his jacket and bend over her shoulder to look at the paperwork she was finishing. His nearness had never failed to fill her senses. Now his absence made her days empty.

Her mother had called more than once to insist that she fly home for Christmas. Kelly had tried to explain that her mare, Happy Talk, could have her foal any day. Her due date wasn't until the second week of January, but Rob thought it was likely the foal would come early.

Happy Talk was too far along to travel and too old to have her foal unattended. It was a task Kelly didn't want to delegate, not to Marcy, not even to Rob. No one would watch her mare as carefully as she would. Happy Talk had lost her last foal, and Kelly intended to make sure that she had this one safely.

But her mother would not accept her excuse. To her way of thinking, Kelly cared more about horses than her family, just as Charlie had, and she'd reminded Kelly of it more than once. In their last two conversations, her mother had sharply criticized Kelly's profession, her father and her values.

To Kelly, going home for the holidays was not an appealing prospect. She realized that her mother's negative attitude had only been inflamed by the sad condition of Charlie's estate and her disapproval of Kelly's reasons for working at Pinetop in the first place.

It was a tense time for all of them. Kelly argued that there would be other holidays they could share happily in the future when the mess at Pinetop was a memory and Happy Talk's foal was delivered safely.

Kelly had told Margaret that Tanner now knew that she was Charlie's daughter, hoping the news would appease her, but it hadn't. Her mother had seized it as yet another reason for Kelly's prompt return, arguing that if Tanner, Kelly and the authorities had not discovered any new evidence by now, they never would.

Secretly, Kelly feared her mother might be right, but she wasn't ready to give up yet. She'd signed a contract to work at Pinetop through the Arkansas Derby, and she was going to honor it.

Hattie had taken it for granted that if Kelly wasn't going home for the holiday, she would be coming to the McCrey house for Christmas dinner. Kelly was looking forward to the occasion with a mixture of apprehension and hope. She told herself that perhaps she and Tanner could set their tensions aside for the holiday and enjoy each other's company again.

As Tanner held the chair for her beside his at the dinner table, Kelly felt the return of the old magic between them. His smile was warm and genuine, and his eyes told her he was glad to be with her. Across the table Rob and Marcy bantered back and forth, and Hattie sat at the end of the table, beaming at them all.

When everyone had filled their plates, the pager sounded its squeal. The guard at Baritone's stall was sending a distress signal. Tanner shot to his feet and crossed the room to switch it off. His eyes locked with Kelly's as she rose. In seconds, everyone was moving, pulling on coats and heading out the door.

Kelly and Tanner ran beside each other to the barn with the others on their heels.

"What happened?" Tanner asked.

The guard was standing at the end of the hallway looking out the back door, his eyes trained on something in the distance. "Fire, boss. Over there." The guard pointed toward the mountains where McCrey timber grew thick.

Tanner took a deep breath, his eyes grimly assessing the dense, billowing smoke on a nearby hillside. "Oh, hell," he said softly. Turning, he glanced toward Baritone's stall. "What about the colt?" he asked.

"He's fine," the guard assured, glancing over his shoulder at the horse. "I thought you'd want to know right away, so I used the pager to reach you."

"How many men do we have on the place?" Tanner asked, already calculating in his head.

"Not enough," Rob said as he came to stand beside him.

"Damn!" Tanner cursed. There couldn't have been a time when he would have been more short-handed than on Christmas Day. Even the volunteer fire department would be hard-pressed to come up with men today. "Rob, get on the horn and call every fire department within fifty miles. Contact the sheriff, maybe he can rustle up more men."

"What can I do?" Kelly asked.

Tanner looked at her. "Run things here," he said, then added in a low voice, "and keep an eye on the colt. I'll need every man on the fire line."

"Then go," she insisted. "I'll make the phone calls."

Tanner nodded and began issuing orders. In minutes he and a skeleton crew were racing to the fire with axes, shovels and tractors from the equipment sheds.

"Stay here," Kelly told Marcy. "Keep an eye on the horse until I get back."

Marcy positioned herself in the open doorway at the end of the barn while Kelly ran to the office at the other end. Quickly she phoned the county fire department and the sheriff.

Minutes later she joined Marcy and peered through binoculars at the fire that had consumed one mountainside and was spreading to another. The wind was whipping the sparks and driving the flames through the forest with amazing speed, while a thick cloud of smoke hovered over the valley.

Hattie rushed into the barn, nearly out of breath. "How bad is it?" she asked breathlessly.

"Bad."

"What can I do?"

"Hook up all the hoses at every barn. . . . Marcy, you help her."

"You don't think it'll spread to the farm, do you?" Marcy asked incredulously.

"We'd better be prepared in case the wind changes," Kelly murmured, then turned and gave Marcy's shoulder a reassuring squeeze.

Marcy nodded, and she and Hattie took off.

Within a half hour, area fire trucks began arriving. Small groups of volunteer firemen and neighbors followed. Through the binoculars, Kelly could see the yellow coats of fire fighters standing out against the stark, blackened landscape around them. Kelly recognized Jared Huxsman's truck as it went flying down the road with a half dozen of his men in the back.

The brood mares in the valley below were running in frantic circles. Birds were swooping low, flitting in and out of the barn without lighting on the rafters. Horses inside the barns were nickering uneasily to each other.

Kelly left Hattie at the barn, while she and Marcy rode to the valley on horseback. Kelly whistled to Happy Talk before she dismounted and opened the gate. Her mare came to her, and the rest of the mares followed, making it easier to drive the brood mares up the hill to a corral that adjoined one of the barns.

The crews fought the fire the rest of the day and through the night. Kelly rotated with Hattie and Marcy. They were busy filling thermos bottles and making sandwiches to send to the fire line while one of them always remained in the barn watching Baritone.

Each time someone came back to the farm, Kelly asked about Tanner. She learned that he hadn't left the fire line for more than a few minutes at a time, and he hadn't left the area all night. They were shorthanded. Too many employees and volunteers were out of town.

Late into the night, Rob returned for an hour's rest. His face and hair were scorched and what he told Kelly made her heartsick. "We're fighting a losing battle," he whispered hoarsely. "I told Tanner we should've sold this damn place a year ago when we had the chance. It's been nothing but bad breaks and heartache since Dad died."

Kelly chalked his bitter words up to the despair that comes with exhaustion and pain.

As men returned for supplies, they brought news of the fire's progress. Fire fighters stayed busy pumping water, digging ditches and clearing fire lanes, but the wind-tossed flames leaping through the treetops were raging out of control.

It wasn't until the following afternoon, when the gusty winds died down, that the fire finally was brought under control.

Kelly had just finished feeding the animals. Walking to the end of the barn, she stooped to pick up a bucket she'd left outside to dry. It wasn't until Tanner's shadow fell over her that she looked up, startled.

He'd come to her first without stopping at the house to clean up. He'd come directly from the charred ruins of his forest to her side. He'd been driven by a need more pressing than hunger or thirst.

An unnamed emotion had drawn him to her side for a kind of comfort and understanding that he could receive from no one else. He sensed that even without words she would know his loss, his heartache. She was the strongest, most resilient person he knew, and it was her strength that he needed from her now.

Kelly stood up, facing him with wide, pain-filled eyes. Her breath caught in her throat. She'd never seen him looking so exhausted and so defeated. She reached up to gently frame his blackened face with her hands. The smell of singed hair came to her, but it didn't matter. He was here, alive, with her.

In that instant, she knew she couldn't have stood it if he hadn't come back to her. She wished she could tell him how frightened she'd been, but he didn't need that now. He needed her support.

She wrapped her arm around his waist and guided him inside. Gently she eased him down onto a hay bale beside Baritone's stall.

He leaned back, looking up at her wordlessly, filling his vision with her. He needed her comfort, her soft touch and gentle words. He was with her at last. It was a need he wouldn't analyze, an emotion deeper than thought, and he'd blocked out all thought hours ago.

She bent over him and smoothed back his scorched hair. "What can I get you?" she asked. "Water, coffee, food? We could go inside, warm up?"

He shook his head, and she caught the flash of anguish in his eyes. He moved his hand and patted a space beside him.

She sat close to him and wrapped her arms around him. As they leaned back against the wooden wall, she was filled with an overpowering need to comfort him.

He rested his head against hers, and she felt an ache of excruciating tenderness. She wanted more than anything in the world to make everything right for him. She loved him with a fierceness she had never known before.

A tired sigh from deep within him ruffled the wisps of hair on her forehead. "We've lost seventy percent of the timberlands, at least," he said hoarsely.

"You saved the horse farm," she said, lifting her head to look into his eyes.

The corners of his mouth lifted slightly, and he barely nodded. "The sawmill is gone, but we managed to move a truckload of lumber to safety. Lost a tractor, but the rest of the equipment and storage sheds are okay. And, thank God," he closed his eyes for a moment, "nobody was killed."

Her arms tightened around him. "I'm so glad you're safe," she whispered with her heart in her eyes.

His mouth curved. "Are you okay?" he asked.

"If you're okay, I'm okay," she assured him, dropping her head to his chest. "You need to rest. I'll walk you to the house."

"I can't. I'm meeting the sheriff at his office in an hour."

She sat up straight and looked into his eyes searchingly. "Why?"

He took a deep breath and exhaled. "There's something you should know."

"What?" she asked, her heart beginning to hammer.

"The fire marshall was here. He thinks the fire was arson."

Her lips parted. "He does?"

"He's going to start an investigation, run some tests. Nothing's certain now, but he said certain dark patterns on the ground and the odors made him think a flammable liquid had been used to start it."

"Oh, God," she said, "who would do something like that?"

Tanner shook his head. "That's what we hope to find out."

Something suddenly clicked in her memory. "Tanner, remember those files I looked at in your office. Wasn't there something about arson in Larson's background?"

"That was nothing, Kelly, a teenage prank."

"Arson is arson," she reminded.

"That happened a long time ago. He and some other kids burned down an old man's haystack. The man dropped the charges, and they did chores for him for a month to make it up to him."

"Where is Larson today?" she asked pointedly.

"In Oklahoma City visiting his mother in a nursing home."

She shook her head. "I don't trust him. I'd get rid of him if it was up to me."

He lightly touched the tip of her nose. "Larson and I go back a long way. There are things you don't know about him."

"Like what?" Tanner was going to have to dig deep to find anything to redeem Larson in her eyes.

"It's a long story, and I don't have time to go into it now." He checked his watch. "I have to go."

"I'll go with you."

"I'd like that," he admitted. He was tempted to keep her with him, but he remembered their responsibilities and how shorthanded they were. "But you'd better stay here," he added softly.

She nodded and reached to cup his cheek with her hand. Gently she turned his face toward hers. She lifted her lips to his and pressed feather-light kisses over his mouth.

A deep moan rumbled from his chest as his arms tightened around her. His lips parted to savor the sweetness she was offering. Her tenderness was like a soothing, healing balm.

He felt as if he could go on holding her, kissing her, touching her forever. He wanted to blot out all the ugliness of the past two days and lose himself in her. But he had so little time. Reluctantly he drew her away. "I have to go."

"I want to help you," she whispered.

"You have," he said, stroking the softness of her cheek with his thumb.

He rose stiffly and walked down the hallway. A moment later she heard his truck drive away.

Chapter Thirteen

Over the next few days, when Tanner wasn't busy meeting with the authorities, he was patrolling the forests with a crew, making sure that the piles of smoldering ash didn't ignite again, clearing debris and calculating losses.

In spite of the demands on his time, Tanner and Kelly managed to see each other every day. The bond between them was growing. With each conversation, he told her more, shared more about what he was doing and what he planned to do.

Kelly listened attentively, making comments now and then. Tanner was more interested than ever in Baritone's progress and the other events in her day.

When they were alone, they'd speculate on the strange events that had occurred at Pinetop, beginning with Charlie's death.

Kelly reported everything that happened to Tanner. She was his eyes and ears at the farm while he was away. They conferred on nearly everything and discussed things they didn't agree upon until they could reach a compromise.

Larson had returned to Pinetop a few days after the fire. Not one to share his feelings, he'd said little except to comment to Marcy loudly enough for Kelly to hear that the owner and trainer at Pinetop were sure getting buddy buddy these days.

New Year's Eve arrived, bringing with it unseasonably warm temperatures. It was a perfect day to bathe the horses. Kelly sent Doug and Marcy to give Mastercharge a warm bath in the indoor washroom.

When Kelly went to Baritone's stall, she discovered a steady stream of water trickling onto the stall floor from the automatic waterer in the corner. The bedding was ruined, and Baritone seemed rather pleased with himself.

The guard told Kelly that he'd heard the colt splashing in the water during the night. Kelly figured the colt had gotten bored and had learned how to dip his nose into the stainless steel bowl and hold down the device that released the water. Perhaps Baritone had gotten carried away and broken the device, she thought.

She showed the waterer to Larson, and he told her that it would be simple for him to repair. She asked him to get to work on it and led the colt to the cross ties in the aisle.

Kelly decided that if Baritone was this restless he needed a longer workout. That morning the colt turned in the best fractions he'd run since Kelly had arrived. She was so delighted she gave him a long warm bath and stood in the steamy washroom, giving him a back rub with a stiff brush, the way he liked.

Kelly left the colt on the automatic walker and went to prepare his stall. She walked to the waterer and saw that Larson had repaired it and had the mess cleaned up. There was fresh bedding on the floor and alfalfa hay in the hay bunk. She checked the feed tub and found that it was filled with the ration she mixed for the colt each day.

When Baritone was dry, she unsnapped him from the walker and led him to the next barn with the guard following closely behind. Suddenly, they heard a strange noise and a terrible crash. They turned and dashed back down the hallway. Mastercharge was lying on the floor of Baritone's stall. From the looks of him, Kelly could see that he was near death.

The guard was running toward them, and Kelly shouted, "Turn on your pager and get Tanner! And call Rob from the phone in the office."

When Kelly looked up again, Tanner was racing down the hallway to her side.

"What happened?" he asked, grasping her arms. "Are you all right? I was headed this way when I heard the pager."

Kelly closed her eyes and nodded, forcing back the queasiness. She looked into his face, hating to heap on more bad news. "Tanner, I think Mastercharge may be dead."

"Dead?" He glanced over her shoulder looking through the wire screen into the stall.

"We don't know what happened, but it was sudden. There was a crash, and he just keeled over."

Tanner swung the stall door open and stepped inside.

"There was a mix-up about the stalls," Kelly continued. "Baritone was supposed to be in here. The waterer was broken this morning, and I asked Larson to fix it."

Tanner stopped in his tracks and looked at the waterer in the corner. "Don't come in here," he warned, "and don't touch anything until I turn off the electricity."

Tanner started down the hallway to the switch box. Mastercharge might have had a heart attack or a seizure of some sort, but from what Kelly had just told him, he had to consider that the horse might have received a lethal shock from a defect in the waterer.

Such accidents had occurred before, usually with electric heaters placed in stock tanks to keep the water from freezing. Tanner had heard about a neighbor's horse chewing through the insulation that covered the wires and dying as a result. Horses were curious, he thought, sometimes too curious for their own good.

Marcy rushed into the barn looking pale. "The guard just told me what happened. He said to tell you he can't get Rob. Hattie says he's gone with Louise to Little Rock for the weekend. He didn't leave a number. Is Mastercharge okay? I just put him in there for a minute while I ran to the bathroom."

"It doesn't matter," Tanner said quietly as he returned. "Rob couldn't do anything anyway. The horse is dead. I'm calling the sheriff."

As Tanner disappeared into the office, Larson rounded the corner and looked into the barn, squinting in the late-afternoon sun outside. "Somethin' wrong?" he asked, starting down the hallway.

Kelly took a deep breath and exhaled, trying to bring herself under control as he approached. "Take a look," she said evenly, "and tell me what you think."

She watched Larson's face carefully as he looked into the stall and recoiled. When he turned around, his face was pale. It was the first time Kelly had ever seen him look shaken.

"What happened?" he asked.

Kelly's eyebrows rose questioningly. "Did you repair the waterer?"

"Yeah, it was workin' fine. Fixed it myself." He looked back into the stall. "You don't think that he got hurt on that, do you?" Larson asked, looking at the horse again.

Tanner appeared again. "We don't know any-thing for sure," he said, "yet."

Larson raised his hands, palms up. "If that waterer hadn't been safe, don't you think I would've gotten it . . . instead of him?"

Kelly tilted her head to study the foreman. Larson had been a puzzle to her since the night she'd arrived.

"You gotta know I wouldn't a hurt a horse," Larson insisted. Looking imploringly at Tanner, he continued, "You know I wouldn't hurt a horse. Man, I raised that stallion from a foal. I couldn't hurt him." Larson's gaze drifted back to the stall.

Tanner glanced at Kelly's tight features. He suspected that she was already blaming Larson. "The sheriff is on his way, Larson. I'll expect everyone to cooperate with him."

Hours later, after a local vet had examined Mastercharge and the sheriff had questioned everyone at the scene, Tanner took Kelly aside. "I've put another guard on Baritone and posted several more throughout the grounds."

"You think Mastercharge was deliberately murdered?"

He placed a hand on her shoulder and nodded. "The vet said he was electrocuted, and the sheriff said the wires had been stripped. He agrees it was foul play."

"Did he arrest Larson?" she demanded in a tone that made it clear she thought he should have.

Tanner shook his head. "He just told him to stick around."

"He should be in jail," she insisted.

Tanner looked her straight in the eye. "Larson swears he fixed the waterer and left. No one was in the barn after that. Marcy and Doug were out giving Mastercharge a bath, and you and the guard were at the track with Baritone. Anyone could have come in here and stripped those wires."

"That was Baritone's stall," Kelly said. "It was just a fluke that he wasn't the one killed."

"I know," he said, his face creased with concern. "That's why we have to talk. Let's go."

Kelly glanced anxiously at Baritone's new stall and the two men standing outside it, each with a revolver on his hip.

"Come on," Tanner said, putting his arm around her shoulder. "There's nothing more we can do here tonight."

He walked her to her cottage, took the key from her trembling fingers, unlocked the door and escorted her inside.

She sank wearily on the sofa, staring into space, trying to sort things out. Tanner walked into the kitchen and put the kettle on to boil.

When he joined her on the sofa, he pressed a mug of hot tea into her hand. "Kelly, I'm concerned about you," he began.

"There's no need to be," she insisted. They had had this conversation more than once recently.

"I think there is. I was on my way to tell you when the accident happened. The sheriff is certain the incident with the hay bales was no accident. Someone was waiting for you."

"For Baritone, you mean."

"Maybe, but since you're with the horse so much, your life is in danger too."

"I wonder," she said. "Someone gave your horse injections, someone rigged the bales to fall, someone started the fire, and someone sabotaged the waterer. Sounds to me like someone is out to ruin you, not me."

"But you could have been killed on more than one occasion. I can't let you continue to take chances like that."

"Well, we can't give in." She chewed on her bottom lip. "Whoever it is must have killed Charlie, too."

"It's possible. The sheriff is working on that angle too."

"For a change," she said.

Ignoring her sarcasm, he reached under her chin and tilted her head to look into her eyes. "Your safety is my main concern right now."

"I'll be fine," she said briskly, setting her mug on the coffee table.

"I know you will because we're going to take steps to make sure of that. Now, since you're finished with your tea—" he glanced at the untouched mug "—you can start packing. Hattie has your room ready at the house."

"Your house?"

He nodded.

"I'm not moving," she stated flatly.

"You're not staying alone," he challenged.

"Look, if I had been staying at your house all along, the same things would have happened. No one has bothered me here, and no one will. *I'm* not the target."

"You have two choices," he stated, and she could see his temper rising, "move into my house or leave Pinetop."

At that moment Tanner wished he'd never heard of Kelly Smith. Her obstinacy was getting on his nerves. "Whichever you choose," he said calmly, "you'd better start packing."

She shook her head. "I'm not moving, and I'm not leaving. Need I remind you we have a contract, binding on both parties, until the end of April? And that contract does not specify that I have to live in your house." She thought of the innuendos Larson had made about her being buddy buddy with the boss. She had earned the respect of the rest of her staff here, and she wasn't going to jeopardize that by moving into the boss's house.

"Forget the damned contract!"

"No!" Her eyes blazed with indignation. "Besides, the one you should be keeping an eye on is Larson, not me. If you'll remember, my father's reputation was ruined on less evidence than you have on him."

Tanner saw the anger in her eyes—and the hurt. He took a deep breath and let the silence build.

"Look, Kelly, I don't want you to leave." He'd lost enough. He couldn't bear to lose her, too. "I only want to protect you."

She blinked back the tears that were pricking the backs of her eyelids. "That's nice, but I'm not the fragile, porcelain type you think I am. Look, I need a little space, all right?"

She took a deep breath. The situation was nearly out of control. If they argued much longer, she thought she'd probably dissolve into tears and look as helpless as he obviously thought she was.

She stood up. "I'm going to check the mares." She lifted her hand briefly as a signal for him to stay where he was. "I don't need a bodyguard to do that."

She walked out of the cottage into the evening shadows and headed to the barn. Within minutes she'd saddled Goldigger and was riding downhill to the valley where the brood mares had been returned after the fire had burned out.

Glancing at the blackened silhouettes that covered the mountains, Kelly felt a pang of anguish. Tanner had lost so much to arson and sabotage. Some lunatic was out to ruin him, and it hurt her to think of it.

Riding had always quieted her nerves and put things into perspective. She was counting on that as she kicked the palomino into a canter.

Most of the brood mares were bunched nearby, under a spreading oak. Straining to see into the gathering darkness, Kelly spotted Happy Talk among them, dozing with one hind hoof cocked, standing nose to tail with a chestnut mare.

Kelly chuckled at the irony, remembering how that same chestnut mare had been the one who'd taken a few hunks of Happy Talk's hide and driven her away from the herd a few months ago.

Such is life, she thought, recalling how things had been when she'd first arrived at Pinetop. Like Happy Talk, Kelly had been accepted by nearly everyone. Pinetop felt like home now, and that's why she'd felt hurt when Tanner had suggested she leave it.

She whistled to Happy Talk, and the mare pricked her ears and swung her head around. Kelly whistled again, and Happy Talk began walking toward her slowly, her swollen sides shifting heavily back and forth. As she drew near, Kelly could see that the mare's flanks had sunk inward.

Kelly tied the gelding to a fence post and slipped through the gate. Placing her hands on the mare's belly, she felt the movement inside. Bending low, she looked under her. The mare was dripping milk. She wasn't due for another month, but Rob had cautioned that he thought she'd deliver sooner. From the signs, Kelly figured the foal would come within the next twelve hours. She slipped a halter on Happy Talk and led her through the gate.

Later, Kelly settled her mare into a double-sized stall used for foaling. She'd washed her with a disinfectant and wrapped her tail with an elastic bandage to make it easier to keep it out of the way. She gathered up the supplies she would need, put on a pot of coffee, and moved a chair from the office to the hallway outside the stall.

Hours later, Happy Talk was moving back and forth in her stall restlessly, stopping occasionally to look at her belly.

Three mugs of coffee later, Kelly watched the mare break into a sweat and begin to tremble. Several times, Happy Talk would lie down for a few minutes and then get back up on her feet. Kelly's heart began to hammer: these were not good signs.

Of all times, she thought, for Rob to be out of town. She phoned two local vets. One was out on call, the other out of town.

When she returned to the stall and looked inside, her eyes widened in surprise. Happy Talk was lying down, and there was Tanner, kneeling beside her in the straw. "Better grab your supplies," he said calmly. "Your mare is ready to drop her foal."

Kelly sighed with relief, her earlier anger forgotten. She couldn't remember being so glad to see anyone before in her whole life. "I'm afraid she may be in for a hard time, and I can't find a vet."

"Well," he said, rolling up his sleeves. "I've done this before, and I imagine you have, too. Together I think we can manage."

Kelly grabbed the items she'd put together earlier and slipped into the stall. She pushed up her sleeves and scrubbed to her elbows with an iodine-based disinfectant.

When the mare began to thrash in labor, Tanner held her head and spoke soothingly her. When her water finally broke, Kelly was relieved to see two tiny front hooves emerging. If the foal's nose followed next, then she felt sure the birth would be normal. Gently, Kelly supported the foal's legs as the mare's contractions pushed them out.

"I can see the nose," she told Tanner with a quick grin.

Happy Talk nickered deep in her throat, and Tanner stroked her neck gently.

"We're okay at this end," he said reassuringly.

Another long push and the foal emerged quickly. Kelly opened the thin translucent sack, peeling it away from the foal's nose and eyes.

Happy Talk raised her head to look back at her new baby, who was batting her damp eyelashes and looking around at the world quizzically. The mare nuzzled her foal, inhaling her scent, and began cleaning her gently.

"Congratulations." Tanner grinned at her.

"Thanks," she said softly, smiling at him. They stayed where they were, not wanting to rush the mare.

After several minutes the mare stood on shaky legs and nudged her foal to its feet. Kelly and Tanner stood back out of the way while the newborn wobbled and toppled a few times.

"I believe you're the proud owner of a beautiful, black filly," Tanner announced, wrapping his arm around Kelly's shoulders and hugging her. "Nice baby, Mama."

"She is that," Kelly whispered.

"Do you have a name picked out?"

Kelly nodded. "This foal was a legacy from my father. When he was happiest, he'd say he was walking in tall cotton. That's the way I want to remember him. Her name will be Tall Cotton."

Gently Kelly guided the foal to her first meal. While it nursed, she held a shot glass filled with iodine under the foal and dunked its navel into it several times to guard against infection.

A few hours later Kelly and Tanner stood outside the stall, sipping steaming mugs of coffee.

"Happy New Year," he said, smiling down at her. "Did you realize that your filly was born at one-thirty in the morning on New Year's Day?"

"Happy New Year." Kelly rose on her toes and planted a kiss on his mouth. "Let's hope it's a better one for both of us," she added.

"Amen," he said emphatically. "Now, what do you think we should do about her?" he asked, nodding toward the foal.

"I'd feel better about leaving her if we got some mineral oil down her first." The foal's system was sluggish, and Kelly feared infection might set in if she remained impacted. "If Rob were here, he'd pass a stomach tube on her."

"Well," Tanner said, "before Rob got his fancy education, we used to put some mineral oil in a pop bottle and tilt the foal's head up and pour some into its mouth."

"I've done it," Kelly said, making a face at him. "Are you game for a struggle?"

He chuckled. "Why should today be any different?"

The foal proved to be surprisingly strong as she tossed her head and thrashed about, eluding their attempts to hold her and pour mineral oil into her mouth.

"Time-out," Kelly called, bending from the waist to catch her breath. The foal would have none of the mineral oil. Tanner agreed, releasing the foal.

Kelly leaned against the wooden wall and slid down to sit on her heels. As she placed the pop bottle next to her, she noticed that she had more oil smeared on her sweatshirt and splattered on her jeans than they'd managed to get into the foal. She glanced up at Tanner and laughed. He didn't look much better. She closed her eyes and smothered another chuckle.

"We know how to have fun, don't we, kid?" he said, wiping his hands across the front of his shirt.

Kelly opened one eye and peered up at him. "Ever have such a good time on New Year's?"

He slid down the wall to sit next to her. "Nah. All those people out dining and dancing, hey, they don't know what they're missing."

She grinned at him, and he leaned closer to rub noses with her. He kissed her once and then again.

It occurred to him that having a bad time with her was still better than having a good time with anyone else. There was something about her that got to him.

She was real and so full of life. He knew without asking that she understood what this farm meant to him. She knew what it was to dream of making a champion.

If he wasn't careful, he warned himself, he might never want to let her go. As he kissed her again, he knew he had already reached that point.

Slowly Kelly drew back. He opened his eyes and looked at her, puzzled. "Something wrong?" he murmured.

"You won't believe this," she whispered.

"What?"

"The foal is licking my hand," she whispered back.

He glanced down. Sure enough, the foal was licking up the oil pooled in Kelly's palm. Slowly, Tanner picked up the bottle and poured a little more into Kelly's hand. The foal looked Kelly in the eye and nuzzled Kelly's chin for an instant, then continued to lick up the oil in her hand.

"I never would have believed it," Kelly said, as the foal tottered back to her mother's side. "We could've saved ourselves a lot of hassle if we'd tried that in the first place."

Tanner made a sound in his throat. "Seems we always go about things the hard way."

He was including their relationship as well, and Kelly sensed it. She nodded. "Truce?" she suggested.

He smiled. "You read my mind." He picked up the bottle and held it to the light to swirl the oily residue in the bottom. "We could drink to that." He cocked an eyebrow.

She made a face. "No thanks."

"Getting picky, huh?"

She nodded. "Mmm-hmm."

"Are you hungry?"

"Starved," she said, realizing she hadn't eaten more than a few snacks in the past twelve hours.

He glanced at his watch. It was almost three. "I'll fix breakfast," he offered.

"You're on." She stood up and worked her knees to loosen the stiffness.

Walking to the cottage, they inhaled deeply of the humid scent of pine bathed in dew. "Where's the guard?" Kelly asked when she saw no one settled into the red rocker on the front porch.

"I gave him the holiday off," Tanner returned smoothly.

Kelly shrugged. "I don't have much in the fridge," she told him as she opened the front door.

"Oh yes, you do."

Curious, she turned to look at him, when her toe bumped into something. She switched on the light and looked down.

"What's this?" she asked. Two suitcases were sitting just inside the door. "You had someone pack my clothes?" she accused incredulously. She knew Tanner could be stubborn, but she never thought he'd go to this length to move her.

"Not your clothes," he corrected, "my clothes."

She looked at him, puzzled.

"I figure if you won't move to my house, I'll move to yours."

"I don't believe this."

"Believe it," he warned. "Now, how about champagne and my specialty, eggs Benedict?" He rubbed his hands together and headed toward the kitchen.

She followed in his wake. "I doubt you'll find the ingredients in there. And," she added wryly, "I'm fresh out of champagne."

He swung open the door on the tiny refrigerator. "As a matter of fact, I asked Hattie to make sure we were well stocked."

She glanced at the shelves crammed full. They'd been nearly empty when she'd left earlier. He grabbed a champagne bottle and closed the refrigerator door with his hip.

Kelly crossed her arms. He hadn't even asked her if he could move in, and here he was taking over. The cottage had only one bedroom and one bath. Just how presumptuous was he? If a man stayed with her, it was by invitation only. "I am not sleeping in that bedroom with you."

He glanced over his shoulder and sent her a flirtatious wink. "The sofa makes a decent bed, as I recall." He popped the cork.

"Then that's where *you'll* stay," she fired back.

"Fine with me," he said quickly, turning on his heel and handing her a glass.

It dawned on her that she'd just been outmaneuvered, or had she outmaneuvered herself, she wondered. She stood there with her mouth open while he filled two glasses to the brim.

"Cheers," he said pleasantly as he clinked glasses and raised his. When she didn't lift her glass, he lowered his. "Ah, come on," he said lightly. "I thought we just agreed to a truce."

She shrugged. "I didn't mean you could move in."

"Humor me. I'm not trying to take advantage of you, but this is an extraordinary situation." The amusement left his eyes. "I'd never forgive myself if something happened to you."

She looked down at her glass and nodded slowly, knowing how awful things had been for him lately, knowing how awful she'd feel if anything happened to him.

A hint of mischief returned to his voice. "Besides, maybe I want to stay here so you'll protect me. Rob is gone for the weekend. Maybe I'm afraid to stay by myself."

She looked up and saw the playful challenge in his eyes. "Okay," she said easily, "but you'll have to play by the house rules."

He smiled and touched his glass to hers. They took a sip and lowered their glasses. "Which are?" he asked setting his glass down and opening a white enamel cabinet.

"I get the bed. You get the sofa."

He shrugged his shoulders, one concession down. He turned on the gas and set a large skillet on the burner.

"You pick up after yourself."

He glanced at her, pretending to look offended. "Of course."

"And I get first dibs on the bathroom."

He lowered his chin to look at her. "We'll negotiate that one."

He'd lived the first five years of his life in the cottage before his father had become prosperous enough to build McCrey house. He recalled that the water heater, as a rule, produced just enough hot water to fill the claw-footed bathtub once.

He dropped a hunk of butter into the skillet and glanced at Kelly. She was leaning against the countertop with her head propped against a kitchen cabinet.

"You could take your bath while I cook."

"Fair enough," she said, setting down her glass.

Kelly filled the tub half full and poured in a generous amount of fragrant bath oil. The luxuriant bubbles served to soak away her tension.

Afterward, the aromas of Canadian bacon and hollandaise sauce drew her to the kitchen.

Walking through the living room, she glanced at the only source of light, the crackling fire he'd built. The heat was gradually stretching into every corner of the cottage. In the kitchen doorway Kelly paused to tighten the sash of her white terry robe.

"Perfect timing," Tanner said, gesturing toward the oak table set for two. "Have a seat," he said, handing her a fresh glass of champagne. "Breakfast is served."

She picked up his glass and carried both to the table while he brought their plates. As she settled on her chair, he set a plate before her. Piled atop a toasted English muffin was a slice of Canadian bacon and a poached egg drowning in a rich hollandaise sauce and sprinkled with chopped ripe olives. On the side were potatoes fried with chopped green peppers and pimientos. Tanner watched as she took a bite of the eggs Benedict. "Mmm, delicious," she said, just a little surprised that he could cook so well.

"Thank you," he said modestly.

After the meal Kelly volunteered to clean up, but Tanner insisted they leave everything to soak. He filled their glasses with the last of the champagne, and they walked into the living room. When he piled more logs on the fire, the flames licked at them eagerly.

Moving to her side, he touched her glass with his. "Happy New Year, Ms. Smith."

"Happy New Year, Mr. McCrey." She looked at him over the rim of the glass as she sipped, and he watched the firelight dance in her eyes.

He felt a tug that was impossible to ignore. Standing close enough to touch, he gazed at her, trying to keep the longing out of his eyes.

The truth was he'd loved her since the moment he'd met her, but he knew that she didn't believe in love at first sight. He was beginning to suspect that he would love her until the day he died, though it seemed she wouldn't be sticking around for the long haul. He'd faced that months ago. But she was here tonight and, for the moment, that was enough.

Gazing into his eyes, she recognized the same yearning that was humming through her. He wanted her; she wanted him. The choice was hers. She knew from his stillness, he was exercising restraint. She could simply walk away. He wouldn't follow.

She knew she didn't want to leave his side, not tonight. A voice inside her whispered that she could have lost him in the fire, never to have known the magic that they could bring to each other. When she'd faced the prospect of losing him, she'd faced the depth of her love for him. What mattered most to her had changed somehow. Tanner was what mattered now.

Slowly she took the glass from his hand and set it on the table with hers. Heaving a sigh, she gave in to something she'd fought for a long time. A sense of inevitability came over her. Taking one small step forward, she moved so close that they were touching from shoulder to knee.

He cupped her face in his hands. Murmuring her name, his lips brushed her mouth, nibbling, savoring the softness of her lips until he could stand it no longer. With a groan, he parted her lips, tasting the hint of wine and something uniquely her own.

He drew back just enough to turn his head and bring their mouths together again. They lost themselves in mindless kisses, which demanded then yielded, searched then gave, stroking a raging need that cried for more.

Her heart racing, Kelly strained closer. She tilted her head back, inviting him to explore.

His lips traveled the tender line of her throat, making her stomach knot with need. He felt her pulse hammering against his lips, and it sped him to the brink. "Soon there won't be any turning back." His whispering breath skittered over her skin, heating her blood, making her shudder with desire.

"Who wants to turn back?" she whispered.

Her mocking tone made his heart pound and his mind cloud. He lifted his fingers and with one deft move, he loosened the sash and her robe fell open.

His breath caught in his throat as the firelight played over her skin. His eyes met hers for an instant and lowered. A tingle raced over her skin, following the path of his gaze. As though he were unwrapping a fragile gift, he lifted the robe from her shoulders and let it fall to the floor.

"So beautiful," he murmured.

She saw the desire in his eyes. And her need grew as well, making her bold. She slipped her fingers inside his collar down to the first button of his shirt, feeling the quick rhythm of his pulse against her fingertips. Her heartbeat speeded up to match his as she opened his shirt to the waist.

The light pressure of her fingers brushing his skin as she worked the buttons one by one was slowly driving him mad. As she peeled his shirt over his shoulders, he reached out and pulled her against him.

With the tantalizing pressure of her small, tilted breasts against his naked flesh he lost all sense of time and place. He was consumed by sensations, beyond thought, beyond reason.

His mouth took hers fiercely, then his ragged breath was against her throat. His lips raced over her. She was on fire everywhere he touched. As his hands moved lower, her vision slipped out of focus.

An instant later they were on the rug. Her scent, her taste, her softness were whirling inside his head. And he was next to her, flesh to flesh.

His hands stroked and teased until her desire became uncontrollable. As she murmured his name, her voice echoed in his mind.

Then they were one, and she was moving with him, matching his strength. He knew the exquisite ache of ecstasy.

Her arms clung to him as wave after wave of pleasure washed through her until she was shuddering at its crest and then floating . . . floating. . . .

Chapter Fourteen

Kelly shifted and snuggled closer to Tanner's warmth. She rubbed her head against his shoulder and drew her leg across his body. Gradually she became aware of her surroundings as the unyielding surface beneath the carpet and the chill air made it hard to find a comfortable position.

She opened her eyes and looked into his. Her slow smile had him breathing a sigh of relief. He hadn't intended to take her so suddenly, so frantically. It wasn't like him to lose control, but then nothing had been the same for him since the day he'd met her.

He stroked her cheek with his fingertips. "I didn't mean for that to happen."

"Oh?" She arched a brow.

The corners of his mouth lifted. "Well, I'd intended to be gentler." His brows lifted apologetically.

"Who's complaining?"

His mouth curved more, and then his expression sobered. "I'd never want to hurt you, you know?"

She sighed. "If you're worried," she said, running her finger down the bridge of his nose, "I think a rematch could be arranged."

Chuckling, he pulled her closer, and they shared a long leisurely hello kiss. Afterward he sat up and rose to his feet. Gently he drew her up, swept her into his arms, and carried her into the bedroom.

The springs creaked beneath their weight as he knelt to deposit her on the bed. The house was cool, and soon they were both scrambling to crawl under the covers. They lay facing each other, embracing and running their hands briskly over each other for warmth.

Soon other needs were arising anew. Tanner gathered her close, wanting this time to explore her more slowly. In the dim light he could see a matching desire in her eyes.

She looked at him, longing for the gentleness his touch was offering. Now was her chance to stretch her soul with giving. Even as it began, she knew this was a moment to cherish.

They made love again, quietly and slowly, with more tenderness than either of them had ever known.

When the first light of dawn filtered through the lace curtains of the window, Tanner awakened and gazed down at her. She looked relaxed and content. His heart swelled with an emotion that he was afraid to speak of aloud. For a long time he lay watching her sleep. Being with her like this filled him with peace, a feeling he hadn't known for many months.

Quietly he slipped out of bed and walked into the living room. The fire had burned down, and the air was sharp. He flipped open a suitcase and dug out a pair of fleece-lined moccasins, then pulled on a pair of faded navy sweatpants.

Kneeling, he stoked the embers until they were red and glowing. Crumpling last Sunday's paper, he tossed it in, along with a few sticks of kindling from an old apple basket on the hearth. After adding a stack of logs, he dusted his hands and headed for the kitchen to put coffee on.

Hopping back into bed afterward, he pulled the comforter over Kelly's shoulders. She stirred slightly as he cuddled her close. He lay waiting, for the percolator to finish rattling, for the fire to warm the corners, for the coffee to lure her awake.

When she finally opened her eyes and looked at him, he smiled. Wrapping her arms around his neck, she snuggled against him. Though her eyes were heavy with sleep, her cheeks were flushed, and he thought he'd never seen her look more beautiful.

He ran his finger through her tousled locks. "You've gone back to your natural color," he said approvingly, "and you're letting your hair grow out."

"I thought I might as well."

"I like it," he said.

"Hmm, that's a wonderful smell," she murmured.

"The fresh-perked aroma of coffee or me?" he said with a teasing smile. Nuzzling her bangs out of the way, he brushed a kiss across her forehead.

"You, of course," she said, feeling absolutely content.

"Like your coffee served in bed, madam?" he asked brightly.

Her eyes narrowed as she stretched like a cat. "If you come with it."

He pretended to look shocked as he groped for her under the comforter. "What kind of man do you think I am?"

Reaching for him, she chuckled. "I know what kind of man you are."

They exchanged a slow smile and several long kisses. The room was light by the time they finally climbed out of bed and Kelly had wrapped up in her robe and padded out to fill the tub.

As she lowered herself into the fragrant bubbles, Tanner tapped at the door. "It's the man with your coffee."

"Come in, by all means."

He pushed the door open and stepped in with two mugs. He handed her one. "How's the water?" he asked.

"Water's fine." She took a sip from the steaming mug. "And so's your coffee."

He leaned against the freestanding basin. "As I recall, the water heater runs low filling that deep tub."

"Fishing for an invitation, Mr. McCrey?"

Sipping his coffee, he looked at her over the rim. "Are you offering one, Ms. Smith?"

She drew up her knees. "Hop in."

"Hot," he hissed as he lowered himself into the

bubbles. The water level quickly rose to her shoulders.

"Of course," Kelly said with a slow smile. She glanced up at a window high on the wall as she heard a popping frenzy against the glass. "What's that?"

"Sleet."

Her brows lifted. "I didn't look out this morning." Usually, checking the weather was the first thing she did after she got out of bed. Today, she'd been distracted.

"Then you didn't see the skim of ice."

"Well, that cancels the workouts," she conceded.

"It's a holiday, for heaven's sake. Don't you ever take a day off?"

She shrugged. "Not very often."

"Then this is the first time I've been happy for sleet." He swirled the coffee in his mug, and his expression hardened. "I could've really used this moisture a week ago when the hillsides were going up in smoke."

"How bad is the damage?" she probed gently.

He shrugged, trying to dismiss it, but the mood lingered. "The forests will come back eventually, but we won't be cutting for a long time."

"I'm sorry."

"Trouble is we have crews depending on us for work. Bad enough to lay them off for a few months. Now we won't have jobs for them to come back to."

"Can they find other work?"

He shook his head. "Minimum wage type work. There aren't many opportunities to make a good salary. This country is scenic, but it doesn't hand you a living. The timber was our mainstay."

"You still have the horse farm."

"And its expenses—more going out than coming in. I had to cancel the bookings to Mastercharge. There'll be no stud fees coming in without him."

"There'll be purses from the races we win."

The corners of his mouth turned up. "If Baritone pans out . . ." His voice trailed off.

"You know I'll do all I can."

He reached for her hand. "Don't let what I've said pressure you. Just do what you can. I knew when I got into the horse business that there are no guarantees."

Kelly was aware that only one in twenty race-horses paid back its investment. And now she understood that the McCreys had been counting on the timber to bankroll the farm until their breeding program was established. "I don't think your horses will let you down," she encouraged.

"Right." He set the mug down on the tile floor. "Except now our trapeze act is working without a safety net."

She nodded as she set her mug aside. Tanner had a cash flow shortage—the horseman's plague. Her father had been proof of that. An idea surfaced, one she had harbored recently. "You know, there's another way you could generate a cash flow."

"I'm listening."

"Well," she said, "you have a marvelous training track here, and your equipment barns are good metal structures."

"And?"

"And there'll be more horses arriving in this area for the season at Oaklawn than there are good facilities for them. Those barns where you're storing equipment could be converted into stalls to board horses. Trainers could stable and train here and haul their entries to the track on race days."

"Would a trainer be willing to do that?"

"Sure," she said, warming to the idea. "Trainers could use your track anytime during the day. At Oaklawn, workout times are limited."

He mulled the idea over, realizing it might work. "You wouldn't mind other trainers working here?"

"Not if it'd help you. Shoot," she said, shrugging lightly, "the competition could be good for us."

His face brightened as he imagined the possibilities. "We'd be selective about who we hired. I'd want you to screen them. You think we'd run a higher risk of sickness in our horses letting others come here?"

"Your horses and stables are on this side of the track, and the equipment barns are on the other side, a good distance away. It might increase our risk, but we do have a good vet on the premises."

He smiled at that. "I suppose I could sell some of the logging equipment to generate capital. We won't be needing it for a few years, anyway." His brows drew together as he concentrated, a habit she found endearing. "We could use the lumber we saved from the fire . . . and the cutting crews could work as carpenters to build the new stalls."

"I could phone other trainers and offer to reserve stalls for them," she volunteered. "Oaklawn Park opens in a month. Think you could have the stalls ready by then?"

He grinned. "Even if the weather turns bad, we'll be working indoors— Kelly, your plan could solve a lot of problems," he praised.

"Tanner?"

"Hmm," he replied, reaching below the bubbles to capture her foot. Slowly, he began to massage it.

"Whoever is trying to ruin you isn't going to like this idea."

"I know." His hands worked her ankle and moved to stroke the smoothness of her calf. "But maybe he'll tip his hand, so I suggest we keep our eyes and ears open and compare notes."

"I agree. . . ." It was becoming impossible for Kelly to concentrate on anything but the sensations consuming her as his hands worked higher.

THE NEXT MORNING Tanner called a breakfast meeting at the McCrey house. Tanner and Kelly sat on one side of the table; Larson and Bud Clark on the other side and the timber crew foreman next to them. After they'd all helped themselves to Hattie's delicious buffet, Tanner explained the plan to convert the equipment sheds into a boarding facility.

Larson set his cup down on the saucer with a clatter. "Our stock is pretty healthy right now," he objected hotly. "Won't bringin' in others be askin' for trouble? There's sure to be more sickness. Besides, my people stay busy without adding more animals for them to see to."

Tanner glanced at Rob. "What do you think about the health aspect?"

Rob shrugged. "It'll increase the chances of infection among the stock, but we've always had more viruses in the spring when the mares booked to Mastercharge started arriving. All we have to do is keep up inoculations and treat early symptoms."

Tanner looked at the large, well-built man across from him. "What do you think, Bud?"

"It could be welcome news for the men. They're all mighty worried about whether they'll have a job this spring." His ruddy face grew brighter.

"After construction is completed," Tanner said, looking at Bud, "we'll need even more men to take up the extra workload. Do you think some of the men would agree to stay on to do the feeding and cleaning in the new barns?"

"I'd be willing, for one," Bud stated. "I'm sure some of the others would be interested, too."

"Then, if there's no more discussion, we'll start building the first of the week."

In a few minutes everyone had cleared the room except Kelly.

"Looks like they're supportive," Tanner noted.

"Except for one," she added wryly.

"He'll adjust."

"Tanner! Larson was the *only* one to object. Why won't you even consider that he could be the one causing all the troubles? He's had every opportunity, and he's carrying around a truckload of resentment."

"Kelly, it isn't Larson."

"How can you be sure?"

Tanner set his cup on the saucer. Staring at the white tablecloth for a moment, he said quietly, "Because of something that happened when Rob and I were kids."

Kelly saw a flash of pain cross his face as he continued. "You know that Rob and I are half brothers. When my father battled Jared Huxsman for custody of Rob, the stress weakened his health. I guess I blamed Rob for that, though it couldn't have been his fault."

"You must have been just a kid then," Kelly consoled, lacing her fingers with his.

"Not really. I was certainly old enough to know better," he confessed. "The summer after I graduated from high school, I was breaking colts for Dad. Guess it was my way of winning his approval. One morning I'd saddled two colts and led them to the stream. The water was running fast and high after a heavy rain.

"Like I'd watched Larson do a dozen times, I tied one colt to a tree and led the other into the water and climbed aboard. The colt tried to buck, but the water slowed him. I heard someone shouting from the bank. It was Rob. He was about six then, and he was cheering me on. When I turned to look, I let the colt get his head down and he threw me." Tanner's face tightened. "I was mad as hell, humiliated mostly, that I'd gotten bucked off and Rob had seen it. I yelled for him to clear out and got back on the colt.

"Next thing I knew, Rob had climbed onto the other colt and untied him. When he hollered for me to look, I saw the colt take off with him. After a couple of jumps, it skidded to a stop and threw him headlong into the stream.

"I jumped down and dove in after him. Rob was caught in the current, and I could see his head bobbing just ahead of me. As I reached to grab him, we slammed into a log, and both of us went under.

"Then Larson was in the water with us, dragging us to the bank." Tanner lifted his gaze and looked into Kelly's eyes. "He risked his life that day to save us. True, he can be rude and bullheaded, but I've known him all my life. He's been like a second father, and no one would ever make me believe he would do anything to hurt Rob or me."

Kelly was convinced that Tanner was the loyal one and that his loyalty in this instance was misplaced. Kelly laid her head on his shoulder. It was the first time in her life she'd ever prayed that she was wrong.

THROUGH JANUARY Tanner was busy supervising construction of the stalls while Kelly continued training Baritone. The weather permitted her to work the colt a half dozen times, and he was steadily improving.

Happy Talk's foal was growing stronger, and other foals were arriving daily.

On the first of February, three trainers arrived to settle their mounts into the new stalls at Pinetop. Everyone was hustling to keep up with new demands, but there was a general mood of optimism. Guards were still in place, but tensions eased as days rolled by without another attack.

Kelly and Tanner tried to see each other as often as possible during the day, but it wasn't usually until late at night, when he slipped into the cottage, that they could really be alone together.

Kelly was aware of the talk about them. From what Marcy had confided, Larson was having a field day, telling everyone that the trainer was sleeping with the owner. Sometimes when Kelly walked into the barns, conversations came to a brisk halt, and Kelly guessed that she was the subject of gossip. She had decided the first night Tanner had stayed with her that what they did was no one's business but theirs. She loved Tanner McCrey, and she would not give up their time together just to squelch gossip.

At the end of March they decided to take Baritone to Oklahoma City for a prep race at Remington Park. Together they led the colt from the saddling paddock through the glass tunnel where thousands watched him and speculated on his ability.

The colt romped home a length ahead of the rest to win a major stakes purse. The press zoomed in for interviews, singing Kelly's praises for conditioning the colt to success. When a journalist recognized her as Charlie Bailey's daughter, the press interest in her increased.

The next day Kelly's picture appeared in the sports section of the newspaper, and before they'd checked out of the hotel, the phone was ringing nonstop.

More than once Tanner handed the receiver to her. Owners wanted to know when she'd be available to train their horses.

Tanner made a flimsy excuse and finally went out for a walk. He'd known he couldn't isolate Kelly at Pinetop forever. She was destined to become a star in the racing world. She had the talent and a charisma that drew the press and excited the fans, but it was her knowledge and skill that appealed to owners, like himself, who wanted winners.

But that wasn't all he wanted from Kelly Smith, Tanner admitted as he took long strides in the crisp morning air.

He wanted her at his side for the long haul. He was in love with her, and it hurt like hell to think she might not stay.

It was more than the difference in their ages. It was the fact that they were at different stages in their lives that worried him.

He'd finally found where he belonged: Pinetop. But Kelly's career was just taking off. To develop it, she should go where the best horses were running for the highest stakes. She would need to be mobile and unencumbered to maximize her opportunities. Like the leading trainers, she would need to travel from race to race, track to track.

In the end he decided that the best thing he could do for her was to enjoy her as long as she was with him, and try to accept the fact that it wouldn't be forever.

She was ready to soar the heights; he was ready to sink roots.

IN THE FOLLOWING WEEKS their loving grew more urgent. Sometimes, when he was holding her, Kelly could feel a desperation rising in both of them.

It wouldn't be long until her contract with him would be up. Job offers were pouring in steadily, offers that would have made her head spin six months ago.

But that was before she'd known Tanner McCrey. Now her dreams had changed. When she'd come to Pinetop, her only concern had been to clear her father's name. That obligation still tore at her heart, but her priorities had changed over the past months, particularly since it had become obvious that most horse people didn't believe Charlie had been guilty.

And now she was deeply in love with Tanner. Helping him, sharing her life with him was her dream now. She was wishing he would ask her to stay. She hoped that if he did it would be for more than a renewal of her contract. But he hadn't asked, and she wondered why.

The staff was surprised by the news that Kelly was Charlie's daughter, but it seemed to elevate her in their eyes, Marcy's especially. It touched Kelly's heart, when the young girl took her aside and whispered, "Kelly, I always fantasized that Charlie was my dad. I guess that sort of makes us sisters, doesn't it?"

"Indeed, it does," Kelly replied.

One day Tanner was ushering Kelly into the McCrey house because Hattie had insisted that she join them for lunch. As their heels clicked across the bottle-green marble entry, Rob bounded down the stairs, singing "Happy Birthday." Hattie joined in from the dining room where she was lighting candles on a huge cake.

"Oh Lord," Tanner said groaning, "I'd forgotten."

"Forgot your own birthday?" Rob chided, clapping Tanner on the back. "Must be getting senile in your old age!"

"I only put on four candles, dear," Hattie soothed, "one for each decade."

"Swell," Tanner muttered. And that was supposed to ease the pain of turning forty?

LATE THAT AFTERNOON Kelly stepped out of Baritone's stall after checking to be sure his leg wraps weren't too tight.

"Hi, there," Tanner called.

"Hello, yourself." She hadn't seen him since breakfast, and she was hoping that his black mood had improved since Hattie's surprise party.

He glanced to see if anyone was watching, then reached out to pull her against his chest. His mouth lowered, and he gave her a long, thorough kiss.

"Hmmm," she said, looking up at him with a teasing light in her eyes, "some things do improve with age."

"Want to explore that idea?" he invited.

She glanced at the doorway for the guard who was always there.

"I sent him to the house for a dinner break." He kissed her again on the tip of her nose.

"Oh?"

"We're all alone." His eyes glowed with mischief.

"What about everyone else?" Kelly fretted, wondering if someone might decide to look for them and find them in a compromising situation.

"Ah, fair lady. I'm not asking for a mere tryst in the hay. I've made dinner reservations for us at Hampton House this evening," he teased, nuzzling her neck.

"Hmmm, dinner at Hampton House?" It was tempting.

"But not till eight o'clock," he said, nibbling his way to her lower lip. "We have a little time now, if we don't waste it talking."

She tilted her head back and looked into his blue eyes. "Seems I recall Doc Andrews saying you loved to play in haylofts when you were young." Her gaze drifted to the loft over the stalls. "Wonder if that still applies . . . now that you're older."

His eyes narrowed in challenge. "You'll find that lots of things still apply now that I'm older."

She walked to the ladder and climbed three rungs before she looked back at him. "Prove it."

He chuckled as he lunged toward the ladder and chased her into the loft laughing breathlessly. Behind a wall of bales, they found a mound of soft hay where broken bales had been tossed aside. As he caught her in his arms, she fell back onto the hay pulling him down beside her. She reached to pluck a straw from his hair and gazed into his eyes.

"No one told me it was your birthday—" she lightly kissed the tip of his nose "—so I don't have a present for you."

He nuzzled her throat. "Oh, I'll think of something you can give me on the spur of the moment."

His lips burned a trail to the hollow where her pulse was beginning to hum.

"But it won't be wrapped."

"I would hope not."

As his fingers worked the second button of her blouse, a noise came to them from below.

Their eyes met guiltily as they slowly sat up and strained to listen. A long silence followed, broken only by the sounds of horses munching and occasionally stomping in the stalls below. Tanner reached for her. Then they heard it again, a sound of wood scraping against wood and then voices.

Crawling to the wall of hay, they peered over the top. Outside Baritone's stall below them, Jared Huxsman handed a small object to Rob.

"Do it now," Jared hissed. "We may not get another chance. The derby is only ten days away."

"There's got to be another way." Rob's voice sounded unusually on edge.

"If this horse runs in the money, Tanner will never sell me that land. This is your future, too. One more setback, and he'll have to sell."

"I don't know, Jared . . ."

"Son, don't quit me now," Jared said, placing his hand on Rob's shoulder. "Let me make up those years when I couldn't be your father. After we turn this farm and mine over to the developers, we can travel the world, enjoy the good life for the rest of our lives. It's what we've always wanted, isn't it?"

"Yes," Rob agreed with little enthusiasm. "But it's Tanner . . . I'm not sure anymore, Jared. Maybe it's wrong . . . there has to be another way."

"Do it. I've already filled the syringe."

Hesitantly Rob accepted the syringe, but both Tanner and Kelly could see the reluctance in his eyes. "Is it the same stuff we used before?"

"Yeah, but this time I doubled the dose." Jared took Rob's hand and wrapped his fingers firmly around the barrel of the syringe. "I paid a fortune for this. Comes from Africa. Hasn't even been identified in the States yet. Do it, son, and we're home free."

Rob took a step back, almost recoiling from what he had to do.

"You're not getting cold feet on me, are you?" Jared demanded in a harsh whisper. "You're in this all the way, remember? You knocked off the old man."

"I didn't mean to kill Charlie . . . I couldn't find his medicine."

"Who'd believe that? Besides, the ransom note was your idea, a real stroke of genius. And then after the old coot was dead, when you tore the last pages out of his journal and erased his last entries in the computer, you sure as hell threw 'em off our track, didn't you? Hell, nobody even thought anything was wrong with the horse until Charlie's kid showed up. Gotta hand it to you, Rob. You thought of everything."

"Not really. You pulled that stunt with the hay bales," Rob accused. "I didn't know a thing about it. You scared the hell out of me."

"I was in another stall," Jared soothed, "watching you, son. I wouldn't have let anything happen to you. It was the horse and that girl I was after. You were a fool to pull her out of the way."

"You promised we wouldn't have to kill anybody. But these stunts are dangerous. They've got to stop. Kelly could've been electrocuted, and somebody could've died in the fire. We're just supposed to be forcing Tanner to sell the land, since I couldn't convince him."

"It's working, isn't it? When this horse dies, Tanner won't be able to hold it together."

"I don't know . . . he's getting by with the boarders here."

"We'll fix that. It'll be a piece of cake. But we gotta do this now while Tanner is gone. C'mon, think about it. Tanner sells Pinetop and the stock— he splits the proceeds with you—we jack the price up and sell this place and mine to my friends in Chicago. They build whatever they want, and everybody's happy."

"Except Tanner," Rob said.

"He'll have half the money from the farm sale,"

Jared reminded. "He can start fresh somewhere else if he wants." He winked at Rob. "A few more weeks shacking up with his lady trainer, and he'll forget all about this place."

Rob heaved a sigh and opened the stall door.

"That's my boy," Jared coaxed, squeezing Rob's shoulder supportively. "Once this horse is out of the way, we can do everything we've always wanted, son. Just think, we won't have to work— we can live the life we've only dreamed."

Kelly glanced at Tanner, heartsick. Tanner pushed her down out of the way as he stood up. "Hold it right there, Rob," Tanner said firmly.

Jared glanced up. Seeing Tanner, he shoved Rob into the stall and reached inside his jacket for his gun. Tanner threw his shoulder against the wall of bales, and the top three rows toppled over the side and tumbled down on Jared, knocking him to the floor.

Scrambling over the remaining bales, Tanner took hold of the mesh screen at the top of a stall, swung over the side and jumped the rest of the way.

"Rob, don't do it," he pleaded, looking through the screen at his brother who stood with one hand clamped onto the colt's halter and the other clutching the syringe.

"Don't try to stop me, Tanner." Rob began backing up with the horse. "First Dad, now you. I can't stand being pulled from both sides anymore."

Kelly dropped the pitchfork from the loft and scrambled down the ladder to pick it up just as Jared rose to his knees. As his hand slipped inside his jacket again, she pressed the sharp tines against his chest. "I wouldn't," she warned.

Jared recognized the fire in her eyes. Her message was clear. Slowly he raised his hands.

Tanner stepped cautiously into the stall. Rob was still clutching the halter, but Baritone was tossing his head and pawing nervously. "Give me the syringe," Tanner ordered quietly. "Whatever you're hoping to accomplish we can talk about. Just don't do anything foolish."

Rob eased another step backwards. "No . . . you never cared about me, so why should I care about you?"

"I've always cared. I admit I've made a lot of mistakes when we were young, Rob, but I've paid for those mistakes. Now put down the syringe, and let's try to work this out."

"Stay back," Rob ordered with a wild look in his eye, and Tanner wondered if Rob was suffering some kind of a breakdown. "I promised Jared . . . now get back!" He moved the syringe closer to the horse's jugular. "Jared is the only family I have . . . he's the only one who cares what *I* want!"

Tanner held out his hand pleadingly. "Rob, come on now, just calm down. This is crazy, and you know it. We're family."

The hand holding the syringe trembled, and

Rob's face began to crumple. "God, Tanner . . . I'm in too deep."

"No, we can get through this together. Whatever happens, I'll be there for you this time." Tanner eased forward. "Give me the syringe, Rob."

"Don't come any closer." Rob shook his head violently.

"Rob, calm down. . . ." Tanner could see the colt was getting edgy.

"Get back!"

As Rob shouted, the nervous colt suddenly shied and spun away. Rob, still gripping the halter, was pulled off balance. Tanner reached out to break Rob's fall, but as Rob released the halter, he was thrown headlong into the corner.

Tanner rushed to Rob's side and knelt, taking hold of his brother's shoulders and turning him over. The syringe was plunged deep in Rob's chest.

For an instant, Rob stared back at him, remorse filling his eyes. "I'm sorry," he whispered hoarsely, "I didn't mean to hurt you . . . never meant to hurt you."

His hand released the syringe and he drew a shallow breath. A moment later, his eyes fluttered shut.

A low sob tore from Tanner's throat as he gathered his brother in his arms and held him tightly.

Larson and the guard rounded the corner and started down the hallway. Kelly caught sight of them and called out, "Hurry, in here!"

The two men rushed down the hallway and took quick stock of the situation.

Kelly glanced at the guard. "This man is armed."

The guard reached into Jared's jacket and removed the gun. Kelly cast the pitchfork aside and turned to Larson.

"Call an ambulance. Rob's been hurt."

Larson nodded and ran toward the office. As Kelly stepped back into the stall, she laid her hand on the colt's neck to calm him. Her eyes moved to the corner where Tanner was kneeling with Rob still cradled in his arms.

Sensing her presence, he lifted his gaze, and his eyes were filled with unspeakable anguish. "Will you help me?" he asked brokenly.

Tears blinded her as she nodded and watched as Tanner scooped his brother into his arms. She helped steady him as he rose to his feet and guided him gently through the doorway.

Slipping out of the stall, she latched the door and walked beside Tanner as he headed down the hallway to the office. He eased Rob down onto the sofa. Kelly glanced up and saw Larson standing behind the desk.

"Ambulance is on the way," Larson relayed gruffly, and she could see tears glistening in his eyes, "so's the sheriff."

She closed her eyes briefly and nodded. "Thank you." Then recalling how Tanner had said Larson had been like a second father to him and Rob, she added softly, "Would you like a few minutes alone with Tanner and Rob before the ambulance gets here?"

Larson nodded as tears began to slide down his weathered cheeks. Kelly reached across the desk and squeezed his shoulder reassuringly, then slipped quietly outside.

Chapter Fifteen

After what seemed like hours, the questions were over. The coroner ruled Rob's death an accident, and the sheriff took Jared Huxsman into custody.

Kelly and Tanner walked wearily to the cottage. Lying together in the darkness, they held each other tightly.

"It wasn't your fault," Kelly whispered, sensing the direction of Tanner's thoughts.

His arms tightened around her. *I've lost Rob, but I still have Kelly,* he thought, drawing her closer.

He realized that he'd tried, perhaps too hard, to keep Rob at Pinetop so they could share a future together.

Am I about to make the same mistake with Kelly? he wondered. *Will I try to hold her here? And if I do, will it destroy her, too?*

The questions plagued him. He loved Kelly, but he knew that it didn't give him the right to mold her future. He had to back off and let her make her own choices.

If she chose to stay, he'd make her glad that she had. But if she chose to go, as he suspected she would, he wouldn't try to hold her back.

Listening to her even breathing, he knew that Kelly was asleep. Quietly he slipped out of bed, and a few minutes later he was standing on the front porch. He would leave her alone to make her choice. She no longer needed him for a bodyguard.

He hurried down the steps before he could change his mind. A heavy snow was falling soundlessly. He trudged slowly up the incline; his footsteps were nearly filled in with fresh snow by the time he reached the house.

Kelly awakened in the cold stillness before dawn. Her fingers traced the dip in the pillow where Tanner's head had been. It was cold. The house was cold. There was no fire in the grate and no fresh coffee aroma. Tanner was gone, and for a moment Kelly felt abandoned.

She knew that Tanner was hurting. People were quick to dismiss the loss of one who'd died on the wrong side of the law. She knew what it was to grieve alone.

She knew that Tanner would want to shut people out in self-defense, but she'd expected that he would make an exception for her. She'd believed they were close enough that he would know he could lean on her.

She knew that tragedy had a way of drawing people closer or pushing them apart. With a sickening dread she began to fear that Rob's death would drive a permanent wedge between them.

In the days that followed, her fear became reality. Tanner avoided her whenever possible. Even at the private memorial service for his brother he was stoic and distant.

Kelly was present when the sheriff drove out to

tell Tanner the list of charges that the district attorney had filed against Jared Huxsman. Even that had failed to draw more than a brief reply from Tanner.

The papers nationwide carried a statement released by the sheriff's office vindicating Charlie Bailey of any suspected wrongdoing. It explained that the ransom note had been planted on Bailey's body to mislead the authorities and that they were now certain Bailey had never intended to kidnap the horse. The story had contained a brief statement from Tanner McCrey that praised Bailey's accomplishments and character. When asked about his brother, Tanner had declined to comment.

Give him time, Kelly told herself as another week rolled by.

Her staff became enthused as derby day approached. The preparations kept her busy, but Kelly took no pleasure in them.

Kelly did manage to arrange a few minutes alone with Tanner. She wrapped her arms around his neck and just held him for a moment. "Thank you," she said.

"For what?" he asked.

"For clearing my father's name."

Tanner shrugged. "The sheriff did that."

She shook her head. "What you said made a difference, especially to me." He held her for a brief moment and then withdrew again.

One day, when she could stand his aloofness no

longer, Kelly marched through the McCrey house to Tanner's office, where he spent most of his time. Kelly knocked, opened the door and walked through.

"We can't go on like this," she said curtly. "Talk to me. You're shutting me out, and I'm sick of it."

Turning from the window, Tanner looked at Kelly briefly before walking to his desk. He scooped up a stack of phone messages and held them out to her. "More of these have come in. Some pretty prestigious stables are knocking at your door, Kelly."

"I don't care about them," she said, casting the notes aside. "I care about you." She walked around his desk to take his arm. "What's happening to us?" Her eyes were imploring him. "Let me love you," she said in a choked whisper.

She saw a flash of anguish in his eyes and then a look of raw need. She slipped her arms around him. He did need her; she'd known it. Her heart flooded with relief.

For an instant, he let himself hold her. Then his arms dropped to his sides.

Bewildered, Kelly looked into his face. There was a shuttered look in his eyes.

"Kelly, you can't just dismiss the opportunities rolling in right now."

"Forget them, will you?" she snapped, her temper rising.

He shook his head. "Owners on both coasts are

calling you, offering salaries triple what I can pay you here. You may never have this chance again."

The only chance Kelly cared about was the chance to stay with him. She wanted him to ask her to stay, but if she had to sacrifice her pride, she would. She loved him that much. "I'd rather stay here."

"You're welcome to stay, of course," he said evenly, "but when you return those calls, I think you'll find a better place."

"This is where you are. So this is where I want to be."

He gazed at her, wishing it could be, but he was afraid she'd change her mind eventually and leave. He'd had all the disappointments he could stand for a while.

"Look, Kelly, we're at different stages of our lives—"

"If you're going to lecture me about age, save your breath," she interrupted.

"It's more than that," he insisted. "It's time for you to take your career and run with it. You turn your back on it now, and someday you'll resent me for it." He scooped up the phone messages and pushed them into her hand. "Look again—" his tone was harsh "—you'll see something you like."

"I'm looking at someone I love." Her heart was on the line now, but she didn't care.

He shook his head disbelievingly and glanced at

his watch. "It's late." His gaze returned to hers. "Maybe too late," he said quietly.

Too late—the words echoed in her heart as he turned and walked out of the room.

He couldn't mean that; he just couldn't.

THE DAYS WENT BY in a blur until the sunny morning of the Arkansas Derby arrived. Kelly was standing with Tanner and Hattie outside Baritone's stall at Oaklawn Park when Louise Cabot walked up.

"Again, I'm so sorry about what has happened," Lousie said, touching Tanner's arm.

He nodded. "Thank you."

Louise fidgeted nervously. "I hope you know that I had nothing to do with what they did. Why, I had no idea . . ."

But everything to gain, Kelly thought peevishly.

"Well," Louise shifted her weight and dropped her arms to her sides, "good luck, Tanner." Louise nodded to Kelly and Hattie before she moved on.

Kelly glanced at Tanner. "Do you believe she didn't know what was going on?"

He shrugged.

Kelly looked at Hattie. "Do you believe her?"

Hattie shook her head briskly. "Of course not. She blinked. Haven't I told you? Liars always blink."

Kelly glanced back at Tanner. His face was

etched with tension. *Maybe it is too late for us,* Kelly thought, *but there is something I can leave you, something you and your father have wanted for years—the derby.*

Kelly watched as Louise walked to stand beside her trainer and began laughing with her friends. In her heart Kelly knew that if there was any justice, Louise Cabot would not win the race.

Jay Moran was approaching, and Kelly reached out and snagged his arm, then hustled him into the stall used for tack storage and closed the door behind them. She wanted to make a few things abundantly clear.

"Keep the colt calm and steady," she began, "and save him for a big stretch run."

Jay nodded. "You've given me the same instructions three times already this morning."

"And another thing," Kelly looked Jay squarely in the eye, "you ride like your career depends on it, because it does. If I even suspect that you're not giving me your best . . ." Her eyes flashed as her voice trailed off with a hint of desperation.

"Don't worry." Jay lifted his chin and regarded her steadily. "I ride to win. You have my word on it."

MARCY AND DOUG led Baritone onto the track. Kelly followed them to the saddling paddock, keeping a close eye on the colt. Gone was his skittish behavior of last year. Head up, ears forward, watching the crowd, he walked boldly with a long swing of shoulders and hips, his hooves plunging deep into the loam.

Tanner joined them in the paddock, and he and Kelly saddled the horse without a problem. When it was time, Tanner gave Jay a leg up and slapped his boot. "Do your best," he told him.

"You can count on it," Jay promised, glancing at Kelly as he spoke.

Doug led the colt to the track where an outrider took the lead rope. Doug and Marcy joined Hattie who was standing at the rail, while Kelly and Tanner climbed a flight of stairs to stand on a platform reserved for owners.

Glancing at the green tote board, Kelly saw that Baritone's odds had dropped, probably due to his recent victory at Remington Park. She noticed that the odds on Claimjumper, Louise's horse, were slightly lower, perhaps because her jockey was a well-known rider from the East.

"The horses are nearing the starting gate." The announcement came over the speaker, and Kelly's heart lurched with anticipation.

Through binoculars, Kelly watched the starters load the horses. Baritone was waiting quietly in the third post position while the others were led into their slots.

"The horses are in the starting gate." The announcement brought a hush. Seconds later a bell clanged, and the starting gate opened. Horses exploded from a standstill to full gallop within strides.

Baritone broke well. Claimjumper hustled from the seventh post position and angled toward the rail, coming dangerously close to brushing another horse as he took the lead on the first turn. Baritone moved to capture a place on the outside, galloping easily, just off the pace.

Baritone was in the middle of the pack as it strung out around the second turn in what would be a grueling mile and an eighth.

"Don't burn him out!" Louise shouted a short distance away. "Hold him!" She lowered her field glasses to glance at her young male companion. "Why, the fool's lettin' him take off like a hijacked jet for Cuba." Her companion patted her hand soothingly.

Kelly shook her head and concentrated on the race. Jay had Baritone galloping down the back-stretch in a steady, fluid stride.

Coming around the next turn, Jay started to let the colt go, passing three horses on the outside. On the final turn for home, Baritone came up behind a wall of horses.

Kelly held her breath, knowing Jay had only seconds to make the critical decision. He could save ground by dropping to the rail and taking a chance on squeezing through, or he could swing wide and go around the horses ahead.

At the top of the stretch, Jay pulled the colt wide

and started around the leaders. Baritone responded and lengthened his stride, pulling for more ground.

One by one Baritone inched past the others. Jay was leaning forward rocking his hands up on the colt's neck, urging him on. Claimjumper was still in the lead, his jockey whipping him on the left. Baritone surged up on Claimjumper's right.

At that instant, Claimjumper's rider switched his stick to his right hand and brought it down hard, aiming for his horse's flank but catching Baritone on the nose instead.

Kelly gasped, and there was a rumble from the crowd. "Did you see that!" she spouted hotly as Tanner swore under his breath.

Jay steadied Baritone and asked him for more speed. The colt responded, flattening his ears and driving for the wire. It was a duel of hearts as Baritone gained ground. Catching Claimjumper in the last seconds, Baritone shot to the wire beside him. The crowd went wild as the tote board flashed a photo finish.

Shivering with goose bumps, Kelly hugged Tanner, squealing with excitement. They had a winner; she was sure of it! Tanner was barraged by well-wishers as they made their way down the steps. Ahead of them, Louise stopped at the rail, her eyes trained on the tote board.

"Well, McCrey," Louise said, looking over her shoulder, "it's you or me."

He nodded, and Kelly grinned. She had faith that

Baritone had done it for them. The seconds ticked by as they waited.

After what seemed like hours, the tote board signaled number three as the official winner of the Arkansas Derby, and the crowd roared their approval.

A cheer went up for Baritone, a horse with the courage to keep going when others would have quit. Jay acknowledged the fans by raising his whip, and they thundered their applause. Tanner took Kelly's hand as they crossed the track to the winner's circle. Jay grinned at them from aboard the colt as a garland of white roses was draped over Baritone's neck and shoulders.

Flashbulbs popped as the governor presented Tanner with the trophy. Joy and pride radiated in his smile as he held the silver cup aloft. Setting the trophy aside, he stepped to the microphone: "I dedicate this victory to the memory of my father Alexander McCrey, who had the dream, and to Charlie Bailey and his daughter Kelly Smith, who helped make that dream come true."

Kelly's eyes filled as she watched him. Somehow she knew that Charlie and Alexander were sharing their joy. Within minutes everyone was moving back across the track as the horses for the final race approached the paddock. Tanner was surrounded by the press and friends offering congratulations. Jay stripped the saddle and carried it to the scale for his weigh-in.

Quickly Doug and Marcy slipped a cooling blanket over the colt's back, and Kelly walked Baritone back to his stall.

After the colt was properly cooled out, she rode back to Pinetop in the van hauling Baritone home.

Her staff was in a festive mood, predicting Baritone as a favorite for the Kentucky Derby in two weeks. While they headed out to celebrate, Kelly loaded her tack into her horse van.

She'd done what she'd set out to do: clear her father's name and win the Arkansas Derby for Tanner. Her missions were accomplished. Instead of feeling elated, she felt incredibly drained. Her contract with Tanner McCrey had expired, and he hadn't offered her a new one.

Instead he'd handed her a fistful of phone messages and told her to pick a new employer. Well, she thought, you win some and you lose some. Her eyes filled with tears as she began to load her personal belongings into her truck.

Her emotions were strung too tightly for any sad goodbyes, so she decided to call Marcy and Hattie and the others after she got back to Shreveport.

She'd returned a few of the phone calls she'd received, but it was too soon to make a decision. She'd called Zack, and he'd offered to let her work with him until she made her choice. She tried to work up some enthusiasm about going home for a while, but it was hopeless.

Slipping behind the wheel, she backed her truck

up to her horse trailer, got out and walked around to the back.

"Going somewhere?"

Spinning around, she saw Larson standing nearby. "Yeah," she said, turning her back on him to wipe her tears on her coat sleeve. She bent to hook the trailer onto the hitch.

"Sorry to hear that," he said evenly.

Surprised, Kelly looked over her shoulder. "I thought you'd be glad."

Larson shoved his hands into his back pockets and shrugged. "Nah—" he tried to smile "—I was just gettin' used to you."

Kelly turned and took a deep breath. "I owe you an apology, Larson. For a long time, I thought you were the one behind all the sabotage that went on here."

"Don't apologize," he said softly, looking uncomfortable. "I thought the same about you."

She shook her head at the irony. "Well, I said some rotten things behind your back," she confessed.

He shrugged. "Couldn't have been any worse than what I said to your face. You see, I knew you were Charlie's kid from the moment I laid eyes on you. He'd shown me a picture one time, and I recognized you."

"Why didn't you tell Tanner?" she asked.

"I'm a lotta things, lady, but I ain't no snitch. I figured at first you might be up to some hanky-panky, and if you were up to no good, I'd find out. Your father and I didn't hit it off, but you're both good trainers. Got that colt ready for the derby, gotta hand it to you."

"Thanks," she said.

"Well, can I give you a hand?"

She shook her head. "No, I've got it."

Larson shifted his feet. It was the first time Kelly had seen him look unsure.

"Good luck," he said.

"Same to you," she replied, watching him climb into his truck and drive off.

Taking a deep breath, Kelly dropped the ramp on the horse trailer and walked to the paddock where Happy Talk stood dozing in the last rays of afternoon sunshine. Tall Cotton was stretched out asleep nearby.

Kelly whistled as she opened the gate. The mare's ears rotated and a shudder rippled over her hide.

She met the mare halfway and snapped a lead to her halter. The foal got to her feet and stretched, then followed as she led the mare to the back of the truck.

Happy Talk walked calmly up the ramp and into the trailer. Kelly tied the mare inside and took another lead with her to lead the filly inside.

By now Tall Cotton was trotting around, delighted to investigate her new surroundings. Kelly moved quietly toward the foal who scampered away each time she came close.

Kelly's patience was beginning to wear thin. Until now, Cotton had always been easy to handle, but she seemed unwilling to forfeit her freedom. Kelly lunged for the foal's halter, realizing as she did it that it was the wrong thing to do.

She desperately wanted to get on her way. Leaving Pinetop was painful enough, so she sure didn't want to stay around long enough to run into Tanner.

As she reached for the foal again, it occurred to Kelly that Tanner was probably out celebrating, and it might be a day or two before he even noticed she was gone.

The realization filled her with despair, and she slumped onto the ramp of the van and dropped her face in her hands.

Weeping quietly, Kelly felt the foal's whiskers nuzzling her face.

"Go away," she sniffed.

"I hope you don't mean me."

Kelly looked up. Tanner was standing beside her. Their eyes met, and her tears flowed faster. "Yes, you go away, too."

"Sorry, I tried but I wasn't very successful at that."

Dragging a handkerchief from his back pocket, he handed it to her. "What are you crying about?"

"Nothing." She sniffed and accepted his offering and blew her nose. She hated herself for acting like this in front of him.

"Nothing is certainly making you sad."

"All right, I'm blubbering like an idiot because I'm leaving." She glanced up at him with pain-filled eyes.

"No, you're not." He reached down to pull her to her feet and into his arms. She laid her head against his chest and bawled even harder.

"I thought I could let you go," he said softly, "but I can't."

Her arms tightened around him possessively. "I don't *want* to be let go."

"Whether you do or not, I love you," he said simply, tipping her head up to meet his gaze. "And I can't give you up. There has to be a way that you can live your life and I can still be part of it."

"I want that more than anything," she whispered with her heart in her eyes.

"We could winter here," he reasoned, "and in the peak season I could travel with you. Hell, I'll sell the place and live like a gypsy if that's what it takes. I love you too much to give you up."

"I love you, too," she vowed, "but I'll never ask you to give up your home. You're far more ambitious for me than I am for myself, Tanner. Haven't you noticed that by now?"

"I only want the best for you, Kelly. I know you're bright and talented, and you have a promising future ahead of you. . . ."

"I'd rather share that future with you, Tanner. None of those things you said about me will mean anything unless we're together."

They gazed at each other for a long moment.

"Are you sure?" he asked.

She nodded, too overcome by emotion to answer him.

"Marry me, Kelly Smith."

Nodding happily, she lifted her mouth to meet his. For a long moment the only world they knew was the one they made together.

Suddenly a clatter startled them. Tall Cotton had scampered into the van on her own, and she blinked at them with wide eyes for an instant before she turned to nudge her mother's side.

"So, now you decide to cooperate," Kelly scolded lovingly, hugging Tanner around the waist as they looked at the colt. She glanced up and met his adoring gaze. "Looks like we're all walkin' in tall cotton, doesn't it?"

He smiled and gave her a look that sent her heart hammering. His mouth slowly lowered to take hers again, and he whispered softly, "The tallest, my love, the very tallest."

Center Point Publishing
600 Brooks Road ● PO Box 1
Thorndike ME 04986-0001 USA

(207) 568-3717

US & Canada:
1 800 929-9108
www.centerpointlargeprint.com